Reckless Abandon
by
Kallie Lane
A Shadow Soldiers Suspense
Book 3

RECKLESS ABANDON: A Shadow Soldiers Suspense Novel

Publishing History

First edition published 2012, The Wild Rose Press, Inc.

Second edition published 2018, Kathryn Donaldson

Third edition published 2021, Kathryn Donaldson

Digital ISBN 978-1-7779233-3-4

Print ISBN 978-1-7779233-2-7

Published in the United States of America

Dedication

To Laurie Donaldson and Rodney Fuller—the real Rocket Girl and Rocket. Although the fictional story takes place in ranch country, Alberta, Laurie and Rod have a beautiful spread in Ontario that they generously shared with me on more than one occasion. Thanks so much for your fabulous hospitality, for showing me ranch life and teaching me about the rodeo, up close and personal. And thank you for allowing me to use your horses' names in this novel, as well as your own rodeo 'handles'. You're the absolute best!

This book is also dedicated to the men and women of the Canadian military, both active and retired. For the sacrifices you've made and continue to make for the rest of us.

Acknowledgments

There are so many people who helped bring this book to life: Coreene Callahan, Fred Donaldson, Marielle Fournel, Rachel Humphrey, Jean Moore, Christian Poulin, Hélène Ste-Croix, and JJ Wilhelm.

Thank you! I couldn't have written this without all of you, and any mistakes are entirely my own.

Chapter 1

The sun blazed overhead as Billie Bradshaw lay sprawled in the dirt, waiting to die. Cold and trembling, agonizing pain shooting through her head, she felt a drip along the base of her skull. She didn't move. Scarcely breathed and didn't open her eyes. Her mind wasn't working right. She didn't know how she'd gotten there. Yet, every instinct she possessed warned her to play dead.

Time ticked by, how much she couldn't tell before she recognized the whine of engines coming over the hill into the valley. Cracking her eyelids, she saw pickups with the *Circle B* insignia pull up and screech to a halt. Her father leapt from the first cab and raced toward her.

"Billie! Christ, we heard a shot!"

What?

He slid to his knees beside her, his body blocking the sun as he cupped her face in his hands. Searching his eyes, her escalating terror lessened a notch. Her dad would keep her safe, make sense of what had happened to her. Carefully, she tested her fingers and toes. They responded okay, she felt them move. She tried to speak but no sound came out. *What happened to my voice?*

"Hang on, love. Help's coming."

Ranch hands circled her, kicking up dust with their boots. Someone shouted loud enough to shatter her eardrums. "Keep your eyes on the hills. Shoot anything that moves!"

Sure, this was Grizzly country, but Billie surmised they weren't worried about bears. She turned her head, a big mistake, and almost fainted from the pain drilling her skull. Her father bunched his jacket into a pillow, lifted her head to slide it beneath her. More pain.

His phone rang. She listened to him yell at someone at the emergency clinic in Hereford before ending the call. "Damn ambulance broke an axle at the turnoff from the highway. A medevac team's on its way."

A few minutes later, she heard the sound of a helicopter clearing the treetops. She breathed in slowly, held tight to her father's hand, and watched it touch down beside the pickups. More dust. More men rushing at her. They wore flight suits, carried a stretcher and—*thank you, God!*—medical supplies.

They slid a board under her and strapped her to it, attached a neck brace and lifted her onto a stretcher. What could only be blood dripped on the board from her head. *Plop, plop,* so much of it...she hated its coppery scent. A man applied pressure behind her ear, began wrapping her head in bandages. She felt woozy again and fought to stay conscious. He asked her questions she mostly understood but couldn't seem to answer. *Why can't I speak? Shock, maybe?*

He was talking, always talking to her.

"How many fingers am I holding up, ma'am?" She held up three fingers.

"Can you squeeze my hand? Wiggle your toes and move your arms?"

She continued to do what he asked. *Now clam up, buddy, and give me some major drugs for this pain.*

Someone else pumped up her arm with a pressure cuff, used a stethoscope to listen to her heartbeat. If only her stupid voice would work, she could tell him her pulse roared through her head like a sonic boom. No need for the stethoscope to get a reading.

A third man hung an IV bag from a metal pole attached to the gurney, its contents dripping through a shunt into her arm. *Whatever you're feeding me, it's not pain meds. My head feels like it's going to explode.*

She coughed, choking on dust. An oxygen mask was placed over her nose.

Her father talked with the medevac team. He wanted a seat on the 'bus' that would airlift her to the hospital. Squeezing her eyes shut, she tried to ignore all of them. *Can't you leave me alone? You've already patched me up.*

"Wake up. Don't go to sleep." A hand tapped her cheek.

"Open your eyes. That's it." Fighting the void of darkness, she lifted her eyelids. Her father's face swam into view; strong, reticent, tense. The pulse at his throat pounded with concern. "Don't worry, darlin'. You're going to be fine. No more accidents."

Accidents? I don't remember...

As she was transferred to the chopper, her father spoke softly to their foreman. "Make the call. Get Rocket here. Now."

What? No! No! Don't call him. Don't...

The helicopter door clicked shut. Billie stretched out her fingers to clutch her father's sleeve. She moaned, trying to get the words out.

"Shh, I know what you're thinking, but you need Rocket. He's the only one I trust to protect you. He'll come. I know he will."

I don't want him. This has nothing to do with that jerk. Don't call him!

The torque of rotor blades and radio noise ended their one-way conversation. She was airborne, heading for the hospital. Her world began to fade from the pain not long into the flight, the seductive pull of unconsciousness blanketing her like a shroud.

REECE 'ROCKET' MORGAN sat on a barstool at *Charlie's*, a resto-bar high in the Laurentian mountains near Silver Lake in Quebec. Life was good, the team celebrating the safe rescue of Theo's lady from some very bad dudes. The fact a couple of good looking females had latched onto him like lint when he'd walked into the bar didn't hurt. Work was done. They wouldn't pile in the chopper for another few hours to head out. He had more than enough time to get to know the women, kick back, and relax.

"Reece, your phone's ringing," Sully, his Commanding Officer, bellowed from the table where some of the crew sat.

"Take a message." Reece kept his focus on the ladies. Seemed they had a thing for military guys. *Hoo-rah.*

"Guy called Pike says it's an emergency."

Reece pulled a hand down his face and groaned. Pike Williams, foreman of the *Circle B* ranch. A voice from his past, he'd taken him under his wing when Reece was nothing but a teenage punk. He owed him, and he'd take his call.

Walking to the table, he grabbed up his phone. "Pike? What's up, buddy?"

"Your girl's in trouble. You'd better get here quick."

"She's not my girl. And she's not my problem. Let her daddy handle whatever trouble she's in."

"She needs *you*, boy. Charley Bradshaw's the one who asked me to contact you. Didn't think you'd come if he called himself. She's in a passel of shit, that's for sure."

Reece laughed aloud at the remark. Billie was the only woman he knew who could bathe in crap and come out smelling like a margarita. "She must be for her old man to want me there. Last time I saw him he threatened to throw me in jail."

"Well, you sure can't blame him for that, Rocket. You shouldn't'a been diddling his little girl. Still, Charley's willing to let bygones be bygones. He's followed your military career—says you're the only one he trusts to help her now."

Pike was right about one thing. Billie Bradshaw had been underage when he'd slept with her. On his eighteenth birthday, they'd been caught in the back of his rusty pick-up behind the barn. That's when her father had threatened to charge him with statutory rape unless he zipped his pants, packed up his gear, and cleared out for good.

Tough call—go to jail or leave Billie. Reece had opted for door number two. Joined the military and never looked back. It still pissed him off he'd been booted to the curb with no chance to explain himself, although he'd deserved it. Hell, if the situation was reversed and he had a sixteen-year-old daughter? But, that was a lifetime ago.

I'm not that dumb ass bastard anymore. And I don't need to prove myself to the Bradshaws.

"Forget it, Pike. I'm not taking the bait. I cared about Billie. She obviously didn't feel the same way about me or she wouldn't have let her father ride me out of town on a rail."

"You cared for her, Rocket? Then why didn't you use protection instead of getting her pregnant?"

Mother of God. They'd only had sex one time. The news stunned him. He willed spit into his mouth to loosen his tongue. "Goddamn. Why am I only hearing about this now?"

"She wouldn't let me tell you, son." There was a pause on the other end of the line. Reece could hear Pike adding a chaw of tobacco to the inside of his cheek. "Besides, there's nothing to tell. She lost the baby four months into the pregnancy. Fell on a trail ride. Hit a rock and miscarried...nearly bled to death herself."

Jesus, Jesus, Jesus. Reece doubled over to catch his breath. He hadn't used a condom, hadn't protected Billie. "You're ten years too late. There's nothing I can do to make this right."

"Now you listen to me, or are you still just some snot-nosed kid who thinks he can take on the world with his fists? Come home, Rocket, and help her. I'm begging here. She won't make it without you, s-son, no matter how stubborn and t-tough she thinks she is."

Reece fought to level his breathing. Pike's voice had warbled, something he'd never heard before from the tough-as-nails foreman. Uneasiness gripped him. "What kind of trouble is she in?"

"Someone tried to kill her. I think they've tried before, but she won't listen to reason. She claims she's just been accident prone lately. But, today they shot her upside the head. She was airlifted to the Foothills Medical Centre Trauma Unit for treatment."

Reece had no choice. He had to go. Not easy for a guy living off the grid. Harder because he still cared about her, and now he knew why she had never returned his calls or answered his letters. Jesus, a baby...loved and lost. He had caused so much pain in her life.

God help him, it was time to man up. "Give me the address."

Reece disconnected the call, turned to tell his teammates he had to boogie. Six pairs of eyes drilled him.

"Morgan, what's happening?" Law asked. "That call sounded serious."

"I have to get to the airport and charter a flight. A friend of mine was shot and needs my protection."

"You want help?" Micah rose from the table, looked ready to join him, no questions asked.

"Thanks. I'll let you know once I have more Intel." Reece slid the phone in his pocket and prepared to leave. "But I'll need a ride to the airport."

"Wheels up, guys." Hawke said. "Let's move."

A short time later, Reece stared out of the helicopter as it approached Montreal Trudeau airport. He needed a chance to clear his head and salvage his sanity. What he got instead was a high octane boost of adrenaline that clenched his jaw and vibrated clear to the soles of his metal-tipped boots.

One lousy phone call and his priorities had folded like a bad poker hand. Another call and he'd chartered a flight from Montreal to Calgary. A Bombardier Learjet 35A waited for him on the tarmac, revving its engines. Time was the enemy. He needed to reach Billie fast.

He also managed to reach his buddy with SARDAA—the Search and Rescue Dog Association of Alberta—to borrow a vehicle. He and Rizzo were tight. Ran into each other from time to time in stink hole situations such as natural disasters. Reece could count on him in a shit storm, the unlimited use of an SUV being the icing on the cake.

Less than five hours later, he was spinning out of Springbank Airport on a cloud of gravel and dust. If he put the pedal to the metal on the Cayenne, he'd make the hospital before nightfall. Hard to believe he burned rubber for the trauma unit. And her.

Billie Bradshaw—the only woman who still held the power to bring him to his knees.

Why does she appeal to me?

"Stupid question, man." He ran his hand over his face as he settled further into the seat.

Smart...beautiful...kind...shot out of his memory banks like a Christmas wish list. All the more reason he wanted to turn tail and run. Not from the potentially dangerous situation, but from the woman. Such was life. No time to dwell on it and even less time to lose. Billie needed him. And that said it all.

Cracking the window, he lit a cigarette—a habit he rarely indulged in anymore—shoved his aviator shades in place and blew out a stream of smoke. Better to die of cancer than go where he was headed now. There would be hell to pay.

BILLIE AWOKE TO DRUMS pounding her skull like a military tattoo. She was woozy and couldn't open her eyes. Her tongue was glued to the roof of her mouth, her throat was parched, and she couldn't reach or see to buzz the nurse's station for help.

She felt along the top of the nightstand until she bumped the plastic drinking cup with her fingers. Clutching it, she bobbled it to her lips. Her arm trembled and spasmed. The straw twirled. Freezing cold water sloshed over her hospital gown before a strong hand wrapped around hers and guided the straw to her mouth for a few quick swallows. "Want...more."

"Let's see how that stays down first."

The voice was deep, safe. *A male nurse?* He stripped off her soaked gown, dried her with a towel, and slipped another gown over her shoulders. The heaviness of a blanket soon cocooned her in warmth. Still, she couldn't hold back a whimper. "Hurts..."

Words became fuzzy, the doctor arguing with someone. "The dose is self-administering. All she has to do is push the button..."

"She can't push the button when she's too sick to open her eyes. Never mind, from now on I'll handle it for her."

"You can't stay here. You're not a relative."

Something started to flow through her veins; a magic elixir quieted the blasts going off in her head and further confused her mind. She drifted off for a while until the harsh voices startled her back to reality again.

"Not moving...phone her father...clear it...can't fend for herself...bodyguard."

So tired. Can't stay awake. Can't make sense of what they're saying. Need to sleep.

THE NEXT TIME BILLIE awakened she was able to lift her eyelids. Her gaze sharpened on a man standing in the doorway with his back to her. Very tall, he was narrow-hipped with faded jeans gloving his backside and long legs ending at a pair of scuffed boots. The black T-shirt he wore delineated powerful shoulders and bulging biceps. Corded sinews wrapped his muscular arms. Longish chestnut hair was secured at his nape by a strip of leather.

Gorgeous. She must be dreaming. Who was he? Some cowboy she met at a bar last night? *Impossible. Drunk or sober, I would remember sleeping with a man like him.*

He turned as if sensing her inspection. She instantly recognized those green, green eyes; his chiselled features; and a five o'clock shadow that seemed to be a permanent fixture on his jaw. Ten years older, he was a breathtaking version of the teenager she'd known. The teenager she'd loved. The teenager who'd scored and bolted, taking her heart along with him for the ride.

It wasn't a dream at all, but her worst nightmare. And why was a gun clipped to his belt?

She cleared her throat and found her voice. "You look like a hundred mile stretch of bad road, Rocket. What are you doing here?"

He cracked a smile displaying white, even teeth. Moving to the foot of the bed, the air around him hinted of sandalwood and peppermint. "It's nice to see you too, Billie. I see you're still styling your hair with a stun gun."

Actually, her hair didn't feel half bad when she ran her fingers through it in a self-conscious gesture. Oh, sure, it was long, wild, and curly, but at least it was brushed—except for where a mountain of bandages was taped behind her left ear. *What is that?*

"Not fair, Reece, like I've had time for the salon." She tried to hide her confusion by pulling herself higher in the bed. Starbursts flashed behind her eyes. Her vision tunnelled and her stomach heaved. "Whoa..."

"Be careful. There were complications—the bullet wound is infected."

Bullet wound?

She didn't move, waited for the dizziness to subside while she soaked up Reece's words. The ache in her head and her sense of helplessness said he was telling the truth.

She opened her eyes again, slowly refocused on pale cream walls, grimy windows with a view of a skyline she didn't recognize, and a profusion of flowers overflowing a credenza in a room that wasn't her own.

"Where am I? The last thing I remember was being out in the west pasture with a broken fence to mend, dragging a roll of wire from the bed of a pickup."

"That was three days ago, before you were medevaced to Foothills for treatment. You've been unconscious most of the time since then."

"I remember...some of it." To her absolute horror, her eyes started to burn, her throat felt tight, and her teeth chattered. She gulped in air but couldn't manage a decent breath. Reece advanced and she held up a hand to warn him away. "Back off. I'm f-fine."

"Nice try, but I'm not buying it." Banding her in his familiar strength, her arms fell around his neck as he lifted her higher against the pillows. Settling her there, the pads of his fingers moved to her shoulders and kneaded them in soothing circles. "Lay still."

Phantom pain, it's what she felt with each stroke of his hands. Her mind and body forgot all about her near-death experience while rekindling the intimate connection she had once shared with Reece. *Don't do this. Leave me alone.*

"Okay, I'm good. You've said hello and now, I want you to leave." God, she couldn't look him in the eye, not while he touched her. She pushed his hands aside. "Thanks for stopping by. Maybe we'll see each other again in another decade or two."

"Wimping out on me already?" Reece cupped her chin in his hand and turned her to face him. "I've waited three days for you to regain consciousness, took care of you while I waited. So now, you're going to humor me."

"I beg your damn pardon." She glared at him, her temper mounting. If looks could kill, he would be writhing on the floor at her feet by now. "Who gave you permission to touch me?"

A low, humorless rumble welled up from his chest. "Here's irony for you. Your daddy sent for me to watch over you. It seems someone doesn't like you, although I can't imagine why, given your sunny disposition. Like it or not, peaches—I'm your bodyguard."

BILLIE SLOUCHED IN the taxi, scanning the hospital entrance for Reece while she buckled up. "Take off now! There's an extra fifty in it for you if we aren't followed."

"Sounds like fun." The sedan shot away from the curb with a screech of tires on the asphalt. "Where are we headed?"

Surprised by the throaty voice, Billie looked up to meet a young woman's gaze in the rear-view mirror. Fine lines creased the corners of her mouth. They made her appear older than she was; competent and tough. A face like hers had stories to tell and not all of them pretty. Satisfied she could handle the cab like a pro, Billie gave her directions to the *Circle B*. "It's normally about a two hour drive from here in traffic. How long before you think we can get there?"

"If I get a speeding ticket, you're paying it, right?"

"Absolutely."

"The name's Rena. What's yours?"

"Billie."

Rena tossed her ball cap on the seat, slid sunglasses up her nose, and flexed tattooed knuckles on the steering wheel. *Prison tats. Oh joy.* A nose ring glinted when she turned in her seat to flash a toothy smile. "Whooeee! I've always wanted to do this, although it'd be lots more fun on my Hog. Still, let's see if I can cut the time down by half. Hold on!"

While Rena accelerated with G-force enthusiasm, Billie slammed back in the seat with a grin. Momentary pain throbbed in her head. Still, it was worth it. Reece would look like an idiot when she pulled up at the ranch house without him. Problem solved, her father would throw the bodyguard out on his yummy butt for not doing his job. He thought he could sneak back into her life, did he?

I think not. Bodyguard my luggage, you jackass.

She lowered the window a few inches to savor the rush of wind on her face and lack of exhaust fumes in the air after Rena gained the highway. They whizzed past cars at breakneck speed, zooming in and out of sparse traffic. Freedom filled Billie with smug defiance as Rena added to the distance between her and Reece. Some bodyguard he was. While he had checked her out of the hospital, gotten her prescriptions, and the requisite wheelchair to take her out of the building, she'd rode the service elevator down to the ground floor, sailed out the main entrance to the taxi stand, and made a clean getaway. She pumped her fist in the air. *A piece of cake.*

Rena shot a glance over her shoulder and brayed like a mule. "Quite the fashion statement you've got going for yourself. I'm more of a Victoria's Secret gal myself."

"What?" Glancing down, Billie realized she was still wearing her *Save a horse, ride a cowboy* nightshirt and *Rootin' Tootin' Sharp Shootin'* slippers Dottie and Pike had brought to the hospital as a joke to cheer her up. *Oops.*

"I was in kind of a rush when I got out of bed."

"Okey dokey." Rena rolled her eyes, looking in the rear-view. "As long as you're wearing your cowgirl underpants on my upholstery."

Billie gave her the thumbs-up sign while still gloating about her great escape. Reece hadn't had a clue, the big sap. He thought she'd fallen in line with his bodyguard gig, end of story. Typical of the man, thinking he could flex his muscles, curl a finger in her direction, and she would do whatever he wanted like Pavlov's dog. She wasn't a star-struck teen anymore.

Sure, there was a time she would have followed the bull rider to the ends of the earth just to admire his champion belt buckles, not that *she* was a buckle bunny. Heck no. She'd been a celebrity in her own right, a champion barrel racer. They had headlined as 'Rocket' and 'Rocket Girl' in their teenage rodeo days. Actually, Billie still headlined as 'Rocket Girl', since she'd built her reputation under the alias. But, no more Rocket. It was hard to believe she'd only had eyes for him back then—fool that she was.

"Cop alert! There's one gaining on our tail. We gotta stop." Rena eased off the gas pedal, pulled onto the shoulder, and came to a rolling halt. She shoved the transmission into park and leaned back against the headrest, speaking out of the side of her mouth. "Be cool and stay quiet. I know how to handle these guys. As soon as he writes me up a ticket, I'll let him pull out in front and we're away again. There's a shortcut off the next exit ramp that'll work fine for us."

"I'm cool." Judging by her prison artwork, Billie guessed Rena knew a lot of shortcuts to stay off police radar. *It could work.* She swivelled in her seat in time to see a shiny black SUV, with bar lights flashing, nose up behind them.

The door opened. *Uh-oh!* She recognized Reece stepping to the pavement wearing black on black boots, jeans, and a polo shirt. A grin rode his face. Sidling up to Rena's window, he removed his shades, tucked them in his neckband, and squeezed past her ample chest to snatch the keys from the ignition.

"Is there a problem, officer?" Rena gulped, looking guilty enough to have a dead body stashed in her trunk. Maybe she did. Or maybe she liked the feel of Reece's arm brushing her boobs. Billie didn't dare ask.

Reece smirked, his emerald gaze dragging up from Rena's cleavage to her face. "Apparently not, since you're still alive. Your cab fare escaped from the psych ward about a half hour ago. Just so you know; the last cabbie she rode with ended up in a ditch by the side of the road with his throat slashed from ear-to-ear."

"You're shittin' me!" Rena leapt from the car and into Reece's arms, no doubt to avoid the Bowie knife Billie must have stashed in her change purse.

"It's okay, you're safe now." Reece patted her shoulders and stood her off to the side. "You'd better stand back though...just in case."

Springing the back door, he wasted no time lifting Billie across the seat and onto the pavement. The second her cowgirl slippers touched solid ground, she wound up and socked him hard in the mouth. "You lying sack of maggots!"

Reece snapped back from her flailing fists, tugged her wrists behind her back, and slapped on the flex cuffs. Flattening her against the car with his rump, he swiped blood from his split lip and angled his chin at Rena. "See what I mean? The woman's got a hard-on for violence."

"Get out of town. I thought she was weird, but the harmless kind, you know?"

"Trust me. There is nothing harmless about her." He jerked his head in Billie's direction. "Shot up a biker bar once because there weren't any western tunes on the jukebox."

"Hates bikers, does she?" Rena's narrowed gaze said it all. *Traitor.* She'd warmed up to the conversation and almost swooned at Reece's bad boy charms. "Looks like you arrived in the nick of time."

"Don't listen to him, Rena." Billie jumped up and down to get a clear view over Reece's shoulder. "I *love* bikers. He's lying, and he's not a cop!"

The woman rolled her eyes. "Listen, Billie, I know cop cars and that's a fancy unmarked he's driving. Besides, anyone who'd wear the getup you've got on has got to be nuts."

Winking at Reece, Rena retrieved her keys and ambled back to the Chevy, squeezing her chest behind the steering wheel. "Thanks for saving my ass, man."

"Goes with the territory to save a pretty woman," he said. "I'm glad no blood was spilled. Yet."

Snorting in disgust, Billie was jerked to Reece's side as he warned her to shut it with a venomous glare. Opening his wallet, he extracted a crisp hundred dollar bill and pressed it into Rena's palm. "Here's for your trouble. I'll collect it from the jerk who let her escape. From now on, you be careful who crawls into your back seat."

"Oh, I will. It's hard enough to make a living without freaks like her twisting in the breeze." Cranking the key, Rena shot Billie the universal finger, waited for a break in traffic, and peeled rubber for her next cab fare. "Nice doing business with yaaaaaa!"

"THAT WAS A NEW LOW, Reece, even for you." Flex cuffs removed, Billie clambered into the SUV under her own steam. She scrambled across to the passenger's seat and huffed at him when he dropped into the driver's side and started the engine. "How did you find me?"

A trained observer, Reece soaked up the hostility of her body language and made an educated guess. Billie was pissed off, although he wasn't sure if it had more to do with the past than his bodyguard gig. She was madder than a rattlesnake caught in the talons of a hawk—and just about as mean.

"Did you hear what I said? I have a right to know." She kicked a foot at the glove box while flailing an arm at his midsection.

Oomph. He sucked in air and rubbed the burn in his stomach. "You have the *right* to keep your hands to yourself, or I'll toss you in the cage. What's it going to be?"

She craned her neck to peer behind them, surveyed the steel mesh enclosure in the back of the SUV, and smirked, dimples riding the corners of her mouth. "You wouldn't dare. That would be too ballsy, even for you."

"Don't push me, peaches. My buddy uses it to transport tracking dogs, but I'll make an exception in your case."

"Bite me."

Oh, he wanted to, and that was the problem. The years hadn't lessened the tightening of his groin when she was within breathing distance. She had grown into herself, her body made for endless nights of lovemaking. Long legs. Rounded hips. Small waist. Full breasts with their little buds peaked slightly upward.

Don't go there.

"Knock it off, Billie."

It wasn't just her body. Or the clean scrubbed face Hollywood actresses would hanker after. Or her amazing scent—all things sultry and fresh. It was the total package, the whole enchilada. Throw in the raw passion for living that shone through those smoke-gray eyes and she was a firestorm.

He should have stayed the hell away.

Couldn't...not with her life on the line. But, the quicker he caught the bastard who had hurt her, the faster he could beat boots out of there. This whole thing made him damned uncomfortable, more so because his stupid brain seemed to connect Billie with home—as if he'd ever had a real home.

He hit the bar lights to turn them off and gunned the engine to escape his meandering thoughts. Billie flew back against her seat, grabbing both the armrest and the dash in a death grip while her feet welded to the floor.

"Jeez, Rocket. Speed limits are more than just suggestions, you know? Is there some reason we're hurtling down the highway faster than the speed of light? A reason other than the obvious one, that you want to get us both killed?"

He didn't respond. A sideways glance revealed her game face—as transparent as the panties she wore beneath that ridiculous nightshirt. Yeah, he had ordered himself not to look when she climbed into the passenger seat, but had ignored his own advice. One way or another, she would bait and harass him all the way to the ranch.

"Did you hear what I said?" Her hand slipped off the dash on a curve of road and came dangerously close to gelding him. In a lightning fast move, he diverted her thrust and may have shrieked like a little girl.

"Pardon me?" she said. "I didn't quite catch that."

Damned woman. It was clear to him now. By the time they arrived at the *Circle B,* she wanted him screaming his head off and out of control. Then she'd pull the ace out of her sleeve, her bullet wound and surgery, and boo-hoo-hoo to Charley Bradshaw about how he'd mistreated her on the drive. Did she really expect her old man to go ballistic and fire his sorry ass? Well, good luck with that. He'd protect Billie with his life, but he wouldn't put up with another minute of her bull roar.

One hand on the wheel, he dialled Bradshaw's cell phone and waited for him to pick up. "It's Reece."

"What's up? Are you heading home with my daughter?"

"On our way. Question—do you mind if Billie sits in back instead of riding up front with me? I have a bed back there. She'll be comfortable, with the added protection of a steel cage."

"Rocket!" The timbre of Charley's voice abruptly changed. "Are you talking about tossing my little gal into a dog crate?"

"Maybe."

"She giving you trouble?"

"You could say that."

He let out an uproarious laugh. "I don't mind telling you, the fruit didn't fall far from the tree when I sired that little hellion. No sireee. Put me on speakerphone."

Reece punched the button and flashed Billie an eat-dirt-and-die grin. She glared, looking like she wanted to singe his sorry hide with a branding iron. "Daddy's on the line."

"Great." She tossed her mane of blond-streaked curls, covered the bandage on the side of her head with a flick of her fingers, and stuck her straight little nose in the air. "Dad, I..."

"Now you listen and listen good, darlin'. Reece has my permission to drag you home any way he sees fit, and I don't care if it's strapped to his hood like a hunting trophy. So, behave yourself, ya hear?"

"But he..."

"I'll see you when you get here. Have a good trip." Bradshaw hung up.

Billie sat stone-faced beside Reece, obviously smarting from her father's lack of sympathy. Her silence bothered him a little until the sting of his split lip, bruised stomach, and aching guy parts reminded him of the cheap shots she'd taken at his expense. Still, she had been through a lot, seemed shocky, and trapped somewhere between mutiny and mistrust.

"I wasn't the one who tracked you down from the hospital. Your father did, and only because he loves you."

She stared out the side window as if it held the secrets to the galaxy. "That's a laugh. He didn't show this much interest in me before I was shot." She turned in his direction, her expression curious. "How did he find me?"

"We both had a hunch you'd bolt and run, since you never really reacted to me being your bodyguard." He ran a finger over her delicate wrist and played with her watch strap. "Remember when your dad came to the hospital and gave you this snaffle-bit watch? It does double duty as a tracking device. I followed you on an app from my iPhone when you took off in the taxi."

"Men and their gadgets." She crossed her arms over her chest and blew a wisp of hair out of her eyes. "I might have known."

"Your father worries about you." Reece slowed for the exit to a secondary road and headed across country. The blacktop would take them through Hereford and on to the ranch. "You shouldn't hold it against him, considering someone tried to kill you."

"You're both overreacting," she said, her voice barely a whisper. "Tell me, how much is dear old Dad paying you to humiliate me?"

"Not one red cent. It's true, he sent for me when you were shot, but I wouldn't take the money he offered. I'm here because I want to be. I'm staying until we catch the creep who's after you."

When they reached Forest Valley, the closest mid-sized town, Reece considered taking a short break at the local coffee shop. A glance at Billie dozing beside him and the getup she wore, he opted for the drive-thru window instead. Sipping his coffee, he tucked a bottled water for her in a drink holder, pulled out on Main Street again, and headed east on the highway.

A little farther out and the local butcher shop triggered a painful memory; he was twelve-years-old and helping his drunken old man haul a deer carcass to the back door for dressing and packaging. His father had later traded the meat for a couple cases of cheap whiskey. Reece had snared a few rabbits that winter, but game had been scarce. So was food on the table, especially after his mother headed south with a passing trucker. She never returned, not that he blamed her. Life as Dad's punching bag had killed the marriage.

He was seventeen when he'd found his old man crushed beneath the wheels of a tractor. The sheriff said he'd been drunk, fallen out, and run over himself. By this time, his father's death had added more weight to the load, and Reece had built a chip on his shoulder a country-mile wide. When Charley Bradshaw heard the news, he brought him to the *Circle B* to live, and Reece had repaid him by being a mean-tempered jerk. Hell, he'd betrayed everyone's trust...especially Billie's.

He understood now that Charley had done his best to help him grow into a man. In those days, Reece figured he'd topped the chart of native sons most likely to end up in jail, or worse. Hell, he owed the man big time. The least he could do now was keep Billie safe. And keep his hands off her.

Plastic-wrapped round bales of hay sat in the fields skirting the highway. The new mown scent haunted him with memories of driving the baler on the ranch. Lunch breaks in the shade of an old maple tree, the taste of thick ham sandwiches with mustard, and sweet-tart lemonade Billie rode out to him on horseback.

Their stolen kisses had led him to take advantage of her trusting vulnerability. Small wonder she hated his guts now—after the pregnancy he'd caused and the miscarriage she'd suffered without him. He needed to talk to her about those things, but now wasn't the time, not until she was one hundred percent healed. She had enough to deal with, without him dredging up painful memories.

He turned onto a gravel road that intersected the entrance to the ranch, hooked a left, and pulled to a stop at the top of the drive. The old homestead looked the same. He guessed it hadn't changed much in over a hundred years or more. She was a proud old gal, chinked log walls faded to gray. Overhanging porches skirted the main house along three sides, a slanted tin roof reflecting the sun's rays in hues of blue that matched the flowerbeds below. Treed windbreaks and wide open spaces surrounded the ranch house and outbuildings as far as the distant mountains.

Horses gathered in the pasture to his right, their whinnies a familiar and welcoming sound. Reece lowered the windows. They broke into a gallop as soon as he touched the gas pedal, easily beating the SUV down the long drive to the house. He chuckled, imagining they smelled Billie curled up beside him on the passenger seat. They were welcoming her home.

Nudging her awake, he watched her stretch like a cat, push open the door, and drop to the ground, her feet flying toward the gate and her beloved horses the instant she laid eyes on them. Panic gripped him. He grabbed the assault rifle from behind the seat and moved to surround her with his bulk as she passed through the fence.

A sparkle in the distance caught his gaze in an instant. Zeroing in on it with the rifle scope, he scanned the terrain for another flash of light. Uneasiness gripped him. Ten seconds. Twenty seconds. Nothing. Still, someone was out there.

Does the bastard want another shot at Billie?

Chapter 2

Alex Banyan dropped and rolled, spitting out dirt as he crashed to a sobering halt beneath a lofty white pine. Winded, he sucked air like a bellows and waited for the rifle retort that never came. *Hell!* He'd almost messed himself when Reece Morgan's gaze locked on him through the scope. As if he'd known he was there. Not possible.

Unless...

Uneasiness coiled his spine like a two-headed cobra. The rumors about Morgan's sixth sense, the same military whispers that said he was deadly—trained to kill in ways that made scumbags slither under rocks—also claimed he had the ability to sense events almost before they happened.

Okay, it sounded like a lot of woo-woo bull crap to him. Still, the next time he had a bead on Morgan, he'd have a C15 sniper rifle bolted under his scope for insurance. He wouldn't rest easy until he blew the man's head off.

It couldn't happen soon enough as far as Banyan was concerned. Too bad Foley had other ideas. He wanted to toy with the prick first, make him pay for what he'd done to them in Iraq, and no one argued with Foley. The guy was several bricks shy of a full load—dangerous as hell.

A few months ago, Morgan had been an unknown. A *ghost* passing through their location with his Special Ops buddies. What were the odds he'd hear something go down and piece the whole fucking operation together?

The bastard had nailed them good, cost them millions in revenue when they had to shut down and cover their tracks. And he'd pissed off their boss, Marcus, which was freaking unhealthy for Banyan's continued state of good health unless he helped fix the problem. Hell, going to jail would be a cakewalk compared to what Marcus would do to him and Foley if they didn't eliminate the threat and resume operations. Banyan knew it was a sure bet he'd be gutted and staked out on the dessert when he returned to Iraq if that didn't happen. Good thing they had a plan.

Yeah, hurting that gal was a real stroke of genius, the only way to get Morgan back home where they could nail his ass without interference. They had him where they wanted him now. Off kilter and worried about his little rodeo queen, with no idea he was the primary target. They would use that to their advantage. Make the woman's life a living hell. And fuck with Morgan until they were ready to kill him.

AT FIVE A.M., BILLIE showered and washed her hair as best she could, considering the bandage. Morning broke early when you worked on a ranch. For her, this was the best time of day. Finger combing the curling strands, she thought about using the hair dryer, maybe adding some makeup and a spritz of perfume. A yellow sundress beckoned from its hanger in the closet. She reached for it and stopped dead, shaking her head in dismay.

Having Reese underfoot brought out her inner bitch. He'd slashed her heart like a notch on his bedpost when she'd been sixteen. Then he'd walked away—more like galloped away—without so much as a "see ya" tossed over his shoulder. Now, she wanted to make him drool to even the score. Make him pay for abandoning her. Maybe stomp on his heart with both feet.

Wow, am I mature, or what?

While she wasn't vain, she knew she'd been blessed with better than average looks. Heck, she could have almost any man she wanted. So, why did her stupid heart still bleed for Rocket? What a pain in her "I-don't-need-anyone" butt. One glance at him in the hospital the other day and her heart had gone bong, bong, bong like a grandfather clock. She had even imagined him in her shower this morning, thought she'd smelled him.

Idiot. What the heck am I doing?

Shaking her head, Billie threw on ratty jeans and a denim shirt instead of the dress, grabbed some paperwork, and headed for breakfast. Clunking down the first few steps in her work boots, she rode the banister the rest of the way to keep things quiet and the others in their beds. Sliding to a stop at the bottom, she peeked around the corner and grinned. The dining room was empty.

Daybreak emerged through the east windows, the sun's early rays sparkling off crystal and silverware. Placemats and napkins were in tones of blue on the polished oak table, the fine bone china a creamy white. An Aubusson carpet in cream and taupe with slashes of blue graced the hardwood floor.

Twelve matching chairs surrounded the refectory table, their cushions upholstered in the same blues and hints of gray that matched the window panels. A long sideboard beneath the bank of windows was the only other furniture in the room.

Billie ran a proprietary finger along the edge of the table. She loved this room. It reminded her of her mother, a Manhattan debutante who had chucked it all to marry her cowboy. *Smart woman*, she thought. Mom and Dad had been madly in love, right up to the day she died in a rodeo accident when Billie was twelve. Her mom had stood on the scaffolding over the bullpens when the boards gave way. Billie hadn't been there to witness the tragedy, but she relived it, time and time again, in her worst nightmares.

And thank God for Dottie, who had moved in with them afterward to run the household and ease the heartbreak of a young girl losing her mother.

Billie sighed, remembered sitting in this room with her mom on stormy days, watching trees bend in the wind and lightning flash, ranch hands scrambling alongside her dad to get the livestock safely tucked away. She and Mom would drink hot chocolate and eat cookies while the men worked, giggling like schoolgirls.

Because of her mother and the decorating skills she'd learned from her, the house was a blend of country chic and understated elegance, with a set of moose antlers thrown in on the wall of Dad's study. The only room he was allowed to decorate himself, the rest of the house fell under Billie's domain.

Tossing her work folder to the table, she followed the delicious aromas to the sideboard, lifting lids off silver serving trays to see what Dottie had prepared for breakfast this morning. Yum, crêpes nestled in buttery syrup, a side of bacon, fruit, yogurt, cereal, and a thermos jug of coffee. The woman would fatten her up yet after the hospital fodder she'd been unable to choke down. She'd lost a few pounds, for sure.

Filling a plate and grabbing a mug, she almost ran to her chair and couldn't wait to dig in, until Reece straddled the seat next to hers and leaned in close. He smelled like sin—clean and seductive—sporting a dark green T-shirt that matched the color of his eyes. His chestnut hair hung straight and loose behind his ears, his face clean shaven. A burn started low in her belly like a pulse. Billie shook her head and went back to her meal, kept her eyes focused away from his lean, hard body.

Fork poised in midair for a bite of heaven, she jumped when his hand swept her chin and brought her face around. Her gaze met the little bump on his nose, a rodeo accident, refusing to land on his unsettling gaze.

"Easy, peaches. The bandage behind your ear is wet. We'll take care of it after breakfast."

"I can do it myself. And stop calling me *peaches*." Tongue-tied and feeling awkward, she flipped open the folder resting beside her elbow and tried to ignore him. "Will you quit staring at me and go count cattle or something? I'll call you when I'm ready to brush my teeth, in case Jack the Ripper's lurking in my bathroom."

"He's not. I already checked." Moving to the sideboard and the coffee jug, his grin flashed in the sunlight. "I thought LeAnne Rimes was singing *Can't Fight the Moonlight* in the shower earlier. Until you belted out the chorus through the steam—slightly off key."

What? She hadn't imagined his spicy scent. "You Peeping Tom, son of a bitch. Stay out of the bathroom when I'm in it!"

"Hey, I'm a gentleman. I turned my back. Nice slide down the banister, though."

Billie could feel heat suffusing her cheeks. He rocked on his heels, watched her, and smirked. Until he caught sight of someone behind her and his expression sobered. Meanwhile, she had smoke pouring out her ears.

"Mornin' darlin.'" Her father brushed a kiss across the top of her head. Claiming his usual seat at the head of the table, he spread the newspaper in front of him and attacked the livestock section.

Dottie shot from the kitchen doing her roadrunner routine as soon as her father's backside hit the chair; wisps of gray hair falling from her topknot, a peasant skirt skimming her sturdy legs. She nodded at all of them while she brought her dad a steaming cup of coffee, fruit and a bowl of cereal. Billie couldn't help but smile. Even Pike didn't get waited on by his sister. Only her father got the complete service deal. Billie suspected Dottie was halfway in love with him.

"How's my little girl today? I heard your mouth revving at top speed a minute ago."

"But, Dad—"

"I don't want to hear it." Her father glanced up from the paper, his dark gaze zeroing in on the folder resting against her plate. He read the label. His moustache twitched, bushy blond eyebrows rising in disbelief. "Beau Valley Productions? Holy hell for breakfast, Billie. Is that what I think it is?"

Crap, she was in for it now. Protecting him from the truth wouldn't be easy. "It is. I signed the contract before my...accident. It slipped my mind until this morning, and I thought I should fill you in on the details."

"Damn it all." His face reddened to match the color of his shirt. "We agreed to talk about this before making a decision."

"What's going on, Billie?" Reece's gaze pinned her from where he leaned against the credenza. In two long strides, he was beside her and managed to scoop up the folder. Jaw tight, he flipped through its contents and slapped it back on the table. Papers scattered in every direction, most of them to the floor. "You leased the ranch out to a movie company?"

"I did. I'm the ranch manager, so I didn't need anyone's permission. Anyway, it's only for six weeks, and they won't have access to all the acreage. The house is off-limits, as well as some of the outbuildings." Billie glared at both men, feeling protective of her project. She also felt guilty for not consulting her dad. "What's done is done. Get over it. Both of you."

Her father stared her down. "Billie, how could you do this without asking me?"

Her heart ached for pulling the rug out from under him, but she held her ground. "You would've nixed the idea. It's a great deal and I didn't want to pass it up. The movie is the pilot for a weekly television show. If the pilot sells, we can look forward to God knows how many years of renting out our pastures to the film company."

"Wrong answer." Her father shoved his newspaper aside and banged the table with a fist. "I don't want a bunch of strangers hanging about, especially after what happened to you."

"Read the contract, Dad, and you'll change your mind. The Brahma bulls and other livestock we breed for the rodeo circuit will be in the film, because our yearly rodeo will be part of the footage. It's all in the fine print. And what happened to me has nothing to do with this."

"Cancel it, Billie." Reece said.

"Hold on a second. Hear me out before you jump down my throat. The studio is paying us big money. We can't afford to pass this up."

"Cancel it," Reece said again, looking grim. "A good lawyer can get you out of the deal. It's too risky. The date on the contract coincides with the attack on you. That's one hell of a coincidence."

It surprised her to feel a little tug in her chest over Reece's concern. But, she wouldn't back down. "Can't do it, Rocket. We're a big operation with bills to pay. The money gives us a fat cushion over expenses."

Reece ignored her and went to work on her father. "Charley, this is not part of our deal. I can't protect Billie like this. It's going to take some serious manpower to check out the film crew and provide security for the rodeo she's talking about. I'll need a list of names of everyone involved. How much time do we have?"

"How the hell would I know? Billie, when are the movie people coming?"

Oops. "Their trailers roll through our gates at sunrise tomorrow."

"For the love of Mike!" Her father tossed his paper in the wastebasket, headed for the door, and hollered for Pike to join him. "Do what you have to, Rocket. Bring in extra people if you need to. But, protect my pig-headed, little girl."

REECE WAITED UNTIL Charley stormed out of the room before bringing his eyes back to Billie. She looked pale and upset. Going up against her father was tough. So, why did she do it?

He clamped her shoulder and turned her in the chair. "I want the real story, and don't leave anything out."

"Are you deaf? I just told you." She tossed her napkin and would have stomped off if he hadn't snagged her wrist, holding her in place.

"You're lying, Billie. I know shit when I hear it. And right now, you're up to your pretty little ears in it. Why did you sign the contract?"

She rubbed her hands down her face and shook her head as if to clear it. "All right...I'll tell you, but you have to keep it to yourself."

"I'm listening."

"I did it because of Satan. Our prize quarter horse is sterile. Dad doesn't know, and I don't want him to find out yet. He's already upset about someone shooting at me. This'll kill him."

"I seriously doubt it. Your father can hold his own, maybe better than you can." Reece grabbed the water jug and poured them each a glass. "What does Satan have to do with leasing out your land?"

"Since we can't use him for breeding anymore, we have to replace him, which will cost thousands of dollars." Billie took a sip from her glass, and Reece noticed her hand shaking. She was a bundle of nerves. "The backbone of this ranch is our ability to produce champions. If we can't use Satan for stud, we have a big hole to fill."

"I understand, but can't you buy semen from other champions?"

"Oh, sure, Reece, and pay about five thousand bucks each time. We've never used Satan to cover all our mares because of bloodlines. It's one thing to buy semen once in a while, and another to pay stud fees on a continuous basis."

"You leased your land to make enough money to buy another champion?" Reece shook his head and leaned back in his chair. "It's a dangerous move, Billie, when we don't know who holds a grudge against you. Letting this film crew on your property is a mistake. Call them and cancel."

Billie gained her feet and headed to the door. "We're done here. I have things to do."

"Hey, where are you going? We haven't finished talking yet."

"Well, I'm finished listening."

She tore up the stairs with him right behind her, along the hallway and into her bedroom. As the door slammed in his face, Reece bounced it back. Billie bounced too, landed on the bed and let out a shriek. The satin bedspread rolled beside her with a life of its own. Something was under there.

"Freaking hell!" Reece hauled her off the bed and palmed his Glock. The ripples in the bedspread changed direction, slithered away from the sound of their voices toward the pillows. "Get out of here. Close the door behind you."

"Wait!" Billie grappled for his gun arm and pointed it to the floor. "Don't shoot until we know what it is. Maybe we can save it."

"Billie, back off. It's a goddamn snake. I'm not taking any chances on it getting loose in the house."

From the time she was a kid, Reece knew she wouldn't hurt a fly. She was all about protecting nature and saving the world. Some things never changed.

"Please, Reece."

Shaking his head, he shook her hand off his arm, raised the gun again, and took aim.

Billie whimpered beside him and touched his back. *Ah, hell, was she crying?* "Don't d-do this. At least t-try to capture it first."

"Capture what?" Charley and Pike must have heard Billie's scream. They cleared the doorway with rifles in their hands. "Crap on a croissant! What is that?"

Reece motioned them to silence with a hand. "It's a snake, Charley, one your daughter is hell bent on saving. Find me something to put it in before it reaches the headboard."

Pike propped his rifle in the corner, dumped a wicker laundry basket with a hinged lid, and tossed it to him. "Here, use this."

"Thanks. Now jack up the air conditioning full blast and get ready at the end of the bed." Sweat broke out along Reece's brow. He had no idea what type of snake it was, but it was a sure bet it wasn't the friendly kind. "Billie, move out to the hallway."

"Not on your life." She ran to the windows instead, ripped down the curtains, and grabbed the curtain rods, passing one to him and clutching the other tight to her chest.

He could see fear in her eyes, but she was determined to stand her ground and rescue the bloody snake. Reece didn't have time to argue as he watched it thrash under the covers. "We only get one chance at this, and I don't want you poking at him. I'm hoping the air conditioning will slow him down."

He handed his Glock to Charley, grip first, and then eased up to the headboard. "Okay, Pike, start sliding the bedspread in your direction. Do it slowly. Charley, you know what to do if the snake coils to strike. And no loud noises."

"You don't need to tell us twice," Pike whispered, easing the cover down the bed, an inch at a time. "Just be glad my sister's downstairs doing the dishes. She'd scream her head off if she saw this thing."

"Slim chance of that." Dottie appeared between Charley and Pike, a gleam in her eye and a wicked blade in her hand. Reece figured the kitchen held a battery of weapons, and Dottie knew how to use them. "Let me slice and dice it first. Then I'll scream."

"Are you crazy, woman? Here, stow the knife and hold this for me." Charley handed her his rifle, moved to the far side of the bed, and took aim with the Glock. "I'll shoot the bastard if it makes a wrong move."

Reece nodded, locked eyes with Billie for about a nanosecond. "Stand clear. The curtain rod's for protection only. Back away from the bed."

She did, and he got the basket in position between his feet. Once he saw the snake's head, he knew they were in trouble. This was a mean bastard, a desert-dwelling species that gave Spec Ops guys full-blown nightmares. Snakes liked to crawl into things like, oh say, sleeping bags, when they got cold. It had happened to people he'd known, and few lived to tell the tale.

Where the hell did this one come from? A desert horned viper, fat bodied with a triangular head and thick scales, it was approximately three feet long, a beige body with brown spots down its back. He'd known a guy who needed his finger amputated after being bitten by one. Reece planned to keep all his digits today.

"Keep pulling the covers off him, Pike," he whispered. "Don't make any sudden moves."

When the viper was fully exposed on the bed, Reece flipped him with the curtain rod, whipped him through the air, and dropped him head-first into the basket in one quick motion. He slammed the lid home and breathed a sigh of relief.

"Better get some ranch hands in here to do a room-to-room sweep. Let's make sure we don't have any more unwelcome guests."

"Right." Pike nodded at Charley and hustled for the stairs. "I'll bring a dog inside to help with the search while I'm at it."

Charley handed Reece his Glock and grabbed the rifle back from Dottie. "I'll start up here while Pike gets the other guys."

Reece nodded and turned to Dottie. "Call Animal Control. Tell them we have a highly venomous species of viper and they should come prepared. Let's hope there's a zoo with a reptile enclosure equipped to house him."

While Reece twisted a piece of curtain rod to secure the lid on the wicker basket, Billie came up beside him and squeezed his arm. "Thanks, Reece. I mean it."

"Don't bother thanking me until I catch the animal who brought you the snake. This isn't over."

He hit speed dial on his cell phone the instant Billie was out of earshot.

Chapter 3

B anyan drove the last vehicle in the convoy, heading north across *Circle B* land; the film site was only a few miles up the road. A chameleon infiltrating the kill zone, he savored the role. But he hated the piece of crap truck he drove. Give him a Humvee any day of the week, or at least something with a decent suspension, something able to withstand the rocky terrain and ease up on the bounce. And for God's sake, let him find a radio station that played hard rock, not Hicksville twang. With a string of curses slicing the air, he felt the truck jerk and pull hard to the left. He'd blown a bloody tire. *Way to stay invisible, idiot.*

No time to bitch and moan because death knocked at his door within another few heartbeats. Winchester primed in the crook of an arm, Reece 'Rocket' Morgan pulled alongside him and stepped out of a fancy SUV. He crossed to the pickup with a hand on the lever action of the 30-30 rifle and pounded on the roof. "Open up."

Sweat trickled down Banyan's spine. What were the chances he'd come face-to-face with the son of a bitch and have nowhere to hide? *Shit.* He palmed the Sig in his jacket pocket and sprang the door.

Morgan leaned in, his gaze searching the cab, his expression unreadable. No hint of 'You're one of the grunts I fubared in Iraq. What are you doing here?'

"What's your name?"

"L-Lakefield. John Lakefield."

"Okay. You need help with the tire, John?"

He shook his head. "I'm good."

The zing of adrenaline slowed down a notch and allowed Banyan's stomach to settle. The bastard didn't recognize him. Thank Christ and all the saints. He'd grown his hair out from the buzz cut and added a moustache since being on temporary leave from the military. Still, would Morgan smell the fear slicking his skin? "Won't take me long to put the spare on. I'll catch up with the others."

Morgan still eyeballed him, stared as if Banyan was an open book and he had photographic memory. Was recall revving his motor? Putting two and two together about his accident-prone rodeo queen? Banyan stared right back. *Want to fry my brains, you son-of-a-bitch? Let's see who has the fastest draw.* His hand tightened on the Sig's grip.

Easing his stance a fraction, Morgan hitched his chin toward the back of the pickup. "You can't change the tire with the generator on the flatbed. The load's too heavy."

"Right." Banyan released his gun and fumbled for the cell phone on the seat. "I'll call for the wrecker. It's up ahead."

"Want me to stick around?"

"Nah, but thanks. The wrecker guys can change the tire. It's their job on location shoots anyway."

"Good enough." Morgan closed the door, tapped the roof again, climbed back in the SUV, and floored it.

Banyan watched his dust trail while making his call to the grease monkeys. He blew out a breath, had the sudden urge to urinate. Hopped out of the truck to relieve himself and zipped up again. Then he laughed out loud. He had worried for nothing. Morgan's sixth sense was total bullshit.

His next call was to Foley. Cell reception was clear and strong—four bars—the call connecting right away.

"Where the hell are you? You should be here by now."

Grumpy pain in the ass. Banyan climbed back in the cab and slammed the door. "Got a blowout and ran into a friend of ours on the trail. No worries; he doesn't have a clue."

Foley's pissed-off voice rumbled against his ear. "If you really believe that, you have shit for brains. Morgan won't show his hand until he's good and ready."

What, are you deaf? "Listen to what I'm telling you, Foley. He didn't make the connection."

"He could still put it together." Foley paused on the other end of the line. "We keep after the woman to throw him off our trail. Stick to the script and stay out of Morgan's way."

Yeah, sure, keep after the woman. Foley was all about terrorizing women—about hurting and defiling them. Banyan had seen him in action before. Wished he hadn't. Figured this part of the vendetta had nothing to do with the plan and everything to do with Foley getting his rocks off. Screw him and his sick appetites. Billie Bradshaw was in for a world of hurt when Foley got a hold of her. And Morgan would go ballistic, which would make him harder to kill.

Marcus, their former Colonel, wanted the creep dead, plain and simple. He was with the Foreign Service now, a heavy hitter with secrets to bury and lots of mercenary muscle on speed dial. He'd kill them all if they didn't get this job done soon.

You want the woman, Foley? Be my guest. But, don't mess up the end game. Or I'll kill Morgan myself. Then I'll deal with you.

REECE PULLED UP IN the ranch's driveway beside a rental car in time to see his buddy, Theo Sauvage, angle out from behind the wheel. He must have boogied getting there because he'd made good time. Theo was a sniper by training and a lawyer by profession—the perfect partner for Reece on this op, because he wasn't there to dispense legal advice.

Reece hopped out of the SUV. They knuckle tapped and punched each other on the arm by way of greeting. "How'd you get here so fast?"

"Hawke flew me out last night, after your phone call." Theo scowled. "We have to stop meeting like this. What's the goddamn world coming to when women are used as human targets?"

"It's SNAFU insane, buddy." The acronym for 'situation normal, all fucked up' said it all, as far as Reece was concerned. His last get together with Theo and other members of his reserve Special Ops squad had been little over a week ago, when a Las Vegas cartel had tried to kill Theo's little pixie. "How is she doing?"

"Why don't you ask me yourself, Rocket?" Melena Salera, a tiny blond dynamo with cobalt-blue eyes, rounded the other side of the rental and charged at him in her size five running shoes. In the blink of an eye, she wrapped herself around him and tugged on his neck to plant a big wet kiss on his cheek. When he heard Theo's warning growl, Reece flat-out laughed. Mel had Theo wrapped around her little finger. He was safe, for now.

"Hey! What about me?" Well, hell, he recognized that voice, too—Breeana McGill. The green-eyed redhead was out of the backseat and moving fast. Theo's brother would kick his ass if he saw his fiancée leap into his arms. Good thing Sully was otherwise occupied, wrapping up a homicide case in Montreal.

Reece's friendship with the two women ran deep; he'd helped rescue Breeana and her son from a serial killer in the not-so-distant past as well. The next thing he knew, he was up to his armpits in sisterly attention, the women squeezing the life out of him.

"Ease up, ladies." Billie bolted from the house and down the stairs. A woman on a mission, she made a beeline for him and his fan club. Curiosity and something else snapped in her gaze. Jealousy, maybe?

If that's what it was, he sure liked the idea. Yeah, it suited him just fine. Bree and Melena were dynamite women. A guy seriously needed an ophthalmologist if he didn't see *that* picture. But Billie was the one who captivated him. Her willowy frame knocked him out, holding his attention in her simple hip-hugging jeans and a clingy T-shirt.

She headed their way in dirt-eating strides, blond-streaked mane blowing in the breeze. Billie the Hammer—he decided the label fit her to a T. Her gaze locked on the women in his arms like a missile zeroing in on its target.

Her eyes flashed a darker shade of gray in the sunlight, a scowl riding a crease in her brow. She strode toward them with both fists clenched. Not good. Reece tucked the two women behind him, just in case. "Hold up, peaches."

He swore he could smell her wildflower scent, and yeah, he waxed poetic in his head while he watched her. Like an auctioneer with a horse on the block in a sale barn—buy this quarter horse, the perfect barrel racer. Great teeth, high set of withers and a well-built neck. And man, she moves like a thunderbolt.

Okay, time to diffuse the situation before someone gets hurt here, namely me. "Billie? I want you to meet some friends of mine."

Reece blurted out the introductions to stop her in her tracks, stressing the Spec Ops angle and how Theo and the women were here to *help* her. She halted, seemed to rethink her fighter's stance. Swallowed her anger and shook hands with the new arrivals while he sucked in a healthy helping of relief.

"I apologize. When I saw you gals crawling all over Rocket, I thought you were with the film crew. Was about to pound the pudding out of you and send you on your way."

"Uh-huh." Bree shot Melena a loaded glance and the two women grinned like Cheshire cats. "You would have laid us out flat because we flirted with Reece?"

"Not exactly. I would have hogtied and dragged you through the dirt behind my horse all the way back to the movie set. This part of the ranch is off limits to buckle bunnies. I can't have my bodyguard...um, preoccupied...while he's on the job."

Well, who would've guessed she had a jealous streak? Nah, it's not possible. Still, Reece couldn't help the grin inching across his face.

Billie glared at him, shook her head, and reversed direction, heading back into the house arm-in-arm with Mel and Breeana. "You guys grab the gear while I show the ladies to their rooms."

"Yes ma'am." Theo whistled, popped the trunk, and handed out two-wheeled carry-ons. They must belong to the women, since Theo had his usual go bag slung over a shoulder. "Whoa, man, you have your work cut out for you protecting that filly. Talk about headstrong."

"Billy's not usually like this. She's just scared. *And,* she hates my guts, which doesn't help."

"Cough it up, Rocket." Theo closed the trunk, turned, and planted his backside against it. Folding his arms across his chest, his gaze narrowed. "Why would she hate you if she hasn't laid eyes on you in years? What did you do?"

Sure, like I'd tell anyone what a punk butthole I was in those days. "Not your concern, man, so stay out of it."

"Message received." His friend held his gaze a moment longer. "I don't know how women do all that soul-baring stuff anyway."

Reece focused on the horses in the paddock, their tails swishing at flies. "I'll let you know if I feel the sudden urge to spill my guts."

"I won't hold my breath." Theo bent to pick up a couple of silver cases. Reece knew they contained the tools of his trade. The guys on the team always prepared for the worst and prayed for the best. "You want to fill me in on the reason why I'm here? Tell me what we're up against?"

"You want the short answer? I think someone wants Billie dead. She was shot a week ago and a venomous snake landed in her bed yesterday. That's when I called Sully."

Theo left the cases where they were, plucked at a strand of wheat edging the driveway instead, checked it and tucked it in his mouth. "Hold up, man. What do you mean—you *think* someone wants to kill her. Don't you already know? It sounds pretty cut and dried to me."

"Yeah, maybe. But let me ask you a question first."

"Go for it."

Sure, and his buddy would think he'd come unglued once he got the words out. They sounded bad enough in his head. "Could you make that shot, Theo? Could you shoot someone on the outside of her skull? Furrow the load along the bone without damaging an ear or penetrating the brain?"

Theo looked at him sideways a second, seemed to realize he'd asked the question for a damn good reason. "Under crosswind conditions? I wouldn't take the chance. It's a hell of a risk."

"That's what I figured."

"Now, under optimal conditions? No wind and a reasonable range to target? I could make the shot exactly as you've described."

A sick feeling roiled in the pit of Reece's stomach. "We need to check the weather report for that day to know all the variables. If we know the circumstances and the exact ground location, we might be able to figure out if Billie's survival was more than just a fluke."

Theo eyed him and something sparked in his gaze. "What are we talking about here, Reece? That's one hell of a shot, especially to just injure Billie. Clipping her wing would've been easier and safer."

"Yeah, but *this* shot guaranteed I'd ride to the rescue, even though Billie and I parted ways ten years ago."

Theo dropped his go bag in the dirt, reached in his shirt pocket for a cigar, and lit up. "You think a mercenary hired on to wound Billie and *not* kill her? Make it look like an accidental miss by not burying a bullet in her brain?"

Reece kicked up gravel with the toe of a boot, inhaled a whiff of Theo's smoke. "When Billie was shot in the head and somehow survived, it made sense I'd show up to protect her. An injury like that indicates attempted murder. And I'd have to make bloody sure it didn't happen again.

"However, a shot in the arm could have been an accident, considering the entire population of Hereford probably has firearms and may hunt out of season—at least they did when I lived here. Whoever's behind this couldn't be sure I'd come back under those circumstances."

Theo tossed the cigar and ground it out under his boot. "You said over the phone the snake in her bed was a desert horned viper."

"Right—a snake indigenous to Iraq and Afghanistan."

"Fuck."

"Exactly. My gut says a terrorist cell is behind this, considering we've reduced their ranks in covert ops and pissed off a lot of tangos. It's easy enough to smuggle a snake into the country when you have the right connections."

"Which makes sense if Billie is the bait—a decoy to smoke you out. God knows, we've all got contracts out on our heads. And you're the original Nomad Man. What's your address in Canada now? A post office box?"

"That's about it. I contract with the military for most of my engineering projects when I'm not with the team, and I float around from base to base when I'm living in country. If someone's trying to get to me, they'll come after her again, Theo. Or if I'm wrong, Billie's been the target all along."

"Bloody hell," Theo growled. "I brought Melena to man the computers and do backgrounds on the movie crew. Then Breeana tagged along, insisted on examining the sterile quarter horse and running some tests. Thinks she can help. I thought you and I could handle the rough stuff. Protect Billie and keep everyone else out of danger. But, with both you and Billie potentially in the crosshairs, we're going to need backup."

"I'll make some calls." Reece knew they needed more members of his Spec Ops squad front and center. Otherwise, something would get missed. And if things got missed, someone could die.

BILLIE SCANNED THE sunroom for landmines before ushering in her guests. The space was airy and tidy, smelled of roses climbing the trellises outside the screens. Wicker furniture was hazard-free; the area rugs vacuumed beneath her feet. Oh, joy, the accent pillows were where they belonged on the sectional sofa and club chairs, not scrunched against the walls behind them. She wondered for a second if she was in the wrong house. Where were the dirty socks, barn boots, hoof picks emptied from jeans' pockets, and newspapers she'd seen in this room an hour ago?

No doubt about it, the men in her family were total slobs when it came to tidying up after themselves. The barns might be neat as a pin, but the house resembled Tornado Alley once Dad and Pike blew through.

She knew what had happened, primo detective that she was. The cleaning fairy—aka Dottie—must have seen their guests arrive and whipped around with dusters on her feet and extra-large garbage bags strapped to her waist to dispose of the fallout. Billie didn't imagine Melena or Bree would give a hoot, but, *she* cared. The "neat freak" gene she'd inherited from her mother was out in full force. And boy, it was a doozy—nothing like scrubbing floors in the middle of the night to help a girl sleep. Just a tad obsessive compulsive? No joke.

Crap. She couldn't haul out the mop and pail as long as Rocket was under her roof, and things weren't getting done quite to her satisfaction. Not that she cared if she disturbed his beauty sleep. Still, the less he knew about her character flaws, the better.

No wonder she felt so damn frustrated. She needed to burn off energy, especially after being hospitalized. Yep, her edginess had nothing to do with Reece—pain in the butt, to die for, bodyguard that he was. Blame it on OCD and get over it.

Breeana and Mel kicked off their shoes, flopped on the couch, and tucked their legs under themselves, patting the seat between them for Billie to touch down. Oh boy, she wasn't exactly "girl power" material. Hoped this wasn't a prelude to sharing confidences and having pajama parties late into the night.

She heard wheels creaking down the hallway and knew she was saved by the tea wagon. Dottie rolled it through the door overflowing with coffee, pinwheel sandwiches, and home baked peanut butter squares. "You ladies must be hungry after the long flight from Montreal and drive from the airport. Help yourselves."

They dug right in and made her housekeeper smile. Billie knew Dottie enjoyed having female company. Well, except for Lorelei Calhoun, an itsy bitsy blond who seemed to have her sights set on Billie's dad. But these gals gave Dottie a chance to stretch her culinary talents past the monthly poker night's chili and beer. Her own lips twitched as Dottie beelined back to the kitchen with a spring in her step.

Billie, on the other hand, wasn't quite sure how she felt about this newfound friendship. She was used to being around livestock and ranchers, not city girls who got mani/pedis. One glance at her own hands and she hid them in her jeans pockets. *Ick.*

After a few minutes, Breeana removed a splint from her right hand and worked it with a squishy ball. Open. Close. Open. Close.

"Wow!" Melena cheered her on, set down her cup to give her two thumbs up. "You have more mobility than you did a week ago."

"I'm pretty happy about it." Breeana grinned, waggled her fingers. "The therapist says another week or two and I'll be able to perform surgery again. Dad never complains, but he's doing double duty at the veterinary clinic. And I miss my critters."

Billie's gaze shifted to the raw scar at Melena's hairline and faded bruises on her face. Whoa. Another banged up lady. Whatever had happened to these women, it had been very, very bad. And by the sounds of it, Reece had played a part in rescuing both of them. Small wonder the bond between him and these two ran deep.

In a purely platonic way, of course.

Anything else and she would have gone kamikaze on them this morning. She shifted in her seat, peeved at herself for almost throttling Breeana and Mel because they'd glued themselves to Rocket. Not her proudest moment.

She could see Breeana wore an emerald the size of a rock on her engagement finger. And Melena was with Theo. She'd made the connection when Reece introduced them. Had a feeling Theo would have restrained her if she'd made a move against Mel.

So, there was nothing to worry about. Not that she cared about Reece anyway. At least, not anymore. If another woman wanted him, she could have him. *Just not under my roof.*

Speaking of the big dope, she heard footsteps thumping overhead. Reece and Theo were up there, the timbre of their voices dialled down several notches. Billie wished she could be a fly on the wall, would love to hear their conversation. They were probably hatching plans Reece didn't want her to know about.

Breeana reattached the splint, leaning forward to drop her squishy ball back in her handbag on the floor. She rummaged around some more and brought out a scary looking needle in a sterile package and some glass vials with rubber stoppers at the ends. Shoving everything in a thermal fanny pack, she clipped it around her waist. "Do you mind showing me Satan? I'd like to take some blood samples and send them to a friend in Calgary for analysis. He's sending a courier to pick them up this afternoon."

"No problem." Billie hopped to her feet and slipped back into her boots. "But, why not use the lab my vet uses to perform the tests? It'll save time. Just don't mark Satan's name on the vials."

"Look, Billie, you're probably right, but this is the way Reece wants it. Since someone shot you and sent you a pet viper, he doesn't want to chance information leaking to the wrong people."

"Did Reece actually say that? Why didn't he talk to me first?"

Breeana splayed her hands, palms up. "He told Sully on the phone after the snake incident yesterday, said we needed to be careful testing the horse."

Rocket was right. Although, someone would have to boil her in oil before she'd admit it to him. She shrugged, moved to the screen door at the end of the room, and opened it. "We can go out this way."

They trooped down the stairs past the barbeque and picnic area, cut across the back lawn planted with blue spruce, and followed along the white fencing to the double doors of the horse barn. Once they were inside, Billie shut the doors again. They walked along the long, wide corridor leading to the opposite end of the barn that opened to the paddock and fields beyond.

"I'm impressed." Breeana moseyed behind her, stopping to peer over the half gates into a couple of stalls. "The place is pristine; fresh straw in the boxes and no manure anywhere. Heck, it even smells nice in here."

"Yes, well, you didn't see it this morning before we let the horses out for the day. It didn't look or smell too great then." Billie laughed, ducked into the feed room to scoop up a can of oats. "Still, I'll tell Dad you gave it your seal of approval."

Satan stood out in the paddock, his long neck extended through the guard rails to munch grass along the outside perimeter. He heard her call his name, the sound of oats swishing in the can, and he trotted right over. Slipping a halter over his head, Billie finger combed his mane while he snaffled the oats. "Come on, I want you to meet some friends of mine."

"He's a Palomino, isn't he?" Melena proffered a tentative hand filled with carrot sticks she must have snagged from the tea wagon. She grinned as Satan's velvety muzzle tickled her palm. Dwarfed by his massive size, she looked like a little china doll standing beside him. "He's so beautiful."

"Yes, he is. I just wish I knew what happened to him." Billie tugged on the halter and clucked, leading Satan down the corridor to a roomy stall. She inclined her head for the women to follow and closed the half door after them. She hooked Satan to cross leads extending from the walls. "He's all yours, Bree. Though I don't know what you hope to find."

"Let me run some tests to eliminate bacterial infections, viruses, possible medication abuse, and a few other things. Then, we'll talk."

"Okay."

Breeana slid her hand along Satan's rump and gave him a pat. Then she slipped on rubber gloves, dabbed his neck with an alcohol swab, ripped open the package, and deftly worked the needle into place. Satan barely gave her a glance; he was so intent on Melena and the carrots.

Sliding a glass vial into the plunger apparatus, Bree began extracting blood. When the vial was full, she capped it, replaced it with another vial, and repeated the process. A couple more vials and she was done. She recapped the needle and stuck it in her fanny pack along with the blood samples.

"I guess you haven't had your vet examine Satan yet, because you don't want your father to know he's sterile. I hope I can find some answers for you."

"Thanks. I'd like to know what we're dealing with before I have that conversation with—"

In a sudden movement, Satan jerked his head and snorted, pulling back with enough force to snap both lead lines.

"Whoa, big guy." Melena attempted to grab his halter. "The mean lady with the needle is all done."

Billie shifted her out of the way. "Stay back. Something's got him spooked."

"What? You think it's the needle?" Breeana glanced nervously at the stallion. Sweat slicked his coat. His eyes rolled white in their sockets. His chest heaved.

And Billie knew.

Only one thing in the world terrified Satan. Bad to the Bone.

A Brahma bull without a soul, he was a rodeo favourite, a bull rider's ball buster. And a killer to boot. He'd tossed a man a few years ago, then trampled him to death in a mad rage.

Damn, she had begged her father to put him down that day. But, the "accidental death" ruling had given him a reprieve. After all, bull riding was dangerous. Participants got trampled and gored. Shit happened...don't blame the dumb animal.

All true, except she'd seen the monster up close and personal—in kill mode. Knew how much he'd enjoyed sweeping in from behind to toss the rodeo clown in the air. He'd gored him clean through. Then he'd bucked around the arena with the body attached to his horns as if he'd won a prize. And after tossing him, he'd crushed him with his hooves.

If she'd had a gun in her hand that day, she would have shot him.

Bad to the Bone was in the barn with them now. Billie could smell him. His heavy footfalls in the corridor vibrated through the soles of her boots. He bellowed. He'd caught their scent, his movements getting closer and closer.

Billie raced to the door and slammed the upper half shut. Wham! A set of horns splintered the panel. She jumped out of the way. The bull reared on its haunches, front hooves flailing inside the stall. He crashed the opening, pawing and snorting, smashing more boards to smithereens.

Satan screamed, raced around his pen in circles, forcing the women to the center of the stall to avoid his hooves. Billie waited for Satan's next pass and lunged for Bree and Melena. She dragged them free, threw them up against the wall separating this stall from the next.

"Climb fast! We're out of here!"

She didn't need to tell them twice. Melena scrambled up like a monkey, was already over the top, and dropping to the other side. Bree climbed one-handed, struggling, her injured hand making it impossible. Billie grabbed her by the waistband and heaved her the last few feet, tossing her over the edge.

Bad to the Bone made it inside the stall a second later and slammed into the wall with Billie still hanging from it. She flew backward, hit on the ground hard. A jumble of broken planks landed on top of her. Pinned, she couldn't move, could hardly suck in air. God help her. She hoped Bree and Melena had made it out of the next stall. Otherwise, they'd be lying under the wreckage with her. Adrenaline seized with a vengeance. Her whole body shook. Or was it terror causing the tremors? Either way, she was finished. Nothing left to do but die an agonizing death.

Two thousand pounds of evil loomed a few feet away. He sized her up. Watched her squirm. Billie recognized the gleam in his eye. Knew he would kill her.

Thank God, Satan managed to skirt around him and get out. She heard his hooves galloping toward the paddock and freedom. Knew he would jump the fence if necessary. Three out of four of them had escaped. Not too bad.

Billie whooshed in a shaky breath and slowly reached out. Her hand found a board, and as she pulled it toward her, her grip tight, her heart hammering, she looked straight at Bad. *Come on, you wild-eyed son of a bitch. Come and get me.*

Chapter 4

"Don't. Move." Reece couldn't see her, but he knew where Billie lay on the other side of the wall. He prayed she heard him and didn't budge an inch. Theo crouched behind her in the rubble somewhere. Rifle primed, the bull locked in his sights, a FUBARed mission if there ever was one—because there was no way Theo could take the shot.

The best case scenario if he did? The bull charged and Theo shot him. But the animal would collapse right on top of Billie, crushing her. And that's *if* the beast dropped when the bullet entered his brain.

Worst case? The Brahma kept on coming for another few seconds after the hit, had time to trample or gore Billie to death, and maybe even Theo. Either way, Billie would die. And Melena? She would have Reece's head on a spike if anything happened to her man. So, yeah, they were SNAFUed times two. Bad to the Bone held all the cards in this high stakes game of life or death.

Pure bullshit as far as Reece was concerned, with no master plan in the Spec Ops manual to override the end result. He gritted his teeth and focused, knew it was up to him to give everyone a "happily-ever-after" to this nightmare scenario. Especially Billie.

Pumped on adrenaline, Reece eased through the opening where the stall doors used to hang; they were nothing but matchsticks now. At the left side of the stall, Billie and the bull only had eyes for each other and didn't see him join their party. They focused deep;

Billie sprawled in the straw while Satan loomed over her like a death warrant.

Oh. My. God. Billie lay about a foot away from the beast's hooves. It was only a matter of time before he got bored with the stare down and finished her off.

Reece's heart lurched in his chest. One hoof plant and Billie would become an obituary notice. *No damn way.* He cared about her. Probably loved her, knew in his gut he'd carried a torch for her since they were teenagers. Did it make him less of a man to admit Billie touched his heart and soul in ways no one else could? That it killed him to know how much he'd hurt her in the past? Hell, if another man had done what he'd done, he would have buried the guy six feet deep. But, if there was the slightest chance she'd forgive him, he intended to spend time making things right. Starting now.

A movement behind Billie caught Reece's attention. He risked an upward glance. Theo signalled him from the shadows of the next stall, brought a hand across his neck in a slashing motion. Okay, bad news confirmed on all fronts; his sniper buddy couldn't make the save. It was time for a kick ass—make that a kick bull—diversion.

Scooping a can off the ground, Reece heaved it at the Brahma. It bounced off the bull's hip bone and hit the far wall, tumbling to the floor with a thud. *Bingo*, it got bully's attention away from his quarry. Bad to the Bone snorted, turned his head, and eyed him with an evil glint. "That's it, you crazy-ass fucker. Focus on me."

Reece fired off a tranquilizer dart next, barely grazing the Brahma's rump, an intentional near miss so the bull wouldn't stagger and fall. It held for about a nanosecond in the skin then dropped to the ground. Mission accomplished. It angered the bull but didn't incapacitate him. The bastard charged him like a battering ram. *Thank you, Jesus.*

Boards flew in every direction as the devil plowed his way out of the stall. In a flash, they were racing up the corridor to the paddock.

Reece was out in front by a hair with Bad to the Bone thundering on his heels like a frigging freight train. He smelled the animal's stench. Felt the heat of its breath on his back. With no time to mess around, Reece reloaded the breech of the pistol on the fly, locked in another 2cc syringe with a 1-1/2 inch needle. *Good to go.*

His shitkickers gained the dirt in the paddock just as a horn slashed his left shoulder. *Shit.* It hurt like stink. Reece twisted right, dove fast, and face planted in a cloud of dust. The bull thundered by an inch off his six. Reece jackknifed to his feet and fired off the round. A direct hit. *Yippee ki-yay.*

While the bull regrouped, the stallion roared past him at break neck speed, apparently not interested in hanging in the paddock with the beast from hell. The horse soared over the fence and moved off to the next pasture in the blink of an eye. *Good for him.* Reece wished he could join him. They'd all had enough excitement for one day.

He bent at the waist and sucked in air while Bad to the Bone tossed his head and bellowed, trying to shake off the dart embedded in his neck. The dart held, for all the good it did. The Brahma didn't even wobble as he circled the enclosure to have another go at him.

"What in the hell does it take to bring this son-of-a-bitch down?"

There'd been no time to check for a higher dose when he'd grabbed the tranquilizer gun and darts from the cabinet in the tack room of the horse barn. After working at the ranch as a teen, he'd known where the guns and medical supplies were kept. He had also remembered helping to immobilize horses when necessary. 2cc's was the average dose they'd used on a horse, depending on the animal's weight and sensitivity to the drug. And that was the only dosage strength he'd found in the cupboard.

Based on the Brahma's weight, he estimated 4cc's of acepromazine was the maximum dose he could safely use on a two thousand pound animal. Which meant he needed another 2cc's buried in Bad to the Bone's hide. After all, he didn't want to kill the brute—just send him to a happy place. Make Bad docile as a lamb while keeping himself on the ground, not sailing through the air on the twister's horns while doing it.

He watched the bull while reloading for the third time. Saw Bad's glance focus away from him to the doors leading back to the barn. Wonderful. Reece didn't have to look to know Theo had Billie moving along the corridor to the opposite doors of the barn, a bull's eye on their backs for the beast tracking their movements from the paddock. Reece lunged for the doors, slid them closed on their tracks. Steadied himself in front of them in a firing stance, and waited.

The Brahma was nothing if not persistent. He'd give the animal that. Bad to the Bone pawed the ground, revved up the gears, and let loose with a head on charge. Thirty feet out, he lost his footing and stumbled, pitched forward enough for Reece to deliver the last ampoule of medication between the shoulder blades.

He dodged to the side when the bull hit. Bad seemed to be woozy now, less interested in killing him, and more inclined to scratch against the barn doors. *Hoo-rah!*

The gates opened at the far end of the paddock, and Charley drove a truck through. Another few minutes and his ranch hands had Bad to the Bone loaded in back and heading off to the bull barn. Charley jogged his way.

Reece's throat was parched, felt drier than dust. Seeing Billie lying in the stall with the bull looming over her had punched his adrenaline straight through the roof. Hell, his hands trembled thinking about it. Good thing the shakes had been slow settling in. Otherwise, he might have missed with the dart gun in the barn. And Billie would be dead. He popped a stick of gum to moisten his lips. "Is she okay?"

"She's fine, Rocket. I owe you big time." The older man tore at Reece's sleeve and checked his injured shoulder. "You're gonna need some stitches. And a tetanus shot to boot."

"Nah, I'm up to date on my shots." Reece winced when Charley prodded. He shook loose from his grip, rotated his shoulder, and then wished he hadn't. The pain was top drawer now that the excitement was over. "Make sure Theo stays with the women until I get back. I don't want any of them out in the open, especially your daughter."

"You can tell him yourself on the way to the hospital." Charley nodded over Reece's shoulder. "They're piled in the Cayenne over there waiting for you. Meanwhile, I'm going to find out who let that bull loose in the horse barn."

"No, you won't. Stay out of it, Charley. I've got enough to worry about without the bastard gunning for Billie taking a shot at you, too." Because if someone really wanted revenge on Billie, what better way to destroy her than killing her father?

BILLIE TOOK THE FASTEST shower in history. Actually, she turned on the jets and didn't shower at all, even if Bad to the Bone had almost peed on her. She should be out there helping Reece right now, and *would* be, if Theo hadn't shanghaied her with Bree and Melena acting as his minions. Hell for breakfast, they'd dragged her back to the house when she should be out in the paddock helping Reece with the bull.

Jerks. She could hear them talking about her down in the kitchen, probably thought she was out of her mind. Too bad. She didn't care because someone needed to help Reece. And that someone was her. *Talk all you want, but you won't stop me.*

Sneaking out the bathroom side door to the guest room, Billie grabbed the rifle off Rocket's bed and loaded it with the 30-30 bullets she found in his go bag. She'd shoot the bull herself. Back in the bathroom again, she moved through the steam and crossed to the far side that led into her own bedroom. Shoving her feet into runners, she slung the rifle over her shoulder by its strap. Climbed out the window and slid down the drain pipe. *Halleluiah!*

She stayed low as she rounded the side of the house, kept to the trees before making a break for the barn. *Damn!* Theo caught her before she even reached the drive. He wrestled the Winchester from her grip. Mel and Breeana latched onto her arm like fungus when she drew back a fist to slug him. "Let me go. Reece needs me!"

"Easy." Theo planted himself in front of her and stared her down. "He can handle things without you. He wants you inside where you're safe."

"I don't give a damn what he wants. The bull's a man eater. It'll kill him!"

"Quit fussing, Billie." Pike hustled toward her from the barn, his lopsided gait slowing him down. "Rocket's got the bull contained, but he's gonna need a doctor for a scrape he got. I'd take him to the clinic, but me and the boys gotta catch the stallion before he runs clear to the highway. The bull spooked Satan real bad."

"Go after him, Pike. I'll take care of Reece." Billie glared at the other blockheads surrounding her. "Get out of my way."

"We'll *all* go. The keys are in the Turbo." Theo palmed his Glock and herded them toward the vehicle. He popped the hatch, unloaded the Winchester, and pocketed the rounds, locking it on the rifle mount while the rest of them climbed inside.

The SUV roared up to the paddock with Theo riding shotgun and Melena behind the wheel. And Reece strode in their direction looking better than fine. Billie breathed easier, the tight knots loosening inside her chest, the sight of him revving her hormones in all four gears. It must be relief kicking in. She refused to believe it was anything else, because he annoyed her.

Men. Trust them to need a doctor with the slightest ache or pain. He sure didn't look injured to her, and they'd be sitting in the clinic for hours, for heaven's sake. She willed her nerves to settle as he passed through the gate, ready to give him a piece of her mind for frightening her so badly. She'd been willing to go another round with Bad to the Bone to rescue him. And she was scared to death of Bad. Narrowing her gaze, she hopped out of the SUV.

Blood soaking Reece's black Tee caught the sunlight the minute he turned to secure the gate latch. *Sweet, sweet Lord.* That was no scratch, no matter what Pike had said. Billie rushed up to him, tugged him the rest of the way to the SUV by his belt, and pushed him inside. She unhooked the first aid kit from behind the seat and got to work. "Strip to the waist, Reece."

"No. I'm fine with my shirt on." He leaned in and whispered in her ear. "But just so you know, if we were alone right now, I'd take it *all* off." His emerald gaze locked on her mouth, did a lazy slide over her breasts and hips before meeting her eyes. "Hell, I'd even throw in a little pole action off the drain pipe if that's what you wanted."

Billie heated up clear to her arctic wasteland with that little speech. Jeez Louise, she fought to control the inferno roaring south through her body. She refused to thaw anytime soon—at least, not with him. Besides, she knew Reece too well. This was his way to throw her off stride, make her quit worrying about him. "Rocket, you're injured. Quit being such a jerk. Get your rear in gear and lose the shirt before I have Theo rip it off."

"Whoa, since you put it that way." He took her at her word and removed the shirt with Breeana's help.

Hot fudge sundae with a cherry on top, Billie couldn't help but admire the view. She'd tried hard over the years to forget Reece was a stunning male specimen. Sinew corded his biceps and triceps, his chest heavily muscled. A delicious six-pack rippled his stomach and an arrow of dark hair pointed south from there to the equipment below his waistband. If anything, Rocket's physique had improved, which hardly seemed possible. Except for the scars mapping his back—lots of them. *Shrapnel, maybe?* Her heart sank. What had happened to the boy along his journey to becoming this man? She swallowed hard, wanted to touch him, and—

Melena hit the gas pedal. Billie jerked, snapping out of her reverie, and the bottle of alcohol bobbled in her hand. The liquid sloshed, then splashed into Reece's open wound. Damn, her hands wouldn't stop shaking.

He jumped in the seat. "Ow! Peaches. Take it easy."

"Hold on. I can fix this." She blew the hair out of her eyes and pushed her patient forward between the front seats, determined to help him in spite of her trembling fingers. "I'll have you patched up in no time."

The stupid bull had gored the back of his shoulder. Billie felt nauseous just looking at the hole. How much pressure should she apply to stop the bleeding? She refused to ask. Wouldn't want Rocket thinking she was a novice in urgent situations. Grabbing a fistful of gauze pads, she knelt on her seat and put her entire body weight behind the force of her hands. Yes, it seemed to work fine. The blood flow slowed, even though Reece grunted like a rutting moose.

"That's a little too much pressure, girlfriend. Here, let me help you." Breeana took over while Billie rolled a dressing to the rough circumference of a quarter. Then she swept Bree's hands aside and drilled it into the circular wound, a few false starts before she got it right. When she was satisfied, she finished off by slapping another dressing over the top and some tape on to hold everything in place.

Huh? Reece didn't move from his slumped over position. *Has he passed out from blood loss?*

"All done, Reece." Billie poked him in the ribs. Still, he stayed where he was.

She glanced over at Breeana, who looked slightly green around the gills. She was a vet, wasn't she? For heaven's sake, the sight of blood shouldn't send her into a tailspin. "Has he fainted?"

Bree peeked at their patient's face and shook her head. "Ah, no. He'll survive. I think."

"Then, what's the problem?"

"Um—"

Reece planted his palms on the console and pushed himself against the backrest between them. Were those tears in his eyes? His shoulders tensed and pain etched his face. Panic took hold of Billie in an instant. Had she done something wrong? She grabbed his hand and squeezed hard. "Say something, Rocket. Please. Is everything all right?"

He levelled his gaze at her while he sucked in a breath. Then a corner of his mouth lifted in a lopsided grin. "You did great, Billie. Hell, I feel better already."

"THE GAUZE IS PACKED in there too tight." The ER doctor poked around with forceps while Reece clenched his jaw.

"Yeah, but it really cut down on the blood loss when I needed it, Doc."

Billie hovered over the physician's shoulder like a mother hen with her chick. "Quit jabbing at him until you freeze the wound. Can't you see you're hurting him?"

"It'd hurt a lot less if you held my hand." In spite of the discomfort, Reece struggled to hide the smile forming when Billie clutched his big mitt in her icy ones. Hell, the injury was little more than a hangnail. He'd survived a lot worse. But he was on top of the heap having her fuss over him. Her reaction gave him hope he could turn her around, maybe win her back. He'd been damn stupid to let her slip through his fingers the first time. It wouldn't happen again, not if he could help it.

After the freezing, stitching, and bandaging, Reece suffered the indignity of having his pants dropped for a shot of antibiotics, and yeah, another tetanus booster. He noticed Billie didn't turn away from *those* procedures like she had for the needlework. Shortly, he was on his feet and heading for freedom with Billie tucked under one of his arms for support. Okay, so he didn't need her propping him up, but he just couldn't help himself. 'Cuz if Billie wanted to play nurse, he'd keep his head in *that* game until she got tired of the job. It felt too damn good having her beside him.

Theo stood outside the door with a mile-wide grin on his face. "He's too much weight for you, Billie. I'll take him from here."

"I've got him, Theo." Billie tightened her grip around Reece's waist. And just like that, he left ground zero and shot straight into hard-on territory. He inhaled her earthy, field flower scent. His senses stirred at memories long buried while his guy parts got with the program behind his zipper fly. Not the time or the place. Still, he refused to let her go.

Reece shot Theo a 'back off' glare. "Keep a lookout for the bad guys while Billie helps me to the car."

His teammate did an eye roll but held his tongue, sort of. He gathered up Mel and Breeana and headed out of the hospital. "Never knew you were such a cream puff, Morgan."

After changing into a fresh T-shirt from an overnight bag he kept in the Turbo, Reece eased into the shotgun seat while Theo cranked the engine. They rolled in silence, Theo watching the road while he scanned the rearview for any signs of trouble. After hitting the access road to the ranch, he nudged his buddy. "Head over to the movie location. I want to pick up the crew roster so Melena can start running those background checks."

"What?" Theo snorted. "You sure you don't want Billie to tuck you in bed? That's quite the injury you've got there."

"Zip it," Reece hissed, easing sideways in the seat to catch Billie's eye in back. "Stay with me while we're at the shoot. I might need you if I start to feel faint."

Sure, like she'd believe that load of crap. Translation—he wouldn't risk letting her out of his sight for one damn minute. But she seemed uncertain whether or not to trust him, and after a moment of hesitation, nodded her head. "You don't have to worry. I won't leave you alone."

"Thanks, peaches." *Fucking A.* Reaching in the glove box, Reece hauled out his Glock and clipped it to his waistband. If he needed to boogey, he'd be good and ready.

BANYAN LOWERED THE gas can to the ground and flipped the switch on the generator. It roared to life accompanied by a round of cheers. God forbid the movie moguls lost electricity for a couple minutes. Time was money. *Yada, yada, yada.* He'd been reamed out good for not checking fuel levels on the power units this morning.

Assholes. He'd had something better to do, like paying off the wranglers who had hauled the bull to the horse barn once rodeo girl was inside. Plus, he'd wanted a front row seat for the action. Mission accomplished on both fronts. The guys had blended right in at the ranch, done the job, and disappeared again like smoke. And judging by the screams coming from inside the barn, Miss Billie Bradshaw was nothing more than a bloody memory now.

Yeah, Banyan was pleased as shit with his handiwork. Foley would keep his head in the kill zone now and his eyes on Reece Morgan, instead of wanting inside the woman's pants all the time. Of course, if Foley ever found out he'd killed her, Banyan would end up dead, too. The prick wanted to play with her more than he cared about icing Mr. Spec Ops. It all boiled down to priorities in the end, and Foley's had needed a major readjustment.

"John Lakefield?"

Holy hell! He knew that voice. The bastard stood somewhere behind him. There's no way he'd tracked him back from the barn. He had been too careful. Wiping his fingers on a rag to stall for time, Banyan slowly grabbed the tools of his trade—an open can of diesel fuel in one hand and a lighter tucked in the other. Worst case scenario? He would give Morgan's pants a soak and toss the flame. Then he'd run like hell. It might not kill his enemy, but it would put one hell of a crimp in his stride, that's for sure.

Banyan swivelled where he stood and almost swallowed his tongue. Morgan wasn't alone. One of his army buddies stood next to him; meaty arms folded across their chests, side arms clipped to their belts, the two of them loomed like giant redwoods. Well shit, so much for Foley's plan of separating Morgan from the rest of his squad. At least one of them had shown. And Banyan could forget his own play with the gas can. They'd shoot him where he stood before he could make a move on either of them.

And wouldn't you know? Billie Bradshaw was sandwiched between them with the other two babes he'd seen at the barn. Freaking hell, the goddamn bull had struck out.

"Yeah, that's me." Banyan knew he was out of ideas. With zero possibility to disappear, he swallowed hard, willing some spit to loosen his tongue. He nodded at Morgan. "Oh, hey, thanks for stopping when I got the flat this morning. Can I help you with something?"

Morgan tipped his chin. "First off, you can screw the cap back on the fuel tank you're carrying. Then you can point us in the direction of the office. The movie set's spread out like a trailer park."

"I know. It's pretty confusing. I get lost myself sometimes." Banyan played it cool, even though his hand shook when he secured the cap on the diesel fuel. He caught the flash of a blue uniform, called out to the head of security making his rounds. "Spinelli, we have visitors. You want to show these folks where the office is?"

Spinelli nodded, paused long enough to hitch his pants over a basketball stomach. Found out Billie and her crew were from the ranch and headed them the hell away from him. Still, Morgan drilled him with a glare as he moved off with the guard. *Fuck.* Heading in the opposite direction and away from the noise of the generator, Banyan hauled out his cell phone and dialled.

Morgan needed to take a dirt nap. Quick.

Chapter 5

"Sweet pea, your hair looks like it was caught in a wind tunnel!"

What? The little man with the falsetto voice sashayed toward Billie from the trailer marked "wardrobe" with both hands glued to his hips. She didn't recognize him, was almost certain they'd never met before. Her gaze cut to the doublewide he'd exited. A luxury coach, it was white with black trim. A patio set—complete with a frilly black umbrella and four matching chairs—sat to the side, a tray of sodas and snacks on its tabletop. A couple of people lounged in the chairs.

He wore tight, red-satin pants with a white organza shirt and a red silk tie looped around his neck. Muted eye liner, penciled brows, and glossy lips telegraphed his disapproval from ten feet away. Diamond studded earlobes winking in the sun, his Louis Vuittons barely touched down before rolling to a stop in front of her.

"And you simply *must* get to wardrobe after you see the hair stylist. Heavens to Betsy, girl, those rags you're wearing will never do. You look like you've been wrestling pigs." *How embarrassing.* To make matters worse, his perfume was expensive, while she smelled like the stable floor.

"Well, I..." Billie knew she was a mess after going head to head with Bad to the Bone. She should have showered and changed before showing her face anywhere, let alone on a movie set. But trim her hooves, she hadn't expected to come face-to-face with a fashionista, not in the middle of Nowhere-ville. She wished the ground would give way and swallow her up.

"You poor thing. Who did this to you? Wait, don't tell me. Let me guess. It was Yvonne. I swear the girl doesn't have a brain in her bupkus. She forgot to check the call sheet, or she'd know we're not mucking out stalls on the shoots today." His eyes left her jeans and tank top to glare at her hair again. "Eeew, did you glop on the gel this morning?"

"No, and you probably don't want to go there." It could be bull drool.

Stylist guy ignored her words and outstretched a hand to the rats nest on top of her head. Reece snagged his arm and held fast. "The lady's not with the film crew. Don't touch."

"Well, halloo gorgeous!"

Bingo! Just like that Billie was out of the hot seat. And Reece was in it—up to his gorgeous green eyeballs.

The little guy greeted Rocket like he was the answer to all his prayers. Batted his baby blues, placed a hand over his heart, and drummed pitty-pat with scarlet-tipped nails. "I just *love* a take charge kind of man. What's your name, stud muffin?"

Yes! How priceless is this? For the first time in their history, Reece was at a total loss for words. Shut down tighter than a nun in a synagogue. He tossed her a glance that screamed "deer caught in the headlights...help me." She didn't bite, wouldn't if her life depended on it. This was way too much fun.

It took a second or two for him to realize she wouldn't jump in and save him. For his mouth to form actual syllables around his tongue, "The name's Reece."

A complete sentence...not too shabby.

"Maurice," the fashionista said, extending a manicured hand. Rocket took the bait, reached out, and got more than he bargained for. Maurice launched into his arms like a ground-to-air missile locked on its target, wrapped him in a hug, and then latched onto his caboose. "Woo-woo, buns of steel in butt gloving denim. Sweet cheeks, there's nothing like a cowboy strutting his stuff to get my blood pumping. And *boy,* is it a-pumping!"

Reece grasped Maurice by the shoulders, peeled him off the front of his shirt, and backed him up a few paces. Early thirties and obviously gay, Billie thought the man was scrumptious. Face it, anyone who rendered Rocket speechless scored big points in her books. Add in Melena and Bree with their mouths hanging open, and the entertainment value was worth its weight in gold.

Theo moseyed over to break up the clinch, and Billie got a bad, bad feeling. Theo's particular skills might not include mediation or bowing out gracefully, although she knew he wouldn't hurt Maurice. Still, this could get interesting. She hauled out her cell phone and started filming. *Lights. Camera. Action.*

"*Stud muffin,* aren't we supposed to be heading over to the office?" Wrapping an arm around Reece's neck, Theo planted a smooch on his cheek and shot Maurice a smirk. "It's nothing personal, honey, but I don't share. So back the hell up and stay away from my poopsie."

Stud muffin? Poopsie? Had Theo completely lost his mind? Billie knew the fists were going to fly the second Reece got him away from the movie set. And she had the reason on film, a one of a kind Kodak moment with lots of blackmail value in case she ever needed it. Oh joy. She panned the cell phone's lens over Breeana and Mel again, with their eyes bugging out of their heads. She had witnesses.

Not that she wanted Reece and Theo to use each other as punching bags. Heck, she'd belt out the chorus of "We Are Family" herself and have everyone join hands if she thought it might make a difference. But it wouldn't. So, might as well gear up for a second trip to the emergency room and keep the film rolling.

And presto, magico, wonder of wonders? Wasn't Rocket doing wonderfully for a guy worried about fainting a half hour ago? His fists were primed and ready to fly in Theo's direction with the next innuendo. Billie stopped filming and stepped in front of Maurice; time to rescue the little guy before he got caught in the fireworks.

Hmm, he wasn't as short as she'd originally thought, had an inch or two over her own five-seven. Maybe he only looked like a small person because of the two gorillas lurking in the background. "Maurice, we'd love to stay and chat, but we really must find the office. Can you aim us in the right direction?"

He took her elbow, pranced around the corner, and pointed. "It's just over there, sweetie. It's the trailer with the adorable little blue and white striped awning."

"Thank you." Billie held out her hand. "It was nice to meet you, and I apologize for my friends. I promise to leave them at home the next time I visit. My name's Billie."

"You do that, Billie, because those guys are waaay too scary for me. Heavens, I thought Reece's lover would resort to fisticuffs to get me out of the picture. How was *I* to know they were a couple?"

Maurice let out a shiver as he shook her hand. He ventured another peek over her shoulder at the two knot heads still staring each other down. "But if you or the other ladies ever want to stop by, I can do wonderful makeovers for all of you. Makeup, hair, the works. Oh, I hope you'll come see me again soon. We could have so much fun! Why don't we plan a tea party?"

"Yes, let's do that. My girlfriends and I will bring little finger sandwiches and cakes. My housekeeper bakes like a dream." While a makeover wasn't exactly what Billie had in mind, a gabfest with Maurice about the film crew could help figure out if there were bad guys in the mix—in a fraction of the time it would take Melena to do those background checks.

Yep, one way or another, she would find a way to come back here without Frick and Frack in tow.

AN HOUR LATER, THEY sat out on the porch waiting for Dottie to prepare lunch. Reece watched the swirl of dust kick from the tires of an old VW van heading down the drive. "On The Road Again," by Willie Nelson blared out the windows. Reece eyed Billie who sat in a swing at the far end of the porch. "You recognize that vehicle?"

"Sure. It's old Gus the courier guy. He must be coming to pick up Satan's blood work."

Reece watched the driver as the van angled to a stop a few feet away. "Either my eyes are going, or old Gus has found the fountain of youth."

"What'cha thinking?" Theo murmured, uncoiling his big frame from the seat next to his by the stairs. He touched the Glock at his waist.

"I'm thinking here comes an assassin in old Gus's messenger mobile."

The mutt was dressed sixties retro, right down to the faded cannabis T-shirt, PEACE symbol dangling around his neck, baggie shorts, and sandals. Hair hung past his shoulders in a greasy tangle. But, he was pumped with muscle, in his early twenties, and built like a power house. Not old Gus material.

Fuck. Beatnik boy was out of the van in a heartbeat. He leapt the porch rail and planted himself in front of Billie before Reece had time to blink.

"Hi, Ms. B..."

Reece tackled him from behind, swung him around, and tossed him at Theo, who locked him in a full nelson. And yeah, the kid looked stunned, which caused Reece to doubt his commando routine and the hippie's intentions. He frisked him anyway and came up clean.

"Let him go. Right now!" Billie was out of the swing and pounding on his back with her fists. Breeana and Mel dragged her to the other end of the porch while she shouted, "I know him. He's Gus's son, Skeeter. Leave him alone!"

Hookay, so Billie knew the guy, but he shouldn't have charged at her the way he had. Skeeter needed to learn some manners.

Short of laying him out flat—which Reece didn't want to do because he was still steamed about the *poopsie* incident and itching to get it on with his fists—there was nothing like the threat of rubber gloves to tear messenger hippie's eyes away from Billie.

"Skeeter, you know what a body cavity search is?" Reece could see Theo crack a grin behind retro guy's thick neck.

"Uh, yeah, but I don't have any weapons or nuthin'. And I wasn't gonna hurt Ms. Bradshaw. So you don't need to do that."

Reece moved in close and snapped the gloves out of his back pocket. Tugging them on, he wiggled his fingers in front of Skeeter's face. "Here's the thing. You come at Ms. Bradshaw again...the way you did just now, and I'll be forced to use these. Understood?"

"Hey man, I can dig it."

"Right answer. I want you to get your butt back in that flower-powered ride and head for the lab with the blood samples, tout de suite, as in get good and gone."

"Say no more. I'm on my way." Skeeter tried to get out of Theo's hold, but it wasn't happening. "Um, can you get your buddy to, like, give me my head back, so I can move?"

"Sure, as long as we understand each other." Reece nodded at Theo, who released retro boy with a nudge.

"Dude, I'm outta here!"

Skeeter thundered for the van. Breeana ran behind him with the goods for the lab. "Wait, you forgot the package. And make sure you drive it straight there. Don't make any stops along the way."

"You got it, little dudette." He scrawled out a receipt and handed it to her through the open window. "So long as rubber glove man ain't riding with the delivery."

The van swerved up the drive while Theo watched through binoculars. "Jeez, I'm getting hungry. How about you?"

"Yeah, I could eat a little something too," Reece said.

Dottie, bless her heart, came out on the porch with their lunch on a tea wagon and set it up on the picnic table.

"A body cavity search. Really? You're unbelievable!" Billie chose a smoked meat sandwich off the platter and smooshed it onto her plate. "I can't believe you did that."

Man, she looked and smelled amazing; he could imagine mist holding the scent of spring after a long winter. She'd showered before lunch and slipped on a yellow sundress that made his mouth water. No great surprise courier guy had leapt the porch rail when he'd seen her sitting there.

Reece wanted to do some leaping of his own, like straight across the table and into her arms. She was something, all right. He was always checking her out when she wasn't looking. Hell, even the pucker marring her brow and anger sparking her eyes sang to him.

I'm losing it, waxing poetic about her puckered brow. No wonder Theo called me a cream puff.

Billie's scowl deepened. "Where did you get the gloves you pulled out of your back pocket? We use those for birthing foals."

Reece couldn't help the grin inching up his face. "Guess that explains why they came up to my armpits to cover my sleeves then. Pike gave them to me on one of my tours through the barns. You never know when rubber gloves will come in handy."

"Oh, for Pete's sake! I thought Skeeter would have a coronary when you whipped those out."

Theo's laugh rumbled from the far end of the table. "No worries, Billie. I saw him light up a roach to calm his nerves when he pulled out of the drive. A couple inhales on that thing, and he'll be feeling mellow again in no time flat."

"Why do I bother talking to either of you when you're both *crazy*?" Billie huffed, pouring herself a glass full from the pitcher of iced tea. "You can't go around scaring people like that, Rocket. Once Theo had him in the whatchamacallit hold, the poor guy really believed you were gonna use those gloves."

"Peaches, he charged right at you. What was I supposed to think? I wanted to put the fear of God in him. Next time, he'll think twice before he comes at a woman like an ax murderer."

Reece absently pinged his water glass with the knife in his hand. Whoops, it reminded him of wedding receptions where everyone clinked glasses to get the bride and groom to plant one on each other. He was always the best man and never the groom, thank you very much. He laid the knife down. "The important thing is Skeeter left here with his teeth still in his head. I could have done worse."

"Idiot," she said, but he didn't miss the smile twitching her lips, pure nirvana to his tortured libido.

Theo's cell phone rang. He took the call, five seconds tops, and disconnected. "Sully's on his way with the others. They'll be here tonight. And he's not real happy about the bull incident."

"Darn it, Theo, you shouldn't have told him." A pout tugged at the corners of Breeana's mouth. "You know how he gets. He worries too much about me."

Right, Reece thought. Breeana had nearly been murdered by a serial killer less than a month ago, but Sully shouldn't worry about her? Good luck with that. He knew Theo's brother too well and didn't blame him for burning rubber to the ranch. "Relax, Bree, I called and gave him the bad news, 'cuz we don't keep secrets from each other. We need the other guys here to give us a hand."

"That seems excessive." Billie stood to pile the dirty plates on the tea wagon, then brushed the tablecloth with a little roller thingie. "I don't get it. Why do you need your whole team front and centre just to babysit me?"

"Because you've got a bunch of strangers on your land. And the rodeo is coming up, which will dump thousands more into the mix."

"Thousands more? Where are you getting those numbers? I expect maybe a thousand people all together."

He tapped her hand, halting its motion across the table with the crumb doodad. "You can plan on at least five times that amount because of the movie shoot. And don't forget the rodeo contestants and vendors who will set up camp for the weekend out in your fields. Add in the organizers, maintenance crew, delivery vans, EMTs, parking attendants, *and* the fans—we need tight security. The tighter, the better."

"Holy Mike." Billie tugged her hand out from under his and sank back in her chair. "I had no idea this would cause so many problems for everyone."

"It's not your fault, peaches. Beau Valley Productions is to blame. They've blasted ads for the rodeo all over the media. I imagine they want the stands filled to capacity when they film the rodeo scenes."

"Oh my gosh!"

"Exactly."

"I'm glad you know now." Melena eased forward and plunked her elbows on the table. "We didn't want to tell you this morning, Billie. The radio stations have already started the promos. We heard a couple on the drive from the airport this morning. They're piggybacking on Calgary Stampede popularity, now that the Stampede is over." Her gaze moved from Billie and sharpened on Reece. "And, *you*. Aside from wanting to thump my man, which he'd rightly deserve, you wanna tell us what's in the playbook for the rest of the day?"

Reece flat out laughed and turned to Theo. "You are one lucky S.O.B., you know that? If I wasn't so scared of Melena, I'd punch you one for that kiss earlier. But since she won't let me, why don't you get her online with your law firm so she can start those background checks? Bree, you can give them a hand setting up. Billie and I need to leave for a couple hours."

"Make sure you bring a camera, pal." Theo wasn't fooled. His buddy knew what the game plan was. "We'll need pics, panoramic views in all directions to determine the intent. I'll check the weather reports for that day, looking at wind velocity, that kind of thing."

"I'm way ahead of you." Reece tossed his napkin on the table and pushed back in his chair. "I've added a video riflescope to the M25. It'll work nicely for our walkabout."

"A primo choice. I'm impressed."

Reece knew why Theo approved. The M25 was a sniper rifle, a favourite weapon in their arsenal of "fighting scumbags" surprises. The fact he'd installed video capability was a bonus. He could film the area where Billie was shot while scanning the landscape for bogeys and open fire with deadly accuracy, if all hell broke loose.

His place on the Spec Ops team might be as an explosives expert, but he was no slouch on the firing range. As a civil engineer on his day job, he maintained a high degree of self-preservation skills, particularly as he contracted overseas with the military. Terrorists loved screwing with roads, bridges, or other structures he developed for friendly forces in off-the-grid hellholes.

It'd be a frosty day in hell when he wouldn't plan for FUBARed while praying for best case outcomes. In this instance, Billie's life depended on it. His gut tightened with a healthy dose of adrenaline. He wouldn't let her down.

BILLIE FELT THE SUSPENSION bounce as the SUV scrambled over potholes. She had been along this dirt road so many times she'd lost count and was used to the bumpy ride. *Today is no different,* she told herself. Except she knew she was lying. The other times she hadn't been scared out of her wits. Seeing the location where someone had shot her opened a door to memories better left buried.

"It happened...over...there." Breath wheezing, Billie gulped in air. Her lungs wouldn't expand. She tried again—still not enough oxygen. Her world started to slide toward loop-de-loop territory. Panicked, she fumbled with the window, managed to lower it, and lean her head out.

"Exhale, peaches. You're hyperventilating." Reece braked to a stop beneath a giant oak tree. Shoving his seat back, he unhooked her seatbelt. He didn't waste time arguing the point, just scooped her up and settled her between his thighs. She had the pliancy of a ragdoll and the wherewithal to match.

"Oh God, oh God, oh God!"

"Relax, honey. There's nothing to be afraid of." Branches overhanging with foliage cocooned them inside the SUV. He eased her head down, his arms solid around her. "I've got you. You're okay. Let the blood rush to your head for a minute."

With no other noise to distract her, Billie listened to the wheeze in her lungs as Reece whispered reassurances in her ear. *Why now? Why should seeing this place send me into a freefall?* Of course, she already knew the answer. Horrible images crowded her head and, Lord help her, she couldn't control the shaking, the fear banding her ribs, or the need for oxygen in her useless lungs. She gripped Reece's arms like a lifeline and held on.

"Easy." His breath fanned her cheek as he pulled her back against his chest. Moved a hand to her abdomen and held it there. "I want you to push against my hand every time you suck in air."

"I-I can't—"

"Jesus, Billie. You can. Breathe through your diaphragm, not your chest wall. Shut everything else out and focus on my hand."

She closed her eyes and tried to do as he asked. Not easy when her mind whirligigged with the God-awful truth. She remembered *everything* now. Walking the boundary line. Seeing the gap in the fence and those cut marks on the wire. Knowing it was deliberate. She could see herself dragging a roll of fencing off the tailgate of the pickup. Hear the loud crack from a rifle an instant before the pain hit her head. But, worst of all, she remembered lying helpless in the dirt. Praying someone would find her in time. Believing she would die.

Reece pressed his other hand against the *bam-bam-bam* of her heart. It pounded like a big bass drum and freaked her out, which made the hammering worse. "I c-can't breathe."

"Trust me," he said, cradling her against him, sweeping her hair aside, and nipping at the pulse point on her neck. He gentled and sucked on her skin, sending laser shocks through her body. His hand moved from monitoring her heartbeat to cupping her breast. Startled, Billie inhaled with him, following the movement of his chest against her shoulder blades—drew in his scent, the hint of sandalwood aftershave—and everything changed. The ache in her lungs eased.

Her crippling fear somehow transferred to want, greedy and pulsing for the man touching her...caring for her. She shifted to look in Rocket's eyes. There was no mistake. He was seducing her, and he wanted her to know it.

"Relax, babe." His mouth brushed her temple, his hand still on her breast. "This is what you need right now. The fact I'm enjoying the hell out of touching you really can't be helped. I want you, Billie."

The plain truth was *she* wanted him. After all the years of trying to forget him, she'd come full circle and was right back where she'd started—in the arms of the only man she had ever loved. Reece's hands and lips on her body felt incredibly right. His actions blanketed out the horror, shifting her focus away from the shock of what had happened to the dress bunching around her waist. His ankle hooked over hers and moved her legs apart. His palm inched along her thigh and slipped under the edge of her thong, teasing the sensitive skin there.

She tried stopping him. She really did. It was impossible to do when he controlled her so completely. When she tried to move, he held her back, locking her against him in a firm embrace.

"Mmm, so sweet, Billie. So gawd damn sweet."

His thumb stroked her sensitive pearl while she whimpered in his arms, begging for mercy. Reece held her, caressing her until she totally lost her mind. Then she shattered in his arms. He sighed and lowered her dress, putting on the brakes as he kissed her neck one last time. "The next time I hold you, it won't be in an SUV. You deserve better."

Why had he stopped? Because they were out in the open or because she'd kept her distance since he'd been back? She knew now, or maybe she'd always known, he was the man who still owned her heart. Yet, she treated him like a stranger because of past hurts. *What am I doing? Don't we both deserve a second chance?*

"If you want to know the truth, this reminds me of the time we made love in the back of your pick-up."

A smile tipped the corners of his mouth. "Hold onto that thought. I haven't forgotten, but this isn't the time, or place, to have that conversation." He eased her onto the passenger seat again, patting her knee. "I need to take a look around."

Reece popped the driver's side door and angled out, reaching behind him to grab a sniper rifle off the gun rack. "Stay inside for a few minutes."

He pressed a button on the rifle scope and Billie saw a light blink on. Stepping away from the tree, he aimed it at the mountains, pivoting in a slow circle as he scanned the landscape around them. After several moments, he turned off the camera but kept the rifle in his hands. He walked to her side of the SUV and sprang the door. "If you're feeling better, let's take a short walk."

Taking her by the hand, he walked her to the place where she'd been shot that day. "Can you tell me what happened?"

"I'd all but forgotten." Touching the healing injury behind her ear, Billie allowed her thoughts free rein. "I remembered brief glimpses when I was in the hospital, but most of it was foggy...until now."

"The meds and your brain's need to protect you probably wiped your memory banks until you were strong enough to dig deeper on your own." He lifted her hand and brought it to his lips, the heat of his mouth against her skin causing her heart to spike. He had the ability to burn her—scorch her—and calm her fears.

"It wasn't an accident, Reece. Whoever shot me knew who he was aiming at." She inhaled a calming breath to steady her voice. "You were right all along. Someone wants me dead."

Chapter 6

It was still light out when they pulled up in the ranch's drive. The setting sun spangled off two rental SUVs parked close to the house. Reece realized the team had arrived, must have landed at Springbank Airport. The local airstrip wouldn't have enough tarmac length for a jet to land. The Challenger 604 belonged to Jake Hawkins, the pilot of their Spec Ops team. A chief investigator with the RCMP, Hawke's pockets ran deep, lined with trust fund millions. He didn't talk about it, but he picked up the tab if they had to boogie to save a life and it wasn't a military sanctioned op.

Reece popped the hatch on the SUV, retrieved the M25, and opened Billie's car door. Damn, she looked shaky. Coming to grips with the fact someone had deliberately shot her had derailed her today. The fact he had been able to help her, and get close to her again, should make him feel like King bloody Kong. But, how could it when she was still so vulnerable? Emotionally bruised, hunted by an enemy he suspected was using her as bait to get to him.

It could be anyone; terrorists wanting to even the score. The family of some lowlife insurgent he'd killed while heading up engineering projects on foreign soil. *Fanfuckingtastic. I could be the reason she's in this mess.*

"Looks like the gang's all here." He hid his worries, eased Billie out of the SUV, wrapped an arm around her waist, and walked her to the porch. "Come on, I'll introduce you to everyone."

They entered the kitchen. Pike was giving Dottie a hand at the stove, spaghetti sauce thickening in the stockpot. *Mmm,* the kitchen smelled awesome. His stomach growled, the scent of parmesan garlic bread ready for the oven reminding him he was hungry enough to eat a water buffalo right about now.

Pike gave them a nod. "Glad you're back, Billie. Satan's bedded down for the night. He should sleep like a baby after racing all over the countryside today. Hell, *I'm* gonna sleep like a baby after chasing him. How's the shoulder, Rocket?"

He shrugged. "It's nothing to worry about. A couple stitches. I'm already back up to speed."

"Spoken like a true liar." Dottie scoffed and swatted Pike's wrist with a ladle when the stirring spoon in his hand headed from the meat sauce to his mouth. "Stop that. Dinner will be ready in thirty minutes. Billie, Rocket, you have time for a drink with your guests first."

"Thanks, Dottie." Billie turned and walked out of the room. She stopped at the bathroom door along the hallway. "I'll be there in a minute."

Reece smoothed a strand of hair behind her ear. He tipped her chin. "You okay?"

"Sure. I'm fine."

Her mouth trembled a little, tugging at his heartstrings. He bent to brush a kiss across her lips. Just a taste, he promised himself, like an alcoholic believing he could take a sip and not drink the whole damn bottle. He should leave well enough alone. Touching her, feeling her response in the SUV today may have eased the ache in his heart, but his guy parts were in trouble with a capital 'T'. If he wasn't careful, he'd cripple himself.

Her hands warmed his chest for an instant before gliding away. She rubbed her eyes, had to be exhausted. "Give me enough time to put on my game face and I'll be ready."

After Billie closed the door, Reece took the stairs to his bedroom to stash the M25. He grabbed a quick shower while he was there and changed his clothes. Then he headed downstairs again. No point in putting it off any longer. Sooner or later, he'd have to face Sully.

"Well, well, if it isn't the bull whisperer." Sullivan turned in his direction, crossed his arms, and widened his stance the second Reece's boots hit the great room floor. Sometimes it was hard to tell Sully and Theo apart, they looked so much alike. But, not this time. Hell, no. There was no mistaking the "endanger my woman again and I'll break your face" warning directed at both him *and* Theo. Theo rolled his eyes but kept silent. Reece understood.

If anyone jeopardized Billie in any way, he'd beat them to a pulp and ask questions later. So, yeah, he and Theo had screwed up big time. They should have paid attention to the women, instead of leaving them alone while they discussed strategy. There was no way Billie, Bree, and Melena should have been in the barn alone. If Reece had seriously thought it through, he would have known they'd take off without a care in the world. Because all three women shared the same personality traits, they were headstrong and gutsy.

"And this must be Billie Bradshaw." Sully walked toward him from across the room, an arm around Bree's shoulders.

Reece felt a hand tugging on his belt and glanced down. Yep, there she was, moving in front of him, looking pumped and ready to defend him if Sully got out of line. While he appreciated the sentiment, he had to conceal the grin tipping the corners of his mouth. Damn, she made him proud. Of course, she wouldn't stand a chance messing it up with Sullivan or any of the other members of his squad. They'd just sit on her and be done with it. Yet, she was willing to take a stand to save him from a possible beat down by his commanding officer.

Sully set his drink on an end table, moving forward to shake her hand. "We're sorry for your problems, Billie. We're here to back up Reece and finish this thing before anyone else gets hurt."

She drilled him with a glare, shot a glance at Breeana who nodded her head persuasively, and accepted Sully's hand. "Rocket *saved* Bree's life this morning. You'll do well to remember that. Otherwise, you can climb in your ride and go back to where you came from, and take the other men with you. Reece saved my life and Melena's too, with Theo's help. You should be thanking them."

"I'm not going to—" Sully grunted when Breeana poked him in the ribs. He sucked in a breath, glanced into her green eyes, and scowled. It appeared Bree had Sully exactly where she wanted him, off his stride and crazy ass in love with her. He cleared his throat. "I'll keep it in mind."

Micah Rivera strolled into the conversation, disengaging Billie's hand from Sully's to brush her knuckles with his lips. "Rocket, are you going to introduce me to this beautiful woman, or should I do it myself?"

Micah was the electronics genius and mechanic of their team. His good looks and boyish charms were seldom lost on the fairer sex, yet Billie shot him down in flames. "Kiss my hand again, without my permission, and I'll knock your teeth out."

"Hookay then." Micah excused himself and headed for the bar, probably wondering where he'd messed up. This had to be a first for their resident Latin lover.

Reece laced Billie's fingers with his, walked her across the carpet to Jake Hawkins, and made the introductions. "I didn't expect to see you here, Hawke. I thought Joelle had a problem brewing in Houston."

"Looks like it could be a false alarm," Hawke said, not elaborating further. He shook hands with Billie and moved off to a corner with Theo and Sully. Something was up.

"Is Joelle his wife?" Billie whispered, once Hawke was out of earshot.

"No, she's Theo's and Sully's sister." Reece placed a hand at her back, guided her to the bar, and poured her a gin and tonic. He added some ice, a slice of lime, and passed her the glass. "I don't know the full story, but I know they're keeping a close eye on her."

"Billy? Come over here and meet these guys." Charley stood with Hunt and Law by the pool table. Billie joined them while Reece headed for Sully, Theo and Hawke. He kept eyes on Billie though, couldn't help but admire the way she moved, the tilt of her head, and the sound of her voice.

Yeah, he was heading into cream puff territory again. Time to quit the poetry routine. The other guys must be wondering what the hell was going on with him, considering he had the reputation for hooking up with the fairer sex in drinking establishments for a couple hours of fun and frolic. A far cry from the way he felt about Billie. He imagined it showed. He just didn't know what to do about it. He'd spent the last ten years living out of a go bag without a permanent address. Billie, on the other hand, called the ranch home and needed to stay there. It would never work between them.

He could hear Charley's booming voice. "Say hello to my daughter, boys. Billie, this here is Hunter Ryan and Law Logan. Law is the 'go to' guy for the team if they need supplies, especially when they're wheels up and in foreign hellholes. And Hunter speaks a bunch of foreign languages. He gets them in and out of hostile territory with no one being the wiser. What do ya think about that?"

Theo's hand gripped Reece's shoulder, bringing his focus back to the group of men. "Melena got a hit on a couple grease balls travelling with the movie crew."

Well, wasn't that interesting? "Tell me."

"Two of their security guards have records. They did time together in the Kingston Penitentiary for armed robbery and assault."

"For Christ's sake. Don't these film people screen their employees?"

"They probably do, but in this case, they hired their security from a reputable firm." Hawke said. "They may have assumed that company had already checked them out."

"It could also be the same security company screening the movie employees," Theo guessed. "In which case, no one's been vetted properly."

"Exactly." Hawke shook his head, taking a swig from his pilsner glass. "There could be a whole nest of vipers working over there."

"What about Spinelli, their head of security? Did Mel find anything on him?" There was something about him that Reece couldn't put a finger on. He didn't feel right, and he didn't like the way he'd looked at Billie when she'd been on the set.

"Nothing so far," Theo said. "Why?"

"I don't like him. The guy gives me the creeps." Reece kneaded the muscles bunching where Bad had gored him this morning, rotating his shoulder to ease out the stiffness. "Jesus, tell Melena to keep digging. She's found two so far. Let's hope she nails a few more."

"I have some other news." Sully leaned into him. "Breeana heard back from the lab where she sent Satan's blood work. According to her buddy who runs the lab, Satan's results are negative for infections and viruses, although they're still waiting for a couple of qualifiers for potential drug abuse."

"So, the stallion doesn't appear to be sick?" Reece thought about it for a moment, not sure what this meant in the bigger picture. "What's your point, Sully? Are you saying if the horse isn't sick, he can't be treated for the sterility issue?"

"It's too soon to tell, but Bree thinks it's possible if Satan's not sick, then he's not actually sterile. She's taking sperm samples tomorrow and driving them to the lab herself. I'm going with her."

"Why not have the courier pick them up? It'll save you the four hours round trip."

"Because, if Satan's not sterile, than someone is damaging his samples before they get to Billie's customers. It could be anyone."

"Can they actually do that?

"Oh, yeah, Bree says they sure as hell can."

"Fuck."

"Yup. That's what I thought you'd say."

HER DAD TOOK ROCKET'S buddies on a tour of the barns after breakfast. Ranch hands had been out there since dawn, clearing the mess in the horse barn and rebuilding the stalls. Billie could hear hammers pounding and saws buzzing through the open windows of the house, which was a good thing while she'd been zinging around downstairs on a cleaning spree. There was no reason for Reece to catch on to how tense she was, or how she solved the problem by scrubbing walls and floors.

The noise ground to a halt as she stowed her supplies and Billie knew why. Breeana needed silence in the breeding shed to put Satan at ease and collect the semen samples. This involved the use of a dummy mare and an artificial vagina, probably not something the Spec Ops guys witnessed every day. Sully would see a whole different side to Bree's veterinary training, and her father would wonder why Billie had given her permission to use the stallion. Reece was right. It was time to tell her dad the truth. Ah, heck, she'd worry about that later, after she had Satan's report back from the lab.

Right now, though, she had something else to do. She walked along the upstairs hallway. Reece and Theo were up to something. She could feel it in her bones. They thought they'd bamboozled her by pulling a disappearing act. Not for long. She snicked open Rocket's bedroom door. Yep, there they were, huddled at his desk and staring at a laptop. The two of them sat shoulder-to-shoulder, blocking her view of the screen.

"So, what's the verdict?" Reece thrummed a steady beat on a thigh with his hand, an action she'd seen him do before when zeroing in on a problem.

"You weren't wrong," Theo said. "Conditions were perfect for an experienced shooter. No wind, no rain, low humidity, and within easy range to target, if we look at the video you filmed yesterday."

"There's no way it was an accident." Reece cursed again. "Considering the trajectory of the bullet, whoever did this fired into the gorge and straight at her."

"An easy shot for a sniper." Theo cracked his knuckles, flashed his fingers across the keys one more time. "I'll cross reference weather data with another site just to be sure."

While Theo worked the laptop, Billie moved into the room to stand behind them. She touched Reece's shoulder as she watched the screen. He glanced up, the look on his face grim. "Why are you checking weather reports for the day I was shot?"

His arm banded her hips and pulled her in close to his side. "I needed to confirm a couple things before we have a chat."

"A chat? About what?"

"I guess that's my cue to leave." Theo stood and offered her his chair. She sat, more like fell into it. Whatever had happened, she knew it wasn't good. "I'll go see how Melena's making out with the employee searches."

The door shut behind him. Reece scooted over on his rolling chair until their thighs touched. She could feel his breath on her shoulder, smell his clean scent. He tugged on a lock of her hair so she'd quit staring at the screen and turn in his direction. His stoic silence and piercing stare said it all. *Lord in heaven, whatever he has to tell me, it's really, really bad.*

"Reece?" She took his face in her hands, the fear in his emerald eyes setting off her alarm bells. "What's the matter? Whatever it is just spit it out."

His gaze locked on hers and held fast, his expression angry and tight. He steadied himself by taking a breath. "I think someone shot you because of me. It's my fault."

"What?" Had he betrayed her? *No, no, no. He doesn't know what he's saying.* "That's ridiculous. You weren't even there when it happened."

"I know I'm right, Billie. You were shot by a pro. Theo agrees with me; we've been over this several times. The bastard shot to wound you—not to kill you. And he did it to get to me."

"You're not making any sense. Why? Why would someone do it? And what could it possibly have to do with you?"

"I have enemies, peaches, bad asses who want me dead. Everyone on the team has a price on their heads."

"Well, of course you do. It's your job to get the bad guys and stop terrorists from hurting people." She tore her gaze away from his and glanced at the screen again. "I guess you do the job well if people want to kill you for it. But how can you think what happened to me is *your* fault? *You* didn't shoot me."

"I may not have shot you, but I'm still responsible. The hit on you could have been a 'divide and conquer' strategy to isolate me from the rest of my team." He laced her fingers through his and raised them to his lips, kissing the back of her hand. "Shooting you brought me here, Billie. Whoever did this knew I'd come back to protect you. He counted on it."

Of all the emotions she expected to feel, anger wasn't one of them. And yet, her blood boiled at the circumstances, at the faceless idiot who had used her for target practice. "That still doesn't make you responsible. And if what you say is true, at least I don't have to worry I have an enemy anymore."

"Maybe not, but you need protection, now more than ever. If I'm right, this guy is a trained killer. He'll do whatever it takes to bring me down, and he'll use you to do it. I'm sorry as hell I brought him to your door."

"He wants you focused on me, doesn't he?" Yes, that's the only thing that made sense to her. "He figures if you're worried about me, you won't see what's coming at you."

Reece touched her cheek, the look on his face so fierce, it was all she could do not to wrap her arms around him and hold on tight. She knew what this did to him. He lived to protect, and he still had a soft spot for her deep inside him. She could feel it. Knowing some lunatic had hurt her, and would do it again, to make him pay must drive him insane. "Yeah, I'm betting that's his plan."

"Well, good. Let's give him a real show, starting today. You're going to the movie set to weed out those scumbag security guards, aren't you? I'm tagging along."

"Not a good idea, and what would it prove?"

"You're going to stumble all over yourself to keep me safe while we're over there, Reece. Let the bastard think he has the upper hand if he's part of the film crew. Make him believe you *only* have eyes for me and have no clue what's happening behind the scenes."

"Okay, I'm warming to the idea." A smile curved his lips. "I stick to you like glue. Meanwhile, the other guys toss the security dudes off the set and scope out the location with fresh eyes. Now that we know the type of man we're looking for, he might be easier to spot."

"Exactly." Billie pulled back and punched him in the arm. "And don't you ever tell me this is your fault again. I'll be damned if you'll drag on a hair shirt every morning, along with your gun and boxers."

"Forget the boxers." He leaned forward, cupped her chin, and brushed her lips with a searing kiss. "I always go commando."

Holy kasmoly! Reece without underwear gave her something else to think about other than the rage and fear twisting her belly. Whoever this creep was, Rocket and his team would catch him.

BILLIE COULD BARELY inhale in the back of the SUV. Reece drove with Hawke riding beside him, while Micah and Law sandwiched her between them like a sardine. At least Micah didn't try to kiss her hand again. Actually, he seemed rather quiet, as if he was off his flirting game, or wasn't sure how to handle her.

Hunt and Theo had stayed behind to keep eyes on the ranch and on Melena. Bree and Sully had headed for the lab straight after lunch. So, it was just her and four of the men. *How many bodyguards does one girl need?*

Reece pulled up beside the office, and they all piled out. The other guys moved away, walking through the rows of vehicles and temporary buildings, and following the signs for today's shoot. Reece took her by the arm and led her around the corner to Maurice's trailer.

"Billie? You brought dessert!" Maurice flew out the door and leapt straight at Rocket, his waxed arms and legs wrapping around him like he was a stripper pole. Reece stayed in control, although he looked like he wanted to toss Maurice over the porch rail.

"Dude, get the hell off me. Now." He staggered back a bit, raised both hands in the air, and shrugged his shoulders. A WTF moment if Billie ever saw one. "Uh, Maurice? I'm not feeling the love here, you know what I mean?"

"Oh, no!" Maurice started sobbing, clinging like a monkey around Rocket's neck. "I-I thought you'd left him for me."

"'Fraid not." Reece patted the little guy on the back and sent her a silent "For God's sake, do something!" plea with his eyes.

Men. How helpless are they?

"Maurice, honey," she said. "You're crushing your lovely canary blouse and miniskirt." *No reaction. Hmm.* "And your thong is showing."

That did it. Maurice unlatched himself, planted his hooker shoes on the ground, and pulled his skirt down over his backside. He cast a furtive glance around to be sure no one was watching and swiped at his eyes. "I'm sorry for making a scene. I'm o-okay now."

Billie took his arm and tugged him inside the trailer, Reece following behind. "We came here because we need your help."

Maurice grabbed a few tissues and blotted tears from his cheeks as he led them to a couch and a couple of chairs. He seated himself on the couch beside her and grabbed her hand, sparing a forlorn glance at Rocket. "What can I help you with?"

Reece leaned forward on his chair and squeezed Maurice's arm. "We'd like you to keep an eye out for anyone you think might not fit in with the rest of the movie crew."

"This is a film set, boys and girls. Everyone who works here is a little off kilter. Can you be more specific?"

Billie wrapped her arm around his shoulders. "We're looking for a bully—a swarthy, macho type—who most likely keeps to himself, but might seem a bit off the beam."

Maurice placed a hand on her knee, exhaling a shuddering breath. "A guy like that can be very scary. I'll keep my eyes peeled, but what do I do if I find him?"

"You call me right away, and I'll come running." Reece scribbled his cell phone number on a slip of paper and handed it to him. "Just keep a low profile and don't get in his way."

"You mean it? You'll really come if I call you?" Maurice batted his eyelashes at Reece. *Keep a low profile, right.* "Jeepers, if there's a slime ball on the set, I'll find him. Have no fear. Maurice is on the case!"

BANYAN STOOD ON A LADDER across from the trailer where he'd seen Morgan and the woman enter. He tinkered with an electrical panel, testing hookups to the generators and wishing he had some Semtex handy, just enough to blow Morgan to hell while he was still inside. Another missed opportunity as far as he was concerned. Goddamn Foley and his "wait and watch" orders. He slammed the panel shut with a bang.

"You need help with that?"

Shit. He spun on the ladder and looked down at the muscle head standing below him. Hands on his hips, a scowl on his face, and a Glock strapped to his hip, a member of Morgan's Spec Ops squad glared up at him. *Hail, hail, the gang's all here.*

Banyan stuck a finger in his mouth and sucked, made quite a show of it. Good thing he'd slashed it earlier on a piece of torn metal from one of the panels. "No, thanks. I just cut myself."

"Better have it looked at." The creep nodded and moved off, turning the corner and heading for the office. Banyan had seen two more of Morgan's team heading that way a few minutes ago with some security guards. Looked like the security guys were about to get their exit visas stamped. Whatever they'd done, they were being kicked off the set.

Spinelli, the head of security, stomped along looking none too pleased. He rolled to a stop beside the ladder, talking around a toothpick lodged between his teeth. "Things are out of hand. I'm losing half my detail. I'll have to replace them with people who don't have prison records."

Banyan climbed off the ladder, folded it, and laid it on the ground. "I might know a couple people."

"Make some calls and get them out here." Spinelli eyed him for a second, spit out the toothpick. "Their backgrounds better be squeaky clean."

"I'll handle it."

Morgan exited the trailer with the rodeo chick and nodded in their direction. Banyan waved back. *Fuck, I hate that cock sucker.* He couldn't wait to blow his head off. Spinelli had hit the nail on the head when he said things were out of hand. With Morgan's team swarming the area, it was time to move on to plan B.

Chapter 7

Reece opened his eyes. The alarm clock read four a.m. Something had snapped him awake. Experience taught him an out of place noise could mean a shitload of trouble. And there it was again, a barely discernible scraping sound.

Stepping into his jeans, he palmed his Glock and paused with an ear to the bathroom door. He remembered Theo saying Billie had climbed down the drainpipe from her bedroom the other morning. Any lowlife could gain access to her the same way. It might explain how the snake had ended up in her bed.

Bastards.

Fear for her amped up his tension, an icy calm belying his unsettled nerves. He exhaled a cleansing breath. He was solid. Good to go. Inching the bathroom door open, the first thing he saw was Billie hunched over the side of the tub. Sick or injured, he couldn't tell. Jesus. If anyone had so much as touched a hair on her head, he'd rip them apart.

Diffused lighting glowed from her bedroom doorway. He slipped past her to peer inside the room. Nothing seemed out of place. The windows were closed. Not a tango in sight. What had happened to her? Shoving the Glock in his waistband at the small of his back, he hit his haunches beside her, touching her shoulder. "Billie, what's wrong?"

She let out a shriek, then toppled back on her butt, wielding a...scuzzy toothbrush? "Crap, Reece, you just about scared me to death."

He hauled her to her feet, searching for injuries. She appeared to be fine. Maybe better than fine. Hair tousled, lips parted in surprise, her body barely covered in turquoise material that passed for a midriff top and skimpy pajama shorts. *Get it together, Morgan. Focus.*

Slipping the toothbrush out of her fingers, he held it up to the light. "This thing is a biohazard. Did you put it in your mouth?"

"Don't be ridiculous." Shooting him an exasperated look, she swooped up to grab the toothbrush out of his hand. He had longer arms. "Give it back."

"Give it a rest." His eyes cut to the bath, where he noticed a bottle of grout cleaner tucked in a corner with the cap unscrewed. The faint scent of chemicals from the toothbrush bristles hit his nose. His lips twitched up in a grin. "Say it ain't so, peaches."

Reece saw color rise in her cheeks, realized she was embarrassed as all get out. Her smoky eyes rounded in an unbidden question. Yeah, he knew about her midnight ramblings—those cleaning marathons of hers he always ignored. He wasn't a psychologist, but he suspected they were less about compulsion and more about putting some order back in her life.

"I was cleaning the grout on the tub. What's the big deal?"

The big deal was they both needed a diversion—Billie from her fears and uncertainty, and him? He was KO'd on adrenaline. His gut-deep worry for her had produced an overload of the stuff in his veins. He needed to decompress before he did something stupid. Like pin her against the wall, strip her naked, shove his pants down, and...

Hell, they'd been circling each other for too long.

Tossing the toothbrush in the wastebasket, he pulled her into his arms and tipped her chin up to feast on her lips. Her reaction was unsure at first, but she hesitated only a second before melting against him. She opened for him, her hands around his neck as he changed the angle of the kiss to delve inside her mouth. Her tongue met his stroke for stroke, tasting like wildfire and honey. Her breasts filled his hands, her nipples pebbling the fabric beneath his fingers.

His own body reacted. Halo jumped into dangerous territory without common sense along for the ride. He craved the touch of her skin, the feel of her beneath him. "Peaches, if you want to stop...tell me now."

Her eyes searched his, and she smiled. Goddamn smiled at him. She inched the silky top over her head and tossed it to the floor. Leaping into his arms, she locked her legs around his hips. "Sometimes, cowboy, you talk too much."

Hoo-rah.

Her hands guided his head to her breasts. He suckled hard, gorging himself on her velvety skin. He lifted her higher against him, his teeth circling and nipping at her navel. She moaned. Head back, eyes closed, and hips rocking, her sweet core pushed against his abs.

He eased a hand between them, slipped beneath the edge of her shorts, and cupped her. Wet. Hot. Home. He was home whenever he touched her, a feeling more powerful inside him than the reasons why he should cut and run. If that made him weak, so be it. But for the life of him, he couldn't get himself under control.

Setting her down on the counter, he unzipped, reached in his back pocket for a condom—wishful thinking, he kept them handy since the incident in the SUV—and suited up. Beyond doing the right thing, he lifted her up and tugged the shorts down her legs. "You sure you're okay with this?"

Desire shone in her eyes, her breathing erratic. "Shut up, Reece."

Crazy. She made him crazy, insane with need. He hauled her into his arms again, pushed into her with all the finesse of a fumbling linebacker. Slammed her with feelings he didn't understand. Didn't want to explore. And not a brain cell in sight to hold him back.

When she climaxed, he followed her over on a hoarse growl. Holding her to him, it was several long minutes before he lowered her feet to the ground. So much for his promise to serve and protect, keep her off limits and safely out of harm's way.

Yeah, I'm a real goddamn prince. "Billie...God..."

BILLIE PADDED INTO her room and switched off the lamp. Moonlight bathed her in shadow, promising pleasant dreams and hours of healing slumber. Crawling into bed, she stretched from toes to fingertips and gathered the pillows beneath her cheek. Her body sated and relaxed, her mind cleared of horrific thoughts, for the first time in a long time she slid off the stiletto edge of fear into warm, comforting sleep.

Mmm, she could still smell Reece on her skin, feel his arm banding her waist, the heat of his body along her spine. Her eyes flew open. She rolled onto her back, stared at the silhouette lying beside her. Not a dream. Not a fantasy. It was Rocket, still clad in his jeans and unclipping a gun from his belt. He moved it to the bedside table.

"Get out of my bed."

"Nope." His lips brushed hers, a hand caressing her throat. "Not until I move the drainpipe outside your bedroom window. It's easy access for any creep who wants to hurt you."

"I have a house full of macho men. I don't see it happening."

"I won't take the chance." His eyes glinted in the moonlight, determination hardening his gaze. "Not with you."

Try as she might, Billie didn't have it in her to object to his line of reasoning. This felt so right. They had shared their bodies. Surely, they could share a bed for one night. Sleep beckoned. She was damnably tired. Surrendering to the urge, her eyes drifted closed again. "Suit...yourself."

He shook her shoulder. "Peaches? Don't conk out on me. We have to talk."

"No, we don't." She turned away from him and snuggled deeper into the pillows, breathing in his closeness. "Men don't want to talk after sex. They light a cigarette or pull on their boots and beat feet for the hills. Quit acting like a girl, Reece."

"But—"

"Go to sleep."

"Well, I'll be snookered."

Billie's next conscious thought was after the sun rose. A hand cupped her breast. A muscled leg straddled her thighs and someone breathed against her ear. *Rocket.* He had surrounded her with his body. She'd slept through the night sheltered by him. And now, here she was lying in the arms of the last man she should be involved with. *Crap.*

"Mornin', sunshine." Moving the hand from her breast to smooth the hair off her face, he kissed her cheek. "Sleep well?"

"I must have." Relieved to see he still wore his jeans, she wondered how she could slip away from him and put things on even ground again. She was naked and he...wasn't.

As if sensing her concern, he tugged the sheet over her and rolled off the bed, plunked himself in the wing chair facing her. "You ready to have that talk now? Or do you want coffee first? I can ask Dottie to bring us a pot."

"Are you crazy?" The last thing she needed was for Dottie to witness this little domestic scene. It was obvious they had rolled in the hay last night, even if it wasn't exactly in her bed. She rubbed a hand along her chin and could feel whisker burn. Holy Hannah, everyone would know what they'd done. "I don't want to talk."

"You have no choice."

"Like hell I don't. I'm not having this conversation with you unless it has to do with bad guys or livestock." She leapt to her feet, dragging the sheet with her and making a beeline across the carpet for the bathroom.

Reece reached out an arm and reeled her back, settling her on his lap. Both his arms came around her, effectively pinning her where she sat. "Pike told me, Billie, that I got you pregnant. How you lost the baby."

"What? You want to dredge up that old news?" She forced a laugh, fought his embrace, struggling to get to her feet again. *Please, please let me go.*

"It's not old news to me." The more she tried to pull free, the harder he held on.

Something snapped inside her in a dizzying rush. Feelings she'd held in check for too long sprang to the surface. Tears spilled over for the baby she had lost. Anger followed for the boy who had left her to suffer alone. She wheeled on him, nailed him in the jaw with a fist. His head snapped back, but still he wouldn't release her. "You son of a bitch! If you'd bothered to keep in touch, you would have known everything without being told by Pike!"

He scooped her up, tossed her to the bed, and eased down on top of her. Pinning her hands above her head, he covered her with his body to keep her flailing legs in check. She squeezed her eyes shut, refusing to look at him.

"You don't want to look at me? Fine. But you're going to listen to what I have to say. I tried, Billie. I phoned, and I damn well wrote."

Her eyes flew open to meet his gaze. Reece may have messed up as a teenager, but she had never known him to lie. "You did what?"

"You heard me. You're all I thought about for months. Hell, I carried your picture in my helmet every time I went wheels up." His heart pounded against her chest. The planes of his face sharpened with anger and frustration. "Whenever I called, the line disconnected. No voice on the other end, just dead air. Do you know how many times I wrote, and you never wrote back? Do you know what that did to me?"

She twisted her wrists, but he didn't loosen his grip. "Please, let me go."

"Not until you hear me out." The intensity of his gaze took her breath away. "Jesus, Billie, what you went through being pregnant...then losing our child. I would have come if I'd known. Taken my chances with your father, and the law, to be by your side."

"Oh, Lord." Finally, after all the years of feeling rejected, thinking she wasn't good enough, she realized he hadn't deserted her. "I never got your letters. Never knew you had called."

"Yeah, I see that now." His mouth brushed hers, his grip easing from her wrists. "I'm only sorry I didn't figure it out sooner."

"It's not your—"

Footsteps and shouts in the hallway drowned out the end of her sentence. Billie clutched the sheet to her chest a second before Breeana burst through the door with Sully behind her. *Good grief!*

"Oops!" Bree stumbled to a halt and Sully bumped into her, almost sent her flying. He snagged her by the waist to hold her upright. Both of them gawked at her and Reece on the bed. Reece held the gun in his hand. *When had he picked it up?*

"Sorry to interrupt, but this is an emergency. Billie, you're needed in the kitchen on the double. Before Dottie kills the 'ass' lady!"

"QUIT CALLING HER THAT, Dottie. Lorelei Calhoun raises donkeys. Calling her the 'ass' lady is downright rude."

"Rude? I'll show you rude."

Quick as lightning, Dottie lunged for the blond's big hair. Hightailing it across the kitchen, Billie tried to wedge herself between them to keep them apart. No dice. Another blond, a younger version of Lorelei, joined in the tussle. Reece took a wild guess that it was donkey lady's daughter. At least, they appeared to have the same hair stylist.

Hawke and Sully hitched their chins at him, grins riding their faces, and their hands in the air, palms up. *Great.* They expected *him* to break up the cat fight. Man, if there was one thing he did not want to do, it was get in the middle of brawling females. He didn't want to be on the receiving end of scratches, bites, and hair pulls. Or get his balls kicked blue.

Yeah, women fought dirty, like a bunch of mangy cats. He'd even seen them try to drown each other in the toilets of fine drinking establishments. The ones where he scoffed back home-brewed whiskey and hoped it wouldn't melt the hair off his chest. He blew out a breath. There was nothing for it. Rolling up his sleeves, he waded in. Grabbing Dottie around the waist, he hoisted her off the floor.

Aw, shit. She threw her head back, tried to butt him in the face. Good thing he was a foot taller than she was. Next came her claws raking across the backs of his hands. *Oompf,* a boot connected with his shin. Damn little he could do other than hold on for dear life. Billie, Lorelei, and the Lorelei lookalike joined the boys watching the show, with Billie shouting "don't hurt her!" when Dottie landed a particularly nasty punch upside his head. "Open the door."

Billie grabbed for it and swung it wide. Kicking like a crazed mustang, screaming words that turned the air blue—yup, Dottie had a mouth on her that did sailors proud—Reece carted her outside, down the porch steps, and onto the driveway. He set her on her feet and backed out of reach.

Dottie tried to get by him. He blocked her path, hoping to God she wouldn't take another swing at him. "Where is she? I'm gonna kill that bitch if she doesn't get her butt in gear and clear out. And take those other asses with her!"

Charley must have heard the commotion all the way from the barn and came running. Billie's father looked dumbstruck to see the crowd gathered and his housekeeper primed to have another go at the donkey lady. "What in blazes is going on?"

Lorelei rushed to Charley's side and burrowed under an arm. "I was delivering the last donkey you ordered. All I did was go into the house to see where you wanted him offloaded. Dottie attacked me as soon as I cleared the doorway.

"Look at me?" she wailed. "My shirt's torn to pieces, my hair's pulled out, and I'm covered in flour."

"Yeah, you got lucky," Dottie said, a sneer on her face. "Next time I'll fry your hide in bacon grease."

"That's enough." Charley patted Lorelei on the shoulder, disengaged himself from her clingy arms, and stalked toward his housekeeper. He raised a hand and pointed to the door. "Go inside and cool off. I'll deal with you later."

"Sure, you do that." Dottie shot another venomous glare in Lorelei's direction. "But get it straight...she's after the ranch and your bank account. And she don't give a cow pie about you!"

Billie placed an arm around the younger woman. "I'm sorry you had to witness that, Jenny Lee."

Jenny Lee laughed. "Don't worry about it, Billie. No harm done. And Dottie's half right. I think my mom does have a thing for your father. She spent a lot of time getting gussied up before we headed over here this morning."

"Well, your mother's a nice lady and she didn't deserve what she got."

"No worries." Jenny Lee said. "I just have to drag her away from your dad so I can head home and get ready for my other job."

Reece smiled at the young woman and spoke to Billie. "What do you say we saddle up and go for a ride until everyone cools down? We still have a lot to talk about."

"Let's do that. Why don't we ride out to check on the horses in the grazing pasture and you can see the donkeys in action? I'll pack us some snacks while Pike saddles Sexy Lexy and Psycho Sally. Meet you back here in five." She said goodbye to Jenny Lee, who had her phone out and seemed to be texting like mad. Billie stopped on the stairs and turned back to him, concern shadowing her eyes. Damn, she hadn't been allowed to ride since he'd brought her home. She deserved a little fun in her life. "Do you think it's safe for us to go out on horseback?"

Probably not, but he'd already decided to send Hunt and Law ahead to scope out the trail and ride shotgun for them. "We'll be fine, as long as we don't go far. Why don't we head out in a half hour? I want to shower first."

She shot him a thousand-watt grin and disappeared inside the house. He took a few minutes to bring the other guys up to speed, making sure Law and Hunt would be armed to the teeth for their little sojourn. Pike was saddling horses and giving the guys directions to the closest trail while he dashed inside to grab a shower, some extra clips for his Glock, and the 30-30 Winchester from his go bag. There was nothing like a relaxing ride in the country to sharpen his reflexes and put him on edge.

Micah stood with Billie outside the barn when Reece caught up to her again. She laughed at something he said. Nice to see they were getting over their differences. While Micah might be the world's biggest flirt, Reece trusted him not to cross the line. Besides, he knew Billie, and didn't think of her as Billie the Hammer for nothing. Used to cowboys coming on to her, she could put their resident Don Juan in his place in no time flat.

Billie patted Sexy Lexy and prepared to mount; Reece caught the name engraved on the sorrel's bridle. Which left him riding Psycho Sally, part thoroughbred and part quarter horse from the looks of her. The chestnut had a white blaze and one white stocking on a back leg from the pastern down. She looked friendly enough, but he had his doubts, considering the 'Psycho' moniker. "Okay, what's the story on Sally?"

He caught the wink Billie sent Micah's way. "She's an ex-rodeo bucking horse Dad converted to calf roping when she stopped tossing and biting riders. Don't worry...she only reverts to her old ways once in a while. You can handle her, tough guy, or did you forget you used to ride wild broncs on the rodeo circuit?"

"That was a long time ago, and not what I had planned for a quiet ride in the country." Still, Reece figured he could deal with whatever Sally dished out. Leaving the ranch years ago didn't mean he'd left his love of horses behind. He rode whenever he could and kept up his skills. Micah shot him an imperceptible nod while giving Billie a boost up in the saddle. Translation—Hunt and Law were checking out the trail.

"Stay behind me, peaches." After a tortuous ride through the first pasture—yeah, Sally tried to buck him off a few times, until she caught the memo he was in charge—they headed into the trees. The sun shone overhead with the promise of a beautiful day. A chipmunk skittered across their path and up the trunk of the nearest poplar. It chattered a warning to the rest of its pals. A breeze whistled through lofty pines, a couple of red-tailed hawks circling, zeroing in on breakfast. A jackrabbit scrambled for cover as they swooped toward him, narrowly escaping a king size set of talons.

No signs of Hunt or Law, but Reece knew they were out there. He hoped their horses wouldn't start nickering and clue Billie in. No reason for her to know about the armed posse escorting her. In spite of wary tension, he forced himself to relax and enjoy the ride. "Man, I've missed being on horseback."

"Tell me about it."

He turned in the saddle to see Billie smile and realized she was the only sunshine he needed in his life. Didn't know why that should surprise him. He'd thought about her long and hard during the past ten years.

"This is the first time I've been out on a horse since...leaving the hospital after the shooting. Except for racing the barrels in the paddock, of course. Cedar and I need to keep up to speed for the rodeo circuit."

"Cedar? That's the horse you use for barrel racing?"

Billie nodded her head. "She's a six-year-old Palomino, a little headstrong but amazing once I got through to her. She bucked me off a few years back. I hurt my shoulder and was off riding for nine months."

"Jeez, Billie. Doesn't sound like a great barrel racer to me."

She laughed. "I sent her to a trainer for a while, took some lessons where she went to boost my confidence, and now we get along fine."

"I don't like it. A horse like that could do real damage if she bucks you while you're racing barrels."

"Don't worry about me, Rocket. I admit I almost got rid of her, but I'm glad I didn't. Cedar's fast. She loves to run and is awesome racing the barrels now. We're winning big on the circuit this year."

Which started Reece's wheels spinning in another direction. He loved Billie and half believed she loved him too. The big question was how could they make their relationship work? Billie was all about the ranch, while he was still about the job. "Where does this trail lead?"

"It comes out over the next ridge. There's another pasture up there where a lot of our horses graze. We sometimes leave them out overnight. That's why Dad bought those guard donkeys from Lorelei. Otherwise, coyotes and other predators could kill off our livestock."

"Guard donkeys? I thought it was a joke. You're kidding, right?" Reece could see a break in the trees up ahead, his mind also registering how animated Billie became when she talked about the ranch.

Yeah, while he roamed the globe doing engineering projects for the military or flying the friendly skies with his spec ops buddies, her roots were buried deep into *Circle B* soil.

Where does that leave us? Can I walk away from her again? Not bloody likely.

The trail widened and Billie cantered up beside him. "It's not a joke, Rocket. We use both gelding and mare donkeys. Not only do they calm the horses, but they protect them from enemies as well. They are aggressive when they need to be. They'll charge other animals that threaten the herd. Wolves, even bears, lose interest and move on rather than go up against them."

Sure enough, as soon as they cleared the trail and entered the pasture, a couple donkeys trotted toward them, braying to beat the band.

"That's Shirley and Flo," Billie said. "Don't let them get too close or they might take a chunk out of you. They don't know you."

"What? These little gals? Give me a break. They look harmless enough, could be wearing sunhats with flowers around the brim." Of course, that was before one of them charged him, full on, its lips curled back and its choppers heading for his leg.

"Come on." Billie nudged her mount's flanks with her heels and galloped for the water tower, shouting over her shoulder. "We'll have our snack over there before we head back. They're used to ranch hands watching the herd from a distance."

Reece touched his heels to his own horse to catch up to her. Attack donkeys—he'd heard it all now. As they neared the water tower, his eyes caught something reflecting in the sun. An explosive device duct taped to the supporting beams of the tower. He'd built enough bombs for the military to recognize it instantly.

Breath froze in his lungs, the sight of Billie racing toward certain death filling him with full blown terror. Reece urged Psycho Sally faster, stretched his mount to come even with hers, lunged for her, and dragged them both free. They hit the ground with the force of a jackhammer. He rolled her beneath him. And the tower blew.

The roar deafening, tons of water and twisted metal hurled around them, hitting the dirt where they lay. *Gawd damn!* White hot metal slammed against his leg. He kicked it off. Billie groaned, didn't move when he shook her shoulder. She didn't appear to be hit, but he didn't know for sure. Hell, she could have broken something when they landed. Reece knew the bomb had been detonated by a remote device, most probably a cell phone, and whoever had done it was out there—close enough to pick them off. *We have to move!*

"Billie? Come on, baby!" No reaction. The horse had galloped off with his rifle. Reece pulled out his Glock, hoisted her over his shoulder, and ran, falling down when searing pain shot through his calf. *Shit!* Scooping Billie up again, he hobbled for the outcropping of rocks edging the tower.

"Put me down!" Billie struggled to set herself upright. "I can walk. I just had the wind knocked out of me for a second."

Once her feet touched the ground, Billie wrapped an arm around his waist and helped him stagger for the rocks. *Jesus, Jesus.* He prayed a bullet wouldn't hit her before they reached cover.

Chapter 8

B anyan left his vantage point on the hill, skidding for freedom like a slalom skier at an Olympic event. Two riders galloped after him up the far side of the gorge, both of them military. *Morgan's special ops pals.* He recognized the breed. They'd spotted him detonating the bomb, charged across the field and up the rise heading straight for him.

He'd seen one of them hoist a M25 sniper rifle to his shoulder. That was his cue to get the hell out. Thank God, the bastard hadn't had the chance to fire off a round before he'd disappeared from view. Man, he didn't want to be on the receiving end when the mutt gained the ridge and let loose, since the weapon had a kill range of 900 meters.

His blood ran cold as his breath sawed through his lungs. What kind of weaponry was the other one carrying? Didn't much matter at this stage of the game; he'd be an easy target for both of them. Goddamn. Death chased his tail, and he couldn't move fast enough to clear out of its path.

Zigzagging between boulders, he kept low to the ground, slithering like a sidewinder for his pick-up hidden beyond the trees up ahead. It was a sure bet they couldn't follow him down the rocky terrain on horseback. Still, if they decided on a foot chase, a bullet in his back wasn't how he wanted this to end. Not with a fat bank account waiting for him in the Caymans.

He dripped sweat, his camo Tee and pants glued to his body by the time he reached the truck. Diving inside, he slammed his

Sig on the seat beside him, cranked the engine, and floored it. The thunk of bullets ripping through trees echoed as he hunched low over the steering wheel, his focus on the rutted track. The last thing he needed was another blowout. A few seconds later a bend in the trail blocked the onslaught of ammo fire.

I'm home free.

He didn't slow down, moving for the highway as fast as the boxy pickup would travel. After swerving to a stop at the intersection, he swung a hard left, easing off the gas pedal to blend with Sunday traffic moseying into town. No point in driving like a maniac and calling attention to himself. His nerves settled as he inhaled, the adrenaline shakes slowly draining from his body.

Should he ditch the truck in Hereford? Nah, it was safe enough. It looked like a thousand other dusty pick-ups in the area. Yeah, welcome to Hicksville. Never thought he'd see the day he'd be driving a bullshit truck and thanking the Lord for it. But, it was rented to the film company and couldn't be traced back to him, so what the hell?

He laughed to himself, pulled into the hotel the movie underlings called home—the "stars" of the show were flown by helicopter to fancier digs in Calgary every night, as per their contracts—and parked underground. Perfect timing. Nothing moved inside the garage, except maybe some rats. His eyes adjusted to the shadows while sweeping the area. No security cameras in the old building, and no one about.

Wasting no time, he stripped out of his clothes and hiking boots, stuffing them in a sports bag. Next, he pulled on a *Beau Valley Productions* golf shirt, pants, and steel toes. He added a touch of cologne and a spritz of mouthwash. Fresh as a daisy, not someone the cops would look closely at if Morgan or the woman died from injuries after the bomb blast. Besides, he'd been there all night with the rest of the crew. No one could prove otherwise.

Locking the pick-up, he whistled as he strolled through the side door of the hotel and up the back stairs. Stopping on the third floor, he used the old key to access his room and toss in the sports bag. He took the Otis down to the lobby.

Spinelli hovered at the reception desk, practically drooling. He clearly wanted more than what was offered in the hotel brochures. The guy was a pig. The receptionist flashed Banyan a smile as he exited the elevator. He grinned back and moved toward her, shot the greasy security guy a scowl until he shoved off. Jenny Lee's pretty face and obvious interest lightened his step as he leaned into her across the counter. Yep, she had it bad for him, which was a good thing. And if Spinelli knew what was good for him, he'd leave her the hell alone.

"Did you see the messages I sent earlier?" A pout graced her silky mouth. "The Bradshaw's housekeeper jumped my mom, and there was a cat fight in the kitchen."

He brushed her hand with his fingers and shot her a wink. Yeah, he'd seen her tweet. As soon as Jenny Lee had mentioned Billie was heading out to show Morgan the donkeys, he'd known where they'd be. He'd had to hustle to beat them to the water tower and set the explosives. "Sorry, babe. I forgot to charge my iPhone last night and it went dead as a doornail. What do you say we meet for drinks after my shift, and you can tell me all about it?"

"See you then," she giggled, a blush creeping into her cheeks.

Dumb country bumpkin. *She has no idea.* Banyan focused on her full mouth. A mouth like that had possibilities. He thought she might ease his tension in other ways, not just by supplying him with Intel. *Why not?* He grinned and headed into the restaurant for breakfast. If he played it right, little Jenny Lee would be warming his bed by midnight.

Helping himself at the buffet, he settled at a table by the window. A waitress came over, poured his coffee, and moved on. *Situation normal, not a fuck up in sight.*

But now that the action was over and the tension had eased, his brain did a walkthrough of the op and wasn't impressed. He should have known Morgan would spot the Semtex in the tower struts. Hell, if he hadn't been so pressed for time, he'd have hidden it better. And not killing him in the blast? That was a freaking disaster. Would a bigger charge have made the difference? No idea, he wasn't an explosives expert. But one thing he did know—he hadn't been equipped with a sniper rifle to finish the job. Yeah, that's where he'd made his dumbass mistake.

Now, he had to make like nothing had happened, that he hadn't just tried to kill Morgan and failed. Foley was obsessed with nailing Billie Bradshaw, and Banyan had almost ruined his chances. He wished he had. If the explosion had killed the woman along with Morgan, it would solve all his problems. *Morgan's dead. Rodeo girl was collateral damage. Marcus is happy. Take a hike, Foley.*

But Foley wasn't a fool. If he got wind of this, he would kill Banyan even before Marcus had the chance. And he knew Marcus would hire someone to slit his throat the second he found out about the screw up, because Morgan was still alive. No matter how he sliced it, he was a dead man if word leaked out.

Tipping his cup, he finished off the last dregs of coffee. *Shit!* He almost had a heart attack when Foley slid into the seat opposite his at the table. Fear tightened his belly. Bile rose in his throat. He wanted to hurl but couldn't afford the luxury. He pushed his plate aside and met the other man's gaze. Banyan held it, determined not to flinch when Foley opened his mouth and growled, "What the fuck did you do?"

GUNSHOTS ECHOED FROM the far side of the ridge. Billie swallowed hard and focused on catching Lexy. No point in screaming her head off and racing around like a girly-girl. But being shot in the head wasn't an experience she planned on repeating. No encores, thank you very much.

"Billie! Get the hell over here. It's not safe."

Jeez, does Rocket have to be so bossy? Especially when it was him who was wounded? Give a girl a break for controlling the panic working its way from her head to her toes. After all, a bulletproof bodysuit and combat gear weren't stashed in her hip pocket for special occasions like these. So, nag off. *I deserve a little credit for not losing it completely.* "I'm just getting the horses."

"It's not you I'm worried about."

"What?" Billie glanced over her shoulder and did a double take. Sure, Reece had his gun out and his eyes glued to the rise where everyone else had disappeared a few minutes ago. But that wasn't what floored her. It was Flo and Shirley. The guard donkeys were trying to propel him along like a foal who'd strayed too far from the herd. The bomb blast must have really rattled them. Shirley kept pushing Reece toward the horses congregated at the far side of the pasture, her head against his back, while Flo brayed at him when he didn't limp fast enough to suit her. "Hold on. I'm coming."

"Make it snappy!" Oh-oh, Flo nipped him in the butt and he yowled. "Get away from me, you horse's ass!"

"Ah, crap." Grabbing Sally's reins, Billie climbed into Lexy's saddle, dug her heels in, and raced across the field to save her knight in battered armor. At least Lexy seemed steady enough after the explosion. She wasn't so sure about Sally, though. While neither horse appeared to be hurt, both were nervous and skittish. Thankfully, the other horses had been too far away from the blast to get hit with flying debris. But Sally was a handful at the best of times. This wouldn't improve her pigheaded disposition. Billie pulled up beside Reece and handed off Sally's reins, which he promptly looped over Lexy's saddle horn.

"You can't seriously expect me to ride that animal in my condition?" He rubbed his butt cheek, limped even with her, and tugged her foot from the stirrup. Next thing she knew, he used the stirrup to heft himself up behind her in the saddle and reached around her to take Lexy's reins. "Let's move before I pass out from the pain."

Sure, what a crock. Knowing him the way she did, he'd rather die than admit he was hurting. Was this an excuse to get close to her? *Bring it on, oh studly one.* Having those strong arms around her and leaning back against his chest felt so fine. The clean, masculine scent of him filled her with unsettling thoughts that teased and confused, but was sharing her saddle really just his excuse to surround her with his body like a human shield? Yep, it made more sense. Darn, it looked like those romantic fantasies were nothing but a pipedream after all.

Fear mushroomed, causing her heart to hammer and hands to sweat. If Reece hadn't spotted the explosive device, they'd be riding through the pearly gates of heaven right now instead of heading for the ranch. And he still protected her with his life, covertly of course, because he didn't want to scare her. Which sounded her internal alarm system with clanging bells; they weren't out of the woods yet. Well, if he could ignore the obvious, than so could she. "No wonder Theo called you a cream puff."

He laughed, planting a kiss on top of her head. "I dare you to crawl into my bed to find any soft spots on this rock-hard body. Guaranteed, they don't exist."

His parted thighs snugged against her backside suggested he'd win that bet. Difficult for her to ignore as they cut across the field for the trailhead, gained the path, and entered the forest. Although his words belied his body language, light and casual, as if they were taking a Sunday canter through the botanical gardens, Reece rode with the Glock gripped in his hand like he expected more trouble. "Tell me a little about Jenny Lee."

Why? Billie felt her back arch like a mama cat's with one of her kittens threatened. *Why would he ask me about Lorelei's daughter?* As far as she was concerned, Jenny Lee was a shy, younger woman who didn't have a mean bone in her body. "Leave her alone, Rocket. She's not involved in this."

He said nothing, swinging the horses about at the sound of hooves pounding the path close behind them. Hunter and Law crashed through the trees and reined in their mounts. "We lost the bastard. He had a pickup stashed for a quick getaway."

"No big surprise there." A scowl rode the planes of Reece's face. "Secure the explosion site until we find the detonation device. Stack the debris behind the rocks where the horses can't stumble on it and keep away from those damn donkeys. They'll bite you soon as look at you."

The men nodded and reeled their mounts, heading back to the field while she and Reece continued for home. They arrived safely some twenty minutes later, with Reece still refusing to go to the clinic. Good thing Breeana had raided the medical supplies cabinet to dress his wound after he hobbled into the house. With a nasty burn on his calf, Bree had to soak his jeans to peel them down his leg. "Lucky there's no muscle damage, big guy. But you're still a stubborn jerk, you know that?"

Reece winced, grinning through the pain. "Yeah, being engaged to Sully's taught you all about stubborn jerks and their minor aches and pains, hasn't it, little girl?"

"Watch it, pal." Sully leaned over the dining room table where Reece lay on his stomach like a roast served up on a dinner platter. "I can always send the ladies to another room and patch you up myself."

"Spare me." That shut him up quick. He didn't say another word until after the wound was cleaned and a burn dressing taped in place. Breeana offered him some pain meds, but he shook his head while he hitched up his jeans. "Get Micah in here. I want his fingers to do the walking on the internet while I head back to the water tower."

The internet? Billie couldn't decide what he meant by that and didn't have time to ask when Sully cut in, his expression grim. "Hawke's waiting for you outside in an SUV. Try to get back here in once piece this time."

Reece tapped fists with him, but didn't say a word. *Of course, Reece could be the real target of the killer.* Panicked, Billie didn't care who watched as she marched up to him, stood on her tiptoes, and kissed him full on the mouth.

REECE HELD THE MELTED remains of a cell phone in his hand—the ignition switch. Another cell phone had called this one to set off the explosion—instant *sayōnara* for anyone hanging around the vicinity—an efficient way of killing off enemies. And Semtex was the incendiary device. Thank Christ, the perp hadn't used enough of the stuff to cause a bigger bang, a goddamn miracle for Billie and him. It was impossible to guess if it was military grade or stolen from a demolition site, but he'd make some calls. Local police would know if anyone had reported a break in.

His cell phone rang. *Billie?*

Reece glanced at the small screen. *Nope, not Billie.* He didn't recognize the number. Hitting the button, he said, "Talk to me."

"Halloo stud muffin." The voice came through the line on a whisper. "I need you."

"Maurice? You'll have to speak up." Jeez, the little guy's timing was off if he'd called to flirt. "I'm in the middle of something, so this better be good."

"It's the shits, lamb chop. I've found a clue to the nasty man we talked about." The squeak of his nasal voice raised an octave. "I'm scared poopless. Need to get out of my spandex before I pee myself. Oops, gotta go."

"Stay inside. Lock yourself in the trailer and wait for me." Reece whistled for Hawke to head for the SUV. "I'll be there in ten minutes."

"Meet me in the parking lot. Don't worry, I'll be undercover." The line went dead.

Reece burned rubber for the movie set, humping the SUV over potholes and through a dried-up streambed to shave seconds off his ETA. Incognito was a misnomer when it came to Maurice. The guy would stick out like a sore thumb, no doubt in ostrich feathers and spike heels if he dressed true to form. So, yeah, that made him a Technicolor target for anyone looking to kill a snitch dogging his heels. Jesus, he shouldn't have asked him to be his eyes and ears with the film crew, a big mistake. Swerving into the parking lot, concern knotted his stomach like a pretzel. He'd never forgive himself if something bad happened to Maurice.

Reece did a quick scan of the other vehicles on the lot. Nada. Nothing moved or breathed, except for the sound of a far-away loudspeaker demanding, "Quiet on the set."

Hawke hitched a glance in his direction. "Did you say your informant would be wearing a disguise?"

"Yeah? Why, you see someone?"

"Check out the giant Easter bunny at two o'clock." Hawke's face split into a wide grin. "There's a pink one hiding in the bed of a pick-up over there. Its floppy ears are sticking up a foot higher than the box."

"For crying out loud. Might have known he'd wear pink. It's in his color chart." Reece reached the truck, popped the tailgate, and grabbed Maurice's arms to slide him on out, gigantic bunny feet plopping to the dirt between his shitkickers. Whiskers scratched through his Tee, big rabbit paws wrapping around his hips to hug his butt. "Cut that out, Maurice."

Hawke mumbled a barely discernible "what the fuck?" then closed his eyes. "Think I'll step over there if you two need a private moment."

"Plant your boots," Reece snarled, not wanting to be alone with the grabby hare. "Maurice has something to tell both of us."

"You sure about that?" Hawke shrugged, lifting his palms in the air. "Just saying."

"What's the rush, sugar bear?" Bunny fur burrowed tighter against him. "Can't we snuggle for a few minutes?"

Reece grabbed his shoulders and tried to disengage. "I already told you...I'm spoken for."

"Right. Theo. The muscle head is still twisting up your sheets and your head. I just don't get it. He's so... uncivilized." Maurice still clung to him like lint, shedding some tears under his armpit in the process. "If you'd only open your eyes and see who's right here in front of you—"

Hawke choked out a growl behind him.

What the hell? Reece glanced over his shoulder at his pal.

"You and Theo, huh? You two timing son of a bitch." Hawke shoved him, nudging him back a couple steps to glare at the bunny. "Get your paws off my man, wabbit."

"*Your* man?" Maurice's eyes bulged from their sockets. "What *is* it with you macho types?"

"Think of us as a band of brothers." Hawke got in his face and gave him the stare down, hands on hips, thumb and forefinger circling the butt of his Glock. The little guy didn't miss the finger action. He looked ready to hop for the hills on his three-foot-long bunny feet. "We eat together, we sleep together, and we keep it in the family. Got it?"

"Roger dodger." Maurice saluted Hawke then backed up a few paces, beckoning him to lift the tailgate back in place, apparently anxious to get the hell out of there. "This is what I wanted to show you. Do I do great spy work, or what?"

"Let the good times roll, Bugsy." A bullet hole lay front and center, puncturing the dusty black paint close to the bumper of the pickup. Reece knelt, running his fingers over it. Judging by the diameter of entry, the gauge could be either a 7.62mm NATO round or a .308 from a Winchester.

And the M25 sniper rifle Law had fired at the bomber used 7.62mm ammo.

Chapter 9

Billie leaned over a picnic table at the rodeo grounds, verifying the checklist on her clipboard. Micah tacked up blueprints on the support beams of the judges' booth for her to study. Man, she didn't have a clue. Should have gnawed on a pitchfork last night instead of bragging to anyone who would listen that she could handle the rodeo set up herself. *A piece of cake...*that's what she'd said.

I'm an idiot.

"Not sure, Mic, but I think you've got some of those diagrams hanging upside down and sideways."

"No kidding? But then again, how in blazes would I know?" He shook his head. "Thought you said you knew the ins and outs of this gig."

"I may have exaggerated a little." Sure, from the bottom of a margarita pitcher everything had looked easy-peasy last night, and she'd flapped her gums. Until her hangover kicked in at the crack of dawn, the same time the rental company's vehicles rolled to a stop at the gate and started honking. And how was she to know it took a convoy of eighteen-wheelers to schlep in the rodeo equipment? *Yikes.*

She'd staggered outside to point them in the right direction—across the road and a half mile down from the ranch house to offload the stuff. "I didn't expect anyone to take me seriously."

"Hmm, guess we all got fooled." Micah gave her a brotherly nudge on the shoulder and almost sent her flying. "Easy there, short stuff. Looks like you've lost your sea legs."

See, that was the problem with drinking too much...it messed her up for days. She'd been stupid to hit the booze last night after surviving the explosion, especially since she didn't usually drink. Now there was nothing but payback in her crystal ball—the shakes, a migraine, and the freaking rodeo grounds to set up.

Of course, Reece and her dad had cackled like a couple of hens with the first blast of a semi's air horn this morning. While she'd held her head in her hands, trying to keep her brain from seeping out her ears, Rocket had carried her to Micah's SUV and sent her on her way.

The big dope. He'd damn well known she was sick as a pup and up to her ears in misinformation if she thought she could handle this alone. Yep, he had worked the rodeo when he'd lived on the ranch. Helped her father with the setup and takedown more than once.

Way out of her element, Billie normally focused on the entertainment and contestants' side of things. She booked live music and caterers, all while handling participants' registration. This was a disaster of major proportions.

"What am I going to do?" Tossing her pen on the clipboard, she scratched her head. A stupid move when even the ends of her hair hurt. "I don't know where to start."

Palms in the air, Micah backed up a step. "Whoa, don't look at me. I'm just the protection detail on this op. You're on your own with the rest of it."

"Coward."

Mic ignored her. Hands on hips, he turned around to eyeball the hills behind them. On the lookout for bad guys? Maybe so, but more likely he was laughing his ass off at the predicament she'd gotten herself into.

Crap. The rodeo set up was her dad's domain, but he'd been focused on protecting the livestock lately, since Bad to the Bone got loose in the horse barn. Then the explosion yesterday had upset him even more. So, fool that she was, she'd offered to take this little gem off his hands to cut him some slack. Yes, she'd downright insisted on it. The fact she'd been celebrating her and Reece's narrow escape from death with a lot of booze didn't really factor into the equation. 'Cuz when Billie Bradshaw gave her word, she kept it. Absolutely.

She gazed at the mess around her. The air was still. Nothing moved, except for the metal poles being tossed from a truck and clanging together, which didn't help her headache. For the love of Mike, there were bleachers to bolt together, tons of them. Lighting towers to erect. Crowd control fencing and parking barricades to assemble. What about the gigantic circus tent that would house the resto-bar? It must be in back of a truck somewhere. And didn't the entertainment stage need to be built inside the tent, which meant the tent had to go up first? She couldn't remember.

Mind spinning, Billie initialed sheet after sheet on the delivery manifest, running her eyes over listings for generators, electrical cables, portable toilets, shower trailers for the contestants, barbeques, propane tanks, ticket booths, and more. Meanwhile, the work crew that came with the trucks stood around waiting for her to give them instructions. If only she had a freaking clue.

A king-size bottle of painkillers and thermos of coffee might help clear her noggin enough to get this show on the road. *Where the heck is Dottie with the goods?* She'd called her an hour ago.

"I am so screwed." She sighed, ready to toss in the towel. Thirty-six hours. That's all the time she had to set everything up. A logistical nightmare. But like it or not, contestants would be rolling through those gates tomorrow night. Not to mention the chefs, waiters, barmaids, tack suppliers, tradesmen, parking attendants, EMTs, clowns, musicians, volunteers, cashiers, farm equipment representatives, and the truck dealership selling tickets for the fully loaded pickup being raffled at the event. The list went on. And on. And on.

Aargh!

Might as well face it, her focus lately had been on the movie set. And the fact someone wanted her and Reece dead, of course. She hadn't thought about the stupid rodeo in days.

"Having fun, peaches?" *Speak of the devil*; Rocket strolled her way looking like the Marlboro Man. Bootleg jeans hugging his thighs. Scuffed cowboy boots on his feet. A navy T-shirt molded to his chest, and a Stetson angled low over his eyes. He'd look mighty fine if she wasn't so pissed at him.

Wow, he evens smells good. Well, at least one of us had time for a shower this morning. Meanwhile, she reeked of the stogie she vaguely remembered puffing last night. Small wonder she'd hurled her cookies. Not one of her finest moments.

"I suppose you came to gloat?"

"Who? Me?" He winked, planted a kiss on top of her head, and dropped a soft-sided cooler and coffee jug on the picnic table in front of her. "Dottie sent me with emergency supplies—coffee, aspirin, and breakfast sandwiches."

"Thank God. I may live after all." Billie grabbed for the coffee jug and poured herself a mug. *Manna from heaven. Yes!*

"Yo, about time you showed up. I was about to kill myself." Micah ambled over and helped himself to coffee and a sandwich. "You never told me Rocket Girl's such a pain in the ass when she's got a hangover. She's no damn fun at all."

"You son-of-a—!"

Reece held her back, shoved the hat back from his eyes, and shot Micah a grin. "Guess she fell for it then?"

"Hook, line, and sinker, my man. Her whining just about did me in."

The two of them high-fived, ignoring her expletives. Reece wrapped an arm around her waist, lifted her off the bench, and swung her around. "Let go of me, you big oaf!"

He pointed a finger dead ahead, pulled off his Stetson, and smooshed it down on her hair. "Wha-what's going on?"

Her dad, Theo, Hawke, Sully, Breeana, Mel, and a bunch of ranch hands headed their way from the parking area, mile-wide grins on their faces. "Fun is fun, babe, but did you really think we'd hang you out to dry?"

"Halleluiah!" She couldn't believe her blurry eyes. "The rodeo is saved!"

"It gets better than that, girlfriend." Bree jogged over, wrapped an arm around her neck, and smooched her cheek.

"Guess what? Satan's got game. I just found out he's not sterile."

Billie was pretty sure her jaw dropped to her boots at that moment.

"ARE YOU SURE?" BILLIE moved her hands to her cheeks as if waiting for the punch line of a bad joke. Reece wasn't sure if she'd heard right, given the fact she wasn't firing on all cylinders this morning.

"Hey, I'm positive. The lab just called. Satan's sperm motility rate is off the charts." Breeana laughed. "Your bad boy has a post-thaw rate of ninety-five percent."

"Holy crap. Satan's not shooting blanks at all."

"Far from it, kiddo. He's the king of any stable with a rate like that."

Billie grabbed Reece around the waist and squeezed him hard. A grin curved her mouth. He hadn't seen her this happy in a long, long time. She sobered after a while, though, and asked the hard question.

"If Satan's not sterile, then what the heck happened?"

"Seth Davis wouldn't lie, darlin'." Charley stepped toward her, kicking up dust with the toe of a boot. "He can't run that fancy Montana spread of his based on anything but the truth."

"Dad? You knew about this?" Billie broke eye contact with her father long enough to nail Reece with an accusatory glare.

He shrugged his shoulders. *Hey, don't look at me. I didn't open my big mouth.*

"Course I knew. Just didn't want to face it." Her father fumbled his words as he raked a hand through his hair. "Seth called me when he suspected a problem with the last order. Guess I was a little abrupt on the phone. Said I'd get back to him, but never did."

"That must be why he called me." She blew out a breath, shaking her head. "His mares didn't impregnate and he was surprised, since he'd used Satan for breeding before. He ordered more straws from another collection of his semen and had them tested. The samples rated at less than thirty percent."

"Hate to break it up, folks, but we've got work to do." Reece didn't like the fact several of the ranch hands hung about, listening to the conversation. Besides, they had a rodeo to put to rights, and he didn't want Billie out in the open any longer than necessary. "We can discuss this later on, when you're not paying a work crew to stand around."

Charley took the hint and began handing out assignments to the men congregated around them, leaving Reece to corral the women.

He swung an arm wide, pointing to his left. "Ladies, the tent will go up over there. Climb up in the judges' booth and enjoy the view until the boys hoist that sucker. Once it's done, you'll be in charge of the sound stage and everything else inside the tent, including the bar."

Sully stepped forward after Hawke and the girls headed off. "Hawke and I will hang out with the women today."

"Good idea. We don't know the work crew this rental company brought in from cow shit. Keep a close eye on Billie for me."

"You're not tagging along?"

"Later, after I'm sure Theo's all set." He wanted him and his sniper rifle up in the hills, in case there was trouble. "And I need to touch base with Micah."

"I'll let you get to it then."

Reece headed for Micah, catching a glimpse of the herd of bucking horses roaming the fields beyond the barn. He watched them nip at each other as they galloped along. A good bucking horse could cost fifteen thousand, or more. And a bucking bull like Bad to the Bone? He estimated forty thousand, easy, not to mention his value in stud fees. The bottom line? Charley and Billie had a ton of money invested in this ranch. And they could lose it all, if Reece and his team didn't get to the bottom of this vendetta. Fast.

Messing with Satan's sperm was bad enough, but what would come next?

Mic worked with a crew out by the barn, connecting steel tubing for the fenced double alley that would safely move livestock from holding pens to the corral for various rodeo events. "Got a minute?"

"Sure." He wiped sweat off his brow with the tail of his shirt. "What's up?"

"First off, thanks for taking care of Billie this morning. I'm sorry if she caused you any grief, but I couldn't resist giving her a hard time after the stunt she pulled last night."

"We've all been there, man." Micah cracked a grin. "At least she didn't throw up on my shoes like she did yours. Besides, she's been riding the edge since this whole thing began. I'm surprised she kept it together for as long as she did."

"Billie's tough. She'll do okay." Reece scrubbed a hand down his face. Hoping she could hold on a while longer. "Listen, did you do the internet search I asked you about?"

"I did. And you were right. Jenny Lee Calhoun has quite the Twitter feed. About twelve hundred people are following her, and all of them with aliases that are almost impossible to trace. She tweeted from the ranch yesterday after Dottie went apeshit on her mother. Sent out a couple tweets actually, including one where she mentions Billie riding out to check on the horses and donkeys after the free-for-all in the kitchen."

"The bomber must have read her tweet. That's how he beat us to the water tower."

"Sure looks that way." Micah scowled. "It's lucky the bastard was pressed for time. He did a lousy job hiding the explosives."

"Amen to that. Otherwise I might have missed them." Reece shoved on his sunglasses. As they settled on the bridge of his nose, he scanned the hills. "Have you seen Theo around?"

"Yup." Mic angled his chin to the right. "Check out the giant elm up on the ridge."

"I don't see him." He took another look. Nothing. No sign of Theo. "Damn, he's good."

Micah shoved gloves on and went back to locking the steel bars in place. "Trust me, he's up there. The man's got a way of disappearing."

"You've got that right."

Climbing the rails to ensure the fencing was stable, Mic glanced his way and laughed like a fool.

"Okay, I'll bite. What's the joke?"

"Maybe he's wearing a disguise. Like your pink Easter bunny informant. Nice going, ace. You really know how to pick 'em."

"Fuck you, too."

Billie looked ashen as death when Reece caught up to her a few hours later. Her shuttered lashes fanned the paleness of the skin on her cheeks. Damn, she looked awful, and yet he still wanted her, a full-blown ache tugging on his heartstrings. He fought the grin itching to form, knowing he reacted to her like a lovesick heifer. She lifted a couple chairs to carry them inside the tent and almost keeled over. He managed to steady her before she lost her balance. "Oops, sorry about that."

"You're done in, peaches." He set down the chairs, wrapped an arm around her, and headed for the SUV. "Come on, you can come out to play with the big kids tomorrow. But right now, I need you back at the ranch."

"What for?" She sighed as she stumbled along, cast a wary glance his way. "It's not something kinky, is it? 'Cuz I'm way too tired."

"I already figured that out." He stopped to tunnel his hands through her hair, running his lips over hers for a quick taste. "Besides, Breeana wants me to take it easy until the burn on my leg heals a little more. I want you to hit the rack for a few hours, that's all. A nap will do you good."

She licked her bottom lip when he released her, which drove him insane. He could nibble on her sweet mouth for a week, without coming up for air, and still not get enough. Too bad she was almost out on her feet, although with the devil riding his shoulder, he wanted to convince her otherwise. Hell no. She was dog tired and needed to catch some shut eye. *Hear that, Mom? I can be a gentleman when I have no other choice.*

"I don't think I can take off right now. Not when everyone else is working their butts off."

"You're the only one with a recent head injury, babe. And you hit the ground pretty hard yesterday when the bomb went off. No one will hold it against you if you grab some down time. Besides, you'll be working tonight."

"I wouldn't call it work, cowboy." Billie winked, stretched up on her toes, and kissed a trail down his neck. "Give me a few hours to recoup and I'll model my sexiest lingerie."

"Be still my aching heart." Reece slapped a hand on his chest and thumped it a few times. "You little flirt. I may not survive until then. But there's something else I'll need your help with first."

"Oh? Like what?" There was definitely suspicion in her gaze now. She knew he was up to something. Problem was, she might not like the game plan.

"How would you like to catch the sperm annihilator?"

Her eyes widened in disbelief. "Tonight? You think we can catch him, just like that?"

"It's a bulletproof plan, peaches. Are you in?"

"You're kidding, right?" Billie climbed in the SUV, turned in the seat to grab him by the collar. "Give me a gun and I'll shoot him in his sperm bank."

BANYAN WATCHED THE uniforms circle the pickup for a third time, snapping pictures as they went, as if they thought more bullet holes might suddenly appear. *Dumb and Dumber*, that's what he called them. They were too cornball to work in the city so got stuck in the back of Nowhere-ville with the rest of the hicks.

"We have reason to believe this vehicle was involved in a crime," Dumb said, pumping up his bulk as he moseyed over to Banyan.

You don't say? Time for the official Banyan shtick on the situation. "I'm sorry I can't be more helpful, officer. But you see, I only use the truck on the job. The bullet hole could have already been there when the film company rented it. It's hard to notice."

"He's got a point." Dumber, a wiry little armpit of a man, bent to slide his finger in the crack below the tailgate. "See here? The hole's tucked right into the bumper seam. Rental company could've missed it when someone else returned the pick-up. Too bad there's no bullet to run ballistics against the guard's weapon at the *Circle B*. Then we'd know for sure."

"In other words, we've got nothing," Dumb agreed, handing Banyan back his license, registration, and rental agreement. "Just stick around for a few days, in case we have more questions."

"No problem. But be sure to note in your report that several employees at the movie site have access to this truck and drive it regularly. I'm not the only one."

The cops nodded and walked off, their cruiser exiting the parking garage a few minutes later. *About goddamn time.*

Spinelli walked out of the shadows and glared at him. He looked as if he wanted to say something then changed his mind and strode back into the hotel. *Weird asshole.*

Banyan climbed in the pickup and keyed the ignition, waiting for a couple of lackeys from the film crew to get a move on and throw their stuff in back. The makeup artist gave him the eye as she crowded him on the bench seat, making room for one of his maintenance cronies on the passenger side. Pulling out of the garage, Banyan headed for the highway and gunned the engine, madder than hell at whoever had spotted the bullet hole and reported it to the cops. He'd nail the chicken shit when he found him. Or maybe not. Better to lay low and keep off the grid from now on. No point in tempting fate before the grand finale.

Rolling down the window, he inhaled deep and almost choked on the smell. Either some farmer was fertilizing his crops with pig manure or the stench came from inside the truck. *Clean Toilets 'R Us,* he thought with disgust, surprised the gal beside him found him so appealing. He suspected he carried the stink of the job on his work clothes, even after he'd washed them. He'd had it with this undercover gig. When he wasn't cranking on generators or tinkering with electronics, he was swabbing the heads. The Ladies' being the worst. *Freakin' women are slobs.*

And those fucking piggies? Thinking they could pressure him into admitting he'd been the one to blow the water tower? *Get real.*

Anyone could have taken the pick-up and done the deed. They had nothing on him, and they knew it. A bullet hole in the bumper meant zip. Besides, he'd be long gone before they caught on to him. Assholes didn't even have his real name, and he'd been careful to wear work gloves inside the truck. No worries. He'd be nothing but a ghost on their radar soon. Wheels up and back to the military. *Salut!*

Foley was the only real threat to him. The freak possessed a wicked sixth sense. He also had a shitload of reasons to suspect him of setting off the fireworks. Still, he wouldn't make a move on him unless he was sure, because he needed him to carry out the plan.

Lucky for me there's been rumblings about other problems at Bradshaw's ranch. Seems there's a disgruntled employee doing some damage over there. Problem is they can't smoke the prick out of his hidey-hole. That ought to confuse Foley for a while. Give him someone else to pin this on.

Speaking of the devil, his phone rang. He thought about letting it go to voice mail but changed his mind. Better to get the yelling over with when they weren't face-to-face. He connected the call. "Yo. I'm in the pick-up, and I've got company."

"Shag it, Banyan. I saw the cops questioning you in the garage. What the fuck did you do? Plant any bombs lately?"

Banyan laughed. "Not guilty."

"That so? Then why were the Five-Oh boys sniffing up your ass? Listen, you little punk. If I find out you made a hit on Morgan without my say so, I'll skin you alive!"

Eat shit, Foley. You'll never know if it was me who blew that tower or Mr. Employee of the Month at the Circle B. You'll just have to deal and move on. "I said it before, and I'll say it again...I have no idea what you're talking about."

"I've got a bullet with your name on it, Banyan. Just want you to know."

"Ease off, pal. There's no reason to—"

Foley hung up. Banyan cursed under his breath. *Trust him to get the last word.*

Wanda, the makeup chick, ran a hand up his thigh, pleasantly refocusing his attention somewhere else. The blood drained from his head straight to his dick. Whoa, she might be a pasty-faced heifer, but she smelled pretty and had definite possibilities. Essence of vanilla surrounded her, making him think of home-baked cookies. What a laugh. Good 'ole Mom had been stoned to the gills for most of his childhood.

Ah, the joys of a happy home.

She trailed her fingers higher up the inside of his thigh, causing his pants to tent. He glanced uneasily at the other mope in the truck. The guy was clueless, gazing out the window at the cows rolling by. Hell, if cosmetic girl played her cards right, he'd let her go down on him at break time. Or hand her over to Foley as a peace offering. *That'd shut him up.*

Nah, he quickly discarded the idea, knowing the bastard would leave marks on her. Or kill her. No doubt in his mind. Sex with Foley was nasty business—burning, kicking, and punching being his way of getting off. And that's when he was in a good mood. Otherwise, it was the bitch's fault he couldn't shoot for the stars. Then the scalpel would come out. Or sulfuric acid.

Banyan cringed, had seen him use both on women during their deployments. Women selling their bodies to feed their children ended up dead or disfigured if they crossed his path. How many times had Banyan heard him say it? "The only good whore is a dead whore."

Jeez, how many women has he killed? No idea, Banyan had only witnessed a few, but more than enough to scrape his insides raw. Foley was insane, depraved. God, he hated the beast. Could never figure out what he had against women. More to the point, why punish Billie Bradshaw for Morgan's transgressions?

He thought about the script again, knew she would replace Savannah Lloyd—the star of the pilot episode—during the flag ceremony at the rodeo opening. He also knew the sniper on Marcus's payroll could wing her off the horse just as easily as kill her, the end result being the same. Morgan would race like thunder to protect her and... *Boom!*

One dead spec ops guy with a bullet planted in his forehead. The only difference being rodeo queen would live to race the barrels another day. A good thing to his way of thinking; their job would get done, either way.

The only question is will Foley go for it? Not in this lifetime, because it didn't involve getting his rocks off by killing Morgan's woman. The scuz.

Banyan eased makeup girl's hand off his fly while mulling over his choices. Should he place a private call to Marcus? If he knew Foley was a danger to the operation, he might pay the sniper a bonus to blow him off the face of the earth.

But...will Marcus believe me?

Chapter 10

Reece and his team stood in the breeding shed, afraid to breathe. Billie and Breeana had made it clear as crystal. No sudden moves and no loud noises when they brought Satan in for his grand performance. Otherwise, they'd have to leave.

Reece was no stranger to the horsy dating game. He'd helped out a time or two in his rodeo days. But when Barry Manilow poured out of the ceiling speakers singing *Mandy*, he almost split a gut holding his laughter in check. Guess the ritual became pansy-ass once the ladies got involved.

"What's the world coming to?" Hawke shook his head in disgust, placing a shit-kicker on the bottom rung of the fence. "Imagine if men couldn't perform without total silence, sweet love ballads in the background, and God only knows what else?"

"I can imagine it just fine." Sully wrapped an arm around Hawke's neck and noogied the top of his head. "It would make it impossible for you to dance naked on the tabletops at *Hanoi Harry's*. And then we couldn't bet on how many bouncers it'd take to toss your perverted ass out the door."

"Fuck you and the horse you rode in on," Hawke snarled, jabbing Sully in the ribs with an elbow. "Besides that was years ago, and I only did it once. It was my birthday."

Silence fell as Breeana entered the shed with a little black mare in tow. A little black mare with pink ribbons threaded through her mane. Had Reece mentioned pansy-ass before? Man, this whole thing gave him a bad, bad feeling. Using a dummy mare to get the stud in the mood was one thing, but the big guy would go crazy with this filly pushing his buttons. And he was way too much horse for Billie to handle.

Sully must have picked up on his anxious vibe. He made a move toward Bree and the mare. She held up a hand to warn him off. *Good luck with that.* Reece knew Sully would be out there at the first sign of trouble. After all, this wasn't a love-starved Chihuahua waiting in the wings for his big event. The stallion was huge, a powerful breeding machine. He'd plow over anyone who stood in his way.

Next thing he knew, Billie came in with Satan straining his lead line. Reece leapt the rail of the visitor's box and was beside her in an instant. "You need another pair of hands. This fella is already raring to go."

"Thanks. I would have asked Dad or Pike to help, but they need to be off their feet after working the rodeo setup today."

"No problem." Reece cocked his head over his shoulder. "I suppose that cute-as-a-button mare over there is Mandy?"

Billie fought the grin itching to form on her lips and lost, big time. "Yep. Isn't she adorable?"

"Babe." His mouth tipped up at the corners. "You and Breeana are messing with us. Barry Manilow singing in the breeding shed...silk ribbons in Mandy's mane...you're cranking our gears."

"Hey, can't we girls have a little fun? Besides, it couldn't happen to a nicer bunch of guys."

The stallion screamed and lunged without warning, anxious to get the show on the road. Whinnies from the estrous mare said she was ready—wanted to dance the merengue with the superstar—*Now!* Reece jumped between them and held Satan back. "Do the wipe down and suit him up while I can still hold him, Billie. We're running out of time."

With Reece straining every muscle in his body to hold the Palomino in check, Billy dove for a bucket and a wet cloth, washing the stud's joystick and then rolling a condom in place to collect the semen. Satan flagged his tail, indicating all systems were go, and Reece introduced him to the fabulous Mandy.

"Jumping Jehoshaphat," Hunt piped up from the peanut gallery. "That is the biggest damn...condom...I've ever seen."

"You can say that again," Sully mumbled. "Hard to believe, but the freakin' stallion outshines me. What's Breeana gonna think?"

"I gotta say, even I'm feeling kinda...small." The rest of them cracked up at Micah's admission. Rumors of his prowess were legendary among the team. Reece figured it was all shitolla wrapped up in a spit shine, but Mic could be counted on to lighten the load in unbearable situations, while filling them in on his questionable exploits.

Reece breathed a sigh of relief once the lovebirds had finished their happy reunion and were separated again. Billy carefully removed the condom and headed for the door. Reece left Sully and the other guys helping Breeana return the horses to the barn and followed her to a small lab in back of the tack room.

He hung back, mesmerized as she pulled on sterile gloves to pour the semen into a glass cylinder fitted with a filter at the top, checking the markings on the side of the container as the liquid flowed through. "70 milliliters; there's enough here for five straws."

"Honey, can you speak English?"

Reece watched her work, couldn't help the pride swelling his chest. Billie was one hell of a woman. She seemed as comfortable in the lab as she was doing everything else on the ranch, including handling firearms. Her degree from a top notch agriculture university allowed her to run the *Circle B* with a blend of modern technology and the old ways of ranching that made the operation a cut above most Alberta spreads.

"Oh, sorry. I was just saying we have enough semen here for five impregnations. Excellent."

Breeana entered the room, donned latex gloves, and helped Billie with the automatic machine that transferred the semen into plastic straws and sealed the ends. "You might want to bank some of these, Billie. I know a reputable sperm bank in Saint-Hyacinthe you can use. The samples will be good for at least ten years, and possibly closer to twenty."

"Dad and I are seriously considering it, Bree. Satan and Bad to the Bone are both top breeding stock. There may come a time, after they're gone, when we'll want to breed offspring from them again for ourselves."

After tagging the straws with plastic labels she pulled off a printer, Billie changed to a pair of lightweight material gloves and moved across the lab to a gigantic thermos jug squatting in the middle of the floor. A little over three feet high, fog swirled from its wide neck as she removed the heavy lid.

"Liquid nitrogen," she explained. "Don't touch it, Reece. Your fingers will fall off. The gloves I'm wearing are designed to protect my hands and arms."

"I'll keep it in mind." He moved forward to peer inside the Cryo-storage system. "Looks like it's mostly vapor in there."

"Don't kid yourself." Billie unhooked a long handle from the lip at the opening and pulled up a round metal canister. She carefully placed the straws inside. Then she wrote the cylinder number, Satan's name, the lot number, and date stamp in a binder. He'd noticed the same info was tagged on the individual straws as well. "We never let the liquid get below a quarter full, since the temperature needs to be maintained at a steady -180°C. There's a monitor on the lid that signals when it's time to do a refill."

"How do you ship the straws to your clients? I imagine liquid nitrogen is far too dangerous."

"You're right. The straws are packed in special containers that contain dry ice so they won't thaw out too much, and we use a carrier who specializes in transporting biological products."

While Billy lowered the cylinder back into the jug, Reece noticed Bad to the Bone's name and info written against another canister number she'd recorded in the binder. Business must be booming. But, did a competitor want to shut them down? Reece had a hunch they were about to find out.

Billie put the lid back in place, removed the cloth gloves and placed them on a shelf. Breeana tossed her latex ones in the garbage. "Okay, boys and girls, we're all done. So what happens next?"

Reece flipped off the light in the lab, closed the door, and led the women out of the tack room. "Now, we wait."

ONCE A MONTH IT WAS poker night at the *Circle B*. Billie could smell the chili simmering in the kitchen. The dining room table had been removed to make room for four oval poker tables topped in burgundy felt. The tables were full of ranchers. Heck, it looked like half the county had shown up. Six cardsharps sat at her father's table when she strolled up with Breeana and Reece. Reece's pals and Melena stood off to the side, munching on pizza slices and watching the action.

"Since it's dealer's choice, we're playing High Chicago. Best hand and highest spade in the hole splits the pot. Aces high, and your best five cards make up the hand." Her dad shuffled the deck, dealing around the table. The first two cards down, the third, fourth, fifth and sixth cards up, betting rounds taking place between each card facing up and the last card down.

"Trust you to change it up, Charley." Dottie folded her hand after one quick glance and tossed it to the table, apparently not liking what she saw. She got up to replenish their beers and pretzels. "Whatever happened to plain ole five card stud?"

Her father flashed a grin. "Now don't be a sore loser, Dorothy."

Dorothy? How weird is that? When had Dad started using Dottie's given name?

"Ah-ha. Read 'em and weep." Pike laid his cards down on the table, a grin wobbling the toothpick lodged between his teeth. "Don't think anyone's gonna beat my full house."

Deke, one of their ranch hands, waved the ace of spades in the air. "And I've got the highest spade."

They divvied up the pot, about five dollars each in quarters and dimes.

Charley glanced up and caught Billie's eye. "How'd it go with Satan, darlin'?"

"It went fine. He's bedded down for the night." She swooped in to grab a few potato chips out of a bowl. "Mandy was the filly of his dreams, Dad."

"Honey, any breathing, red-blooded mare is the filly of Satan's dreams. Still, I can't wait to hear from Seth after we send him this new batch tomorrow." He paused to take a pull on his long neck bottle. "That ought to dispel any rumors about him shooting blanks. The way I figure it, there was a breakdown with the courier service, and they didn't report it; maybe didn't want to file a claim on their insurance. The straws must have heated up during transit."

"That's what I think, too." Billie gave her father a hug and a kiss on the cheek. "The shipment was damaged somehow. I'm going to talk to our sales rep. I want it in writing it won't happen again."

"Good idea." Her father patted her hands still circling his neck and eyed Reece. "Hey, any of you folks wanna play? We've got room for a few more."

"Thanks, but we'll take a rain check, Charley." Reece looked around at the rest of his crew shaking their heads and then at Breeana and Mel feigning yawns, their hands covering their mouths. "It's been a long day for all of us and we have to finish the rodeo set up in the morning. Guess we'll grab a nightcap and turn in early."

"Sure. Suit yourselves."

They left the dining room and walked down the hallway to the family room. Billie shut the door after everyone had moved inside. Hunt and Law handled the bartending, Mel slicing lemons and limes, and Hawke filling the ice bucket. "You guys really think it will work?"

"The word's out, peaches." Reece passed her a gin and tonic. Wrapping an arm around her shoulders, his breath fanned the top of her head. "Everyone knows about the new sperm samples, and the fact they're leaving here tomorrow. The guy has to make his move tonight."

"Don't worry, it's a shoe in." Sully agreed, clinking his glass with hers. "We'll nail the bastard by morning."

Billie and Reece were alone in her room a while later. He watched as she changed out of her boots, deciding her Nikes were better suited for a stealthy walk through the stables. While Reece never made a sound when he moved in his shit-kickers, her boots tended to creak with every footfall. Maybe she should oil them. Tying up her sneakers, she wrung her hands, her heart hammering with the knowledge they were about to catch the traitor inside *Circle B* ranks. Not a happy thought when she considered most of these people family.

She moved to the window, watching a sliver of moon rise against the inky night. Stars winked in the distance, reminding her of a childhood song about wishing on stars. *If only.* She expelled a shaky breath, dreading the upcoming confrontation. "Okay, I'm ready."

Reece turned her around, sensing her mushrooming concern. "You don't have to do this."

"Yes, I do. I need to face it head on. Let's go."

"In a minute." His eyes swept over her, catching the anxiousness of her gaze. Lingering on her breasts that moved with every panicked gulp of air, he pulled up her shirt and eased his arms around her. "I need to touch you first, skin to skin. You were one hell of a turn-on in the breeding shed tonight."

"Rocket, I—"

His mouth claimed hers, hungry and hot, sending liquid heat to her core. His lips trailed to the sensitive spot behind her ear as he cupped her bottom, splaying her against the bulge of his cargo pants. "I wish I had time to taste all of you."

"I wish you did, too." Billie burrowed against him, wanting to breathe in his heat, move to the bed, forgetting about the samples in the lab and the turncoat planning to destroy them.

How can one of my own people hate me so much?

His lips covering hers again and his tongue delving deep, Reece's hands traced her ribcage to settle against the sides of her breasts before pulling away. Voice soft with concern, he reached out, tucking her hair behind her ears. "Whatever happens, we'll handle it together. It will be all right."

Billie nodded, about to respond when Melena and Theo edged through the bathroom door from Reece's room. Mel looked like a pint-sized ninja, dressed in black from head to toe. Billie almost giggled looking at her. She sure wasn't much of a threat, unless you looked at the man watching her back. Theo overshadowed her, a big, brawny warrior packing lots of muscle and a gun at his hip.

He moved forward to join Reece. "I'll go down first and make sure no one's hanging about at the bottom. I just wish these gals would stay put and leave this to us."

Mel stood on tiptoes, smoothing the frown lines on his brow with a fingertip. "You worry too much, Sparky. We're going, either with you or without you. 'Cuz Billie and I want to kick ass for a change."

He laughed, shook his head, and moved to the window—their point of exit—the only way for them to leave the house without being noticed. How else would they catch the culprit in the act?

Melena and Billie crowded in behind Theo, determined to be next in line. He edged out, grabbed the pipe, and started down. First in line, Billie watched him go. Steel creaked, rattling against the side of the house. *Holy crap!* The supporting clamps tore away from the wall. Billie didn't think; she lunged for the pipe as it swayed further out. Next thing she knew, she was halfway out the window with her head pointing toward the ground. She stared in horror but couldn't let go. If she did, the pipe would spin out of control. Theo could break his back or worse when he hit the ground.

"Hold on!" Mel wrapped her arms around Billy's waist and they both slid farther out the window. A steely hand gripped her leg and held fast. *Reece.* He somehow managed to hold both of them while hooking the drainpipe with his other hand and pulling it back against the wall. Terrified, Billie now found herself hanging with nothing to hold onto, not even the blasted pipe.

Once Theo reached the halfway point, Reece released the pipe and whisked Melena back inside. Strong arms circled her next. "Easy. I've got you."

Feet planted on the carpet inside her bedroom, Billie wrapped her arms around his neck. "Guess the drainpipe couldn't handle Theo's weight."

"No shit, Sherlock." Reece ran his hands down her arms, checking for injuries. Apparently satisfied, his mouth curved in a grin. "Jeez, you sure know how to scare the bejeezus out of a guy. Do you ladies want to call it quits for tonight or do you think we can try this again? Without the *Cirque du Soleil* aerobatics this time."

Honestly? I'd rather hide under the covers and sleep through this whole nightmare. Except Billie had never been one to let other people handle the tougher problems. No, the trouble was hers and she'd deal with it. Worry about the fallout later.

"Stuff it, Rocket. I'm next in line." Reece shot her a nod of approval, giving her the moxie she needed to climb out on the ledge.

"You'll be fine, babe. I won't let you fall."

He was right. She grasped the pipe and shimmied down without any effort, easy as pie. Theo lifted her to the ground when she neared the bottom. Next came his little pixie, sliding down like a pro. Theo wrapped an arm around Melena when she landed, ruffling her spiky blond hair. "Sugar, you took another three years off my life when you nearly fell out the window. Will you quit doing that stuff?"

She patted his jaw. "No worries, big man. Billie and I had it under control."

He rolled his eyes, squeezing her hard against him. "Yeah, I noticed."

They looked up to watch Reece climb on the ledge. Billie wondered how he'd make it with no one holding the pipe. *Stupid question.* He dove through the air, catching a limb of the old maple tree swaying about ten feet out from the house.

For the love of Mike! The branch miraculously held, Reece swinging along it toward the trunk. Climbing to the bottom in half a minute, he brushed leaves from his clothes, wrapped her around the waist, and brushed his lips against her forehead. "Let's go."

"Show off." She placed her hand in his and followed his lead.

Keeping low, they kept to the shadows while crossing the field, entering the barn from the paddock side. Reece went in first, with her and Mel squished in the middle, and Theo bringing up the rear. Billie swallowed a startled cry when she saw lights click on in the tack room up ahead. A door snicked open and closed, the door to the lab. Their culprit was already inside doing his dirty work.

She inched closer and came up against Reece's back. When she tried to move by him, he held her back. Shrugging out of his grip, she dodged under his arm to peer through the glass door to the lab. *Oh. My. God!*

The last person she expected to see stood inside. Billie shook her head, not understanding. What the hell did her father think he was doing?

BILLIE SHOT THROUGH the lab door like a thunderbolt. "Dad!"

Reece dogged her heels, signalling Theo to stay in the tack room and keep watch with Melena. Once he was inside, he ground to a quick halt, the tension in the air thick enough to stop an Abrams tank.

Jesus, Mary, and Joseph. This didn't look good.

Charley faced off against his daughter without saying a word. The look he gave her—more like a stare down—spoke volumes. He was hiding something.

Reece did a quick scan of the lab, relieved to see the lid still on the Cryo-storage unit. Nothing seemed out of place. No semen straws floating in hot water at the sink to damage their contents. Computer and lab equipment looked A-okay. Lab books, files, and binders all neatly stacked on the shelves where Billie had left them a few hours ago. The low hum of overhead lighting was the only sound in the room, except for a refrigerator whispering in a far corner.

"What are you doing in here, Dad?" Billie's voice wobbled as her fists tightened at her sides, a sure sign she was stressed to the max. Small wonder, considering dear old dad was giving her the silent treatment. Reece wanted to uncurl her fingers, ease the anxiety hunching her shoulders with a long, slow massage. Unfortunately, this wasn't the time or the place.

Charley finally moved away from the wall with Dottie trailing behind him. He tugged her alongside him, the two of them acting as guilty as sin. One glimpse at the glance they exchanged pretty much told the tale. They were up to their eyeballs in horseshit and going under for the third time. At the very least, Billie deserved to hear them admit it. He leaned on the truth buzzer with an intimidating growl. "Which one of you wants to tell us what's going on?"

"It was me." Dottie almost shouted. She clung to Charley's hand as though he was her lifeline. Reece had to give her credit, though, when she stared straight at Billie and didn't pull any punches. "I damaged Satan's sperm in those shipments."

Her words cut through the air like a stiletto. Billie fumbled for a comeback. He could see the heartbreak in her eyes and wanted to ease the hurt. Dottie had raised her from the age of twelve, for Pete's sake. It must be impossible to imagine her doing this kind of harm for no good reason. "Why would you do such a terrible thing? You're my family. I've always loved you like a mother."

"I'm sorry, and that's all I'm gonna say." Dottie focused on the toes of her scuffed boots. "You can call the sheriff. Press charges. I won't give you any more trouble."

"She didn't do it to hurt you, darlin'," Charley said, heaving out a breath. "She did it to get back at me. And I deserved it."

Reece took Billie's arm, leading her to the computer chair before her legs gave out. She was pale as a ghost, her hands shaking in her lap. *Damn it, Charley, what the fuck did you do to cause your daughter so much pain?* He eyed him with a cold stare. "Since Dottie's clammed up, you'd better start at the beginning and fill us in on the details."

"Don't say anything!" Dottie jumped to Charley's defense. "Keep your lips zipped. *I* did it and *I'll* pay the price."

Bingo, and there it was, as obvious as a jet stream across a clear blue sky. Dottie loved the father *and* the child. And she would do anything to hide Charley's screw-up from Billie. Hell, she'd even go to jail if it meant keeping Charley's and Billie's relationship intact.

Billie's no fool. She'll figure it out. Her father's in this up to his armpits and sinking fast.

"Dad? Tell me what happened, or I swear I'll never talk to you again!" Billie was on her feet and zeroing in, fire burning in her eyes and icy determination hardening her heart. Reece couldn't help but feel a surge of pride. When Billie declared war, she didn't take any prisoners. It was *do* or *die* time for Pops.

And goddamn if he didn't see a flash of pride in the old man's eyes, too. He might be facing the firing squad, but he'd die happy knowing he couldn't best his little girl. "It's not easy to confess I messed up, least of all to you. I ain't proud of it, believe me."

"Charley!" Dottie warned him again, a scowl riding her expression.

"Keep quiet woman and let me say my piece." The old man watched his daughter again, seemed to know his goose was in the roasting pan unless he came clean. "When you were shot and lying unconscious in the hospital, I was scared shitless you wouldn't make it."

"I get that. Go on." Arms crossed over her chest, Billie tapped the floor with a nervous foot, no doubt wanting him to move along with the newsfeed.

Charley shoved his hands in his jeans pockets and hung his head. "I hightailed it out of the trauma unit when Rocket arrived to guard you that night. Headed for home, but ended up at a bar instead. You see, praying didn't make the worrying stop, Billie, and I figured a whiskey might take the edge off. I wanted to lose the pain for a couple hours."

"And this is a bad thing?" Billie's glare at her father eased a fraction. "You were entitled to let off some steam after that nightmare. Heck, Dad, you were there for me. You kept me sane when I was scared to death. Held my hand and smiled at me. Convinced me I'd make it through, even when I half believed I still might die. I remember all of it, before I passed out. But none of this has anything to do with Dottie going berserk and destroying the samples."

"If you'd let me get this off my chest, you might think otherwise." Charley raked a hand through his hair, looked like he'd rather be having his teeth pulled, without anaesthetic, than standing there choking on what was stuck in his craw. "I didn't just have a few drinks, my girl, I got hammered to the freaking gills. And Lorelei was there. She drove me home."

When Billie remained silent, he glanced at Dottie, wrapped an arm around her shoulders, and pulled her against his side.

Reece's inner radar pinged, more like bonged, to attention.

"The truth is Lorelei offered me more than just a ride to my door. And she didn't need to ask me twice. I slept with her...here, in the house...though I don't remember doin' it. But, she was with me when I rolled out of bed the next mornin'. And Dottie saw her."

Billie slid her gaze from her father to Dottie. Reece could see it in her eyes, hear it in her voice when she spoke. She'd connected the dots. "You're in love with my father."

Dottie nodded her head, swallowing hard, her feelings for the man almost flashing in red neon across her forehead. "I've loved him since the day I arrived here, fifteen years ago, but knew I couldn't act on it so soon after your mama died. So, I held on. Kept hoping he'd come to think of me as more than a housekeeper."

"And when Dad slept with Lorelei under our roof, you snapped." Billie kept her voice soft. One woman talking to another—daughter to surrogate mother—an understanding passing between them that surpassed their age differences, and even Dottie's wrongdoing. "I'm so sorry."

"Don't be. What I did was wrong. I can understand a man having affairs, but not where I live. And not the man I love...not after he claimed to love me back." Tears swam in her eyes. Dottie batted them away in a fierce gesture. "I blamed Lorelei, too. That's the reason I attacked her the other morning in the kitchen. I'd already punished Charley by damaging Satan's straw samples. I finally got even with both of them. But I *never* wanted to cause you pain."

"Oh, Dottie."

Reece doubted he would ever understand women and their soul-baring moments for as long as he lived. It didn't make sense to him that Dottie and Billie were suddenly crying and hugging each other. Behaving as if they were still the best of buds. Meanwhile, he knew Dottie needed to take responsibility for her actions. Otherwise, there could be a repeat performance.

Like the next time Charley stopped in at the *Silver Spur* for a few brewskies and came home with his fly undone. Even if he just forgot to zip it after using the head. Dottie, of the sharp knives and vengeful spirit, was liable to think he'd made another kind of pit stop and perform surgery on his privates. Or kill him. Hell's bells, he'd seen Dottie handle a knife when someone put the snake in Billie's bed. She knew how to use it and was fully capable of doing serious damage.

Reece didn't like it. He'd already guessed Billie wouldn't banish her stand-in mother from the *Circle B*, no matter what she'd done. And guilt-ridden Charley sure as hell wouldn't push Dottie out the door, especially since he strongly suspected she was sliding between his sheets. They needed a plan to keep a tight lid on things, or home-sweet-fucking-home could turn into a house of horrors. *Holy shit.* The woman he loved lived there.

Silence reigned as Billy paced the lab. Even the fridge complied, clicking off its cycle for a few minutes. It was quiet enough to hear a pin drop, or the wheels spinning inside her head. After Reece counted the floor and ceiling tiles, a ghost of a smile nudged at the corners of his mouth. Billie was up to something. He could feel it. The quirky little vibe, gut feeling, little voice in his head, that always tuned in to Billie's channel, ticker-taped the news to him like the Dow Jones Average. It was a sure thing. Never wrong. He took a mental step back and waited for the bombshell he knew was coming. Charley wouldn't escape his daughter's wrath without battle scars. Neither would Dottie.

Because Billie the Hammer was about to lay down the law.

Peaches, just be sure to include a straitjacket for Dottie in the fine print at the bottom of the contract. We wouldn't want her slicing and dicing in the middle of the night.

Chapter 11

Billie gazed at her father standing shoulder-to-shoulder with Dottie across the small room. In all her years, she had never thought of him as being less than perfect. After Mom died, he'd done everything he could to make her world right again. That included sending for Pike's sister, bringing Dottie home to live with them and take care of her. Heck, he would have done anything to see her smile. The trouble was he had always been so strong in mind and body, she hadn't understood how much he still missed his wife or had needs of his own that weren't being met.

And Dottie? Well, she wasn't Mom. An introvert, she had a rough edge that bordered on uncertainty. But, she'd made the world a better place for Billie as she grew up in a man's world. Otherwise, she might have forgotten everything her own mom had taught her. Dottie had ensured it never happened and protected her with the ferocity of a mother guarding her own child. Especially after Billie lost her own precious baby. She suspected it was Dottie who had stopped all communication with Reece, and for the right reasons. They'd been a couple of kids, far too young to continue a relationship that might have ruined both their lives.

But Reece stood beside her now, unwavering support in his pensive green eyes. He linked his fingers with hers, letting her know he'd go along with whatever she decided to do about Dottie's confession and the damage she had caused. He was a far cry from the teenager he'd once been, heading for the hills at the first sign of trouble. No, this man was her port in a storm. *Her rock.* She squeezed his hand and held on tight.

"Dad?" Her voice rasped in her throat like a chain smoker's, emotion tightening her vocal cords. She tried again. "Do you love Dottie?"

He gazed at the woman beside him, a smile curving his lips. "I do. Guess I just haven't gone about showing her in the right way."

Billie held her breath, wanted to be sure she understood her father correctly before she went any further. "Do you love her enough to marry her?"

"I dunno. What do you think, Dorothy?" He wrapped his arms around her waist. "You figure September is a good month for a wedding? I love you, Dot, and I'd be honored to have you as my wife."

Dottie tugged his face down, her eyes filled with tears as she kissed him full on the lips. It felt a bit odd seeing her father and Dottie professing their love for each other, and yet, it somehow felt right. "It's only a few months away. But if Billie's willing to help with the planning, I think the end of September could work out fine."

Billie wanted to do a happy dance. *"Congratulations"* was on the tip of her tongue when Reece gave her a nudge with his elbow. Heck, she wanted to avoid this next bit, but realized he wouldn't give her an inch of wiggle room. "I'd love to do that. And there's something else I'd like to help you with."

"Oh? I can't think of anything, offhand." A note of suspicion crept into Dottie's voice, her expression suddenly subdued. "What did you have in mind?"

"I want you to learn to take better care of yourself. Build up some confidence." Billie licked her lips, hoping she said this right. "You have to cope with your feelings better, Dottie. Anger isn't healthy. Attacking Lorelei and destroying our property only made things worse."

"Does this mean you want me to see a shrink?" Dottie glanced at her father and back at her again. "I'm not against it, exactly, but I don't fancy driving to Calgary on a regular basis. It's a long trip, especially in winter."

"There's a good therapist living here, in Hereford now. I've heard she's semi-retired and takes appointments a few days a week."

"I don't know what I'll say to a head doctor. Still, Lord knows I could do with someone to talk to, and I want to make sure this marriage sticks. Thank you, Billie, for giving me this second chance. I'll try real hard not to let you down again."

Reece stepped forward, wrapping his arms around Dottie and her dad. "Let me be the first to congratulate you. I wish you all the happiness you both deserve."

Billie added her own joyful wishes to Rocket's, after giving her dad and Dottie a big hug. "And let's keep what really happened to Satan's samples just between us. If anyone asks, we'll say it must have been a shipping mix-up. The damage will be undone once Seth receives the new samples and tests them."

They shook on it and turned off the lights, with Dottie and her father taking the lead as they all headed to the house.

"You did good, peaches," Reece whispered as they followed Theo and Melena out of the barn. "I was a little worried you might not push the therapy angle with Dottie, but you stuck to your guns. I'm proud of you."

"Thanks." *Jeez Louise, I'm proud of myself. But knowing how he feels makes victory a little bit sweeter.*

BILLIE SURVEYED THE rodeo grounds with a critical eye. They had accomplished an incredible amount since yesterday. Pike had worked through the night with a full crew and the results were amazing. A few last minute touches and they'd be ready when the gates opened for registration tonight.

"Billie! Billieeeee!"

That sounded like... "Maurice?"

Sure enough. He was dressed to the nines, although he walked a little funny. More like staggered across the corral in a slinky, black cocktail dress, sequins winking in the sun. His arms windmilling as he swatted at horse-flies trailing along behind him.

His spike heels sank in the dirt with each wobbly step—it was a miracle he didn't trip and break an ankle. By the time he managed to reach her, his fake cleavage heaved with exertion, and Billie wondered about the enhancements in his bra. Whatever they were, his breasts looked real enough to have ranch hands whistling and making lewd gestures. It was obvious they'd missed the Adam's apple and size eleven feet. Or, maybe not.

"Ooh, I'm so glad I found you." Cocking a hip, he wrapped an arm around her and air-bussed her cheeks. Letting go of her to swipe at another fly, he stomped it under his Jimmy Choos. "Vicious bloodsuckers. They've been dive bombing me since I got out of the car."

Billie shook her head with a laugh. "You can't wear hair gel and perfume and expect them to ignore you, Maurice. They're flying off the horses in the paddocks to get at you."

"Hmm, that's not the kind of attention I had in mind." He pouted ruby-glossed lips, rotating his neck to scan the area around them. "Where's my hunka?"

"Your hunka what?"

"My hunka, hunka burning love, of course." Slipping on jewel-trimmed shades, he kept his eyes on the lookout for Reece. "The man is primo real estate, you know what I mean? I wore this sexy dress to make him drool."

"Uh-huh."

Maurice looked fabulous, his hair and makeup exquisite. Billie hated to admit it, but she really should ask him for some fashion advice. Heck, even his ankle bracelet oozed sex appeal, drawing attention to his shapely legs. Perfectly waxed and tanned. Might as well face it; the fashionista put her and just about every other woman she knew to shame. "I think Reece is involved with someone else. Just letting you know so you don't get disappointed."

"You don't know the half of it, sweet pea." He leaned in and whispered conspiratorially in her ear. "I hear he's mixing it up with a whole lot of someones...namely the other eye candy from his military team. But, one look at me in this Dior knockoff and it's hallooo mama, cha cha cha."

I don't think so, little guy. Actually, Billie wondered where Rocket was herself. He never left her alone, even with Theo up on the hill and the other guys watching her from a distance. He must be hiding from you-know-who. "What are you doing here, Maurice, besides looking for Rocket?"

"I'm working. Some of the film crew are here, too. They're starting to set up for the shoot tomorrow. And I wanted to bring you your costume. Come on. We'll get it out of my car and you can try it on."

"Now wait a minute." Billie dug in her heels. "No one told me I'd be wearing a costume."

"Heavens to Betsy, girl, lose the snooty attitude. You're standing in for Savannah Lloyd on the rodeo takes, remember? That poor woman doesn't know a horse from a surf ski, so you're doing all the riding and horsy shots." He tugged on her wrist, heading for the parking lot on three-inch spikes. "The two of you have to be dressed the same or it won't work for the close-ups."

"What's wrong with that picture?" Billie allowed him to drag her along, amusement tingeing her voice. "You people are making a frickin' pilot for a drama set in ranch country and your female lead can't even sit a horse? That's just dumb, Maurice."

"Sweetie, it's stupid as shit, but I don't call the shots. *And*, I didn't hire the cast. I just dress 'em up so they look the part. I'm the best in the biz. They don't call me the wardrobe queen for nothing."

Guess not. Actually, Billie figured he'd earned the title for a couple of reasons.

They crossed the road to the parking lot, more like parking field, and she felt the little hairs stand up on the back of her neck. She turned and caught a glimpse of Spinelli disappearing between two studio trucks. *Is he following us?*

Just as they reached the pick-up, Reece appeared out of nowhere. He didn't look happy to see her in this isolated spot with only Maurice for company. *Tough patooties*; he could have been with her if he hadn't been so busy avoiding the little guy. "Ladies."

"Sugar bear!" Maurice tore around the tailgate and launched himself into Reece's arms, his hands zeroing in on Rocket's butt for a quick pat down. "I *knew* you'd find me."

Disengaging from the clutch and grab, Reece planted the diva firmly on shaky stilettos. "Behave yourself."

"Do I have to?" False eyelashes fluttering, Maurice gazed at Reece as if he wanted to drink the man in like fine wine. And God help her, Billie thought he was too delicious for words. "Did you miss me?"

"Cut it out. And what's the deal bringing Billie back here to your truck?"

"Relax, cowboy. We'd never go anywhere without you." He popped open the cab, handing Reece a garment bag and white Stetson. "I was just getting her rodeo costume. How about we cuddle while she tries it on? I have a blanket in the truck. We can laze in the shade over by the picnic tables, and—"

"Not today." Reece hefted Maurice bodily into the truck, closed the door, and leaned against it. "Billie will let you know if the gear doesn't fit."

Maurice lowered the window, staring at Reece with woeful eyes. "But, baby cakes—"

"We'll see you tomorrow. Don't hit any potholes on your way out." Swooshing the hat down on Billie's head, Reece slung the garment bag over his shoulder and took her hand, watching a sad Maurice drive out of the parking lot.

She let go of his hand to wrap an arm around his waist. "That wasn't very nice."

"Yeah, I know, but I keep hoping he'll latch onto some other guy and move on. I'm not about to trade you in for Maurice."

"Whew, that's a relief."

Reece bent his head and fused their lips with enough energy to make her toes curl. Too bad she had a problem to solve, or she would drag him to the picnic area herself. Push him down on the grass, and...the thought made her toes curl even more. "I have to go. There's something I need to take care of."

His mouth touched down again, smoothing the frown lines on her forehead. He tipped her chin with a finger. "What's up?"

Billie sighed, refocusing on the current crisis and wondering how she could fix it. "It's the bareback rider I hired for the halftime show. She fell off her horse at rehearsal today and wrenched a shoulder. I need an act to replace her."

"Say no more." A smile crinkled the corners of his eyes as he moved to the sensitive spot behind her ear and got busy. An inferno shot to her core in about half a second. *Wowzers*, talk about a mindless diversion.

"I'm serious, Reece. I don't know who I can get at such short notice. Millie's a popular act and I can't think of anyone who would give as solid a performance."

"I can help you with that." He pulled back and cracked a grin. "In case you haven't noticed, I'm not just a pretty face."

"Maurice would agree," she said. "He thinks all of you is beautiful."

He threw back his head and laughed, maybe a touch too hard. Was it her imagination or was eluding his personal fan club taking its toll? Funny how Reece could face off against unseen enemies, but a guy chasing him in a dress totally threw him off his stride.

"Seriously, I have a friend who's a member of the Search and Rescue Dog Association of Alberta. He also contracts to the military and various police forces to train dogs and their handlers in tracking techniques, drug sniffing, and attack procedures. Hell, Rizzo even teaches them to parachute into war zones. Guaranteed, he'll put on one hell of a show."

Hooked by his enthusiasm, Billie had her built-in calculator whirring a mile a minute in her brain. "I can't afford to pay him much. Do you really think he'll do it?"

"He'll come." Reece shifted his stance, looking distinctly uncomfortable. "I've had him on standby since I first flew out here."

"Why?"

He shrugged, looking like a kid caught with a frog in his pocket at the dinner table. "No particular reason."

Nuts, she didn't need a crystal ball to know he'd been holding out on her. His closed-mouthed military style drove her crazy, especially when he made decisions about her wellbeing without so much as clueing her in. "Rocket, is this one of those need-to-know things that you arbitrarily decided *I* didn't need to know? 'Cuz if it is, then *you* need to know I'm moving your stuff out of my bedroom."

Reece studied her for a minute, seemed to understand he either spilled his guts or slept in the doghouse. "I hear you, peaches, loud and clear. I guess we should talk."

No kidding? Honestly, were all men complete idiots when it came to sharing the important stuff? She'd compare notes with Breeana and Mel as soon as she got the chance.

BANYAN FOLLOWED BILLIE into the field designated as a parking lot, veering off into the trees when he saw Morgan dogging her heels. He moved silently through the forest, found a log, and settled down to take a cigarette break. Too bad Morgan was following the woman, or maybe it was a good thing. As long as the tough guy kept eyes on her, Banyan figured she would be safe. Of course, that depended on his own people holding off until tomorrow before taking G.I. Joe out, like they'd been ordered. If they went after him today, she'd be too close and end up as collateral damage. No choice in the matter.

He didn't have the stomach for it. Knew he'd cut her a break if he could. Grab her himself and stash her somewhere until it was over. And keep her away from Foley.

The plan was the plan, was the plan, according to Marcus. The big question being would Foley obey orders or ignore them and do what *he* wanted, such as grab the girl and send Marcus a one-two-fuck-you message? If that happened and Morgan got away, Marcus would kill both of them. The boss didn't give a crap that Foley was a freak who would take what he wanted, when he wanted, and to hell with everyone else.

When Banyan reasoned it out that way, it made sense he'd want to see Billie Bradshaw protected. As long as Foley couldn't get his hands on her, he was saving his own skin. *Right?* Wrong. It was a boldfaced lie and he knew it. Hell, why did he care? Maybe he was tired of getting blood on his hands. He hadn't signed up for this. All he'd ever wanted was to make some fast cash for his retirement fund. And suddenly, he was neck deep in Marcus's operation and part of a bona fide murder squad. And, yeah, he understood Morgan needed to die to protect all of them. But, the woman? *Fuck.* Why couldn't they give her a free pass?

Whatever happened, he knew now wasn't the time for him to grow a conscience. Not when they were so close to the wire. Hell, Banyan didn't even know who all the players were. It wasn't much of a stretch to assume the movie set crawled with them. A couple of the rodeo mopes probably worked for Marcus, too. A lot of new hands had been hired within the last few days to handle the livestock brought in for the show. He sighed. Maybe it was a good thing he didn't know about the others. Foley was enough to keep him awake and sweating most nights.

And what was Spinelli doing here with the camera crew? He'd even brought along a couple of his lackeys for the ride—the new guys he had told him to hire. The jerk was a brainless dickweed to show his face. Hell, if anyone bothered to check, there'd be a lot of explaining to do, considering the movie company didn't handle security for the rodeo. He supposed they'd make up some excuse about guarding the camera equipment. What a crock?

What about the film crew? How many of them were on Marcus's payroll? Christ, he was paranoid. He wanted out in the worst way. While he might not recognize everyone on Marcus's team, he knew who they were up against. A suicide mission if he ever saw one. Given half a chance, Morgan's guys would kill them all.

Banyan's cell phone rang. Foley's number popped up on the screen. Just what he needed, another call from the lunatic fringe. He crushed out his cigarette and answered. "Yeah?"

"Banyan?"

"What's on your mind, Foley?"

"You've been following Billie Bradshaw around like a lost puppy. Planning to nab her for yourself, boy?"

Okay, goat-fuck time. If Foley thinks I have designs on the woman, he'll slit my throat. "Someone's sending you the wrong message, pal. I've been keeping an eye on Morgan, not the rodeo queen. The fact they're together can't be helped."

"I don't believe you."

"Then go fuck yourself."

"You have a mouth on you like a stink hole." Foley laughed into the phone. "Have you forgotten I have a bullet with your name on it?"

"Did you forget I don't give a shit? I'm sick and tired of your goddamn threats." Foley got scarier every time he made contact, and Banyan vowed he would never work with the bastard again. Meanwhile, he'd keep pushing back. It was the only thing the asshole understood. Showing fear was the worst thing he could do right now. "Go hassle someone who gives a crap."

He disconnected the call, turned off his phone, pulled open his pack, and lit another cigarette. His nerves calmed as he drew smoke into his lungs. The shaking in his hands eased as the adrenaline rush caused by Foley's harangue slowly ebbed from his bloodstream.

He closed his eyes, vivid images of him with a garrotte around Foley's neck calmed him further. Yeah, that's what he'd do...kill the prick after tomorrow's mission. No one would care, not even Marcus, as long as they hit Morgan first. Who knew? He might even get a bonus.

"Banyan."

His eyes popped open. Foley stood in front of him, a silencer screwed to the muzzle of his gun. Oddly, Banyan's last thought was how much he regretted not being able to save Billie Bradshaw. Foley would destroy her. That was the thrill for him.

"I'll see you in hell, Foley."

"You first."

He pulled the trigger.

Chapter 12

Rodeo registration snarled traffic on the main road. Per Reece's instructions, security stopped every vehicle coming through the gates, requiring proof of entrant's fee. Looking like a caged bear, Hunt sat in the SUV at the entrance with the bar lights flashing, his eyes glued on the hired security as well as the vehicles in the line-up. Checks and balances, that's all he and his team could do. Reece hoped it was enough.

He stood behind Billie, keeping his eye on her as she did her job, checking and rechecking the participant lists and handing out registration packets.

Reece rested his hands on her shoulders. "You need help with anything?"

She tipped her head back and smiled. "Looks like we've got it covered. You don't need to be here if you've got something else to do."

"You're kidding, right?" Sure, like he'd leave her alone for one damned second. "I'm enjoying myself. There are a lot of familiar faces in the crowd. It feels like old home week."

Klieg lights from the film crew glared down on them, allowing him to catch facial expressions of the passersby and watch for body language. Anything out of the norm and he'd spot it. Like the guy who moseyed up to Billie a few minutes ago with his tongue hanging to his knees. He hovered over her like a bad smell, trying to cop a feel with the back of his hand when he reached for his registration papers. Reece grabbed his thumb, twisted it with a try-to-touch-her-again-and-I'll-snap-it-off promise in his eyes. Touchy-feely got the message, pulled back his aching digit, and moved along to his truck.

He glared at the next guy in line. "Move it, buddy."

Billie frowned at him. "Was that really necessary?"

"Just setting the mood, peaches. And it most definitely was."

She shook her head and went back to work, trying to conceal her smirk. For the most part, everybody greeted Billie like an old friend. Excitement over the weekend's activities seemed to build with a lot of backslapping and shoulder nudging. Reece knew why. He remembered those icy Alberta winters with little to do but watch the snow fall and reminisce about the fun times. It was the summer get-togethers like rodeos that made ranching worthwhile. A lot of people even remembered him from his circuit days. Each shook his hand and asked if he was coming back.

No thanks. Bull and bronc riding were dangerous sports. He'd given up the life a long time ago. Hell, he'd take his hat off to anyone brave enough—or stupid enough—to go up against a man-eater like Bad to the Bone. But he'd keep his own feet on the ground, and his body parts in one piece.

He watched the crowd head back to their pick-ups and trailers, continuing on to the campground to get settled in. Some of them hauled campers, most would pitch tents, and a few had those fancy horse trailers with built-in sleeping quarters. The smell of horses and the occasional shuffle and bump from inside a trailer brought it all back to him. Even the horses greeted each other, their whinnies floating on the cool night air.

A western band rocked through loud speakers from the tent a quarter mile away, getting its groove on for tomorrow's festivities. He assumed tonight would be fairly quiet, although his team was on high alert, making rotations through every inch of the rodeo setup. The heavy drinking shouldn't start until tomorrow night, when fists would probably fly. Familiar with the rodeo scene, he knew some of these folks wouldn't make it through the qualifying rounds in the morning, but they'd stay over the weekend to socialize and cheer on their pals. By tomorrow night, a few would be drunker than skunks—just in time for the barbeque and dance.

Yup, he'd written the playbook on that one. He'd been a teenage punk with a penchant for booze and trouble.

The rebel rousers would be looking to put the beat down on some idiot spectator with a heckling mouth, no brains, and even smaller balls to back up his bullshit. Reece knew the type, too stupid to cut and run after they'd spent the day jeering and laughing in the stands, usually after some poor devil snapped a limb during an event. Getting tossed off a horse or a bull was no picnic. Participants sometimes died. And cowboys hated assholes.

Reece laughed to himself, remembering how he'd been one of the horse and bull jockeys, looking to even the score with whichever poor sod had laughed a little too hard and a little too long when someone had gotten hurt. Spectators tended to forget contestants didn't stay up on those broncs and bulls forever. They had lots of time between events to eyeball someone in the crowd making an ass of himself. By the end of the day and after a little liquid libation, a smart mouthed heckler would be wise to move on, unless he wanted his eyes blackened.

"Yo, Rocket, you've got company." He turned to see Law stroll up behind him, accompanied by Nick Rizzoli. Reece watched the other man's approach, realizing he'd been dubbed the friendly giant long ago with good reason. The guy had forty pounds on him and a couple extra inches in height. Built like a mountain, Rizzo was an ex-marine. And like the members of his Spec Ops team, a man who could hold his own in mind-fuck situations—while being an unbelievable softy when it came to women, children, and animals.

"Rizzoli. It's about time you showed up."

"Good to see you too, man." Rizzo slapped him on the shoulder and moved in for a knuckle tap. "I flew the Herc here, left her at the little airstrip on the other side of Hereford. If one of you wants to play pilot, I thought McGee and I could parachute in for the halftime show tomorrow."

Reece knew the Hercules C-130, had jumped from it—or one just like it—a gazillion times. Rizzo used it to train military dogs and their handlers. "I'll fix it with Hawke, since he flies the most. That will be one hell of a show stopper, my friend."

Billie swivelled in her chair at the commotion. She smiled the second she laid eyes on Rizzo's companion. "That is the biggest, most beautiful German Shepherd I've ever seen!"

Rizzo laughed at her remark as he leaned down to give the dog a pat. "This is McGee, ma'am, and he's a three-year-old Shiloh Shepherd, the largest of the Shepherd breed. He weighs in at a hundred and sixty pounds."

"Oh my Lord. I think I'm in love." Billie rose from her chair to introduce herself properly. Nick straightened to shake her hand. "May I pet him?"

"Sure, Billie. Just let Rocket make the introductions. He and McGee have been pals since he was a pup."

"*Friend*, McGee." Reece hit his haunches, closed Billie's fist, and brought it to McGee's nose so he could take a whiff. Once his thick tail began to wag, he eased back and let them get acquainted. McGee was smart as a whip and a handsome devil to boot, standing thirty-four inches at the shoulder with a plush silver and black coat. A thick mane extended from his neck to his chest. He was a lady killer and knew it, already washing Billie's face with his tongue. After a couple minutes, he eased her arms from around McGee's neck, pointing in Rizzo's direction again. "You're hurting Hank's feelings."

"Hank? Hank who?" She turned on her heels and nearly fell over. "I don't believe it! A Bloodhound? Oh, look at his sad, droopy face."

Rizzo laughed. "Don't be fooled, Billie. That's Hank's natural expression. Reece, you wanna introduce her to Hank while you're both still low to the ground?"

"Glad to." He repeated the same steps, placing Billie's closed hand under Hank's nose. It took barely a second for him to memorize her scent. Bloodhounds had an extraordinary sense of smell, and Hank would never forget her. He was a little smaller than McGee, but still a brute of a dog. A red-head, his sleek coat shone beneath the lights like burnished copper.

Pike motioned a hand at Billie, shaking his head and making a tsking sound. Guess old Pike figured if it wasn't a horse, it wasn't worth looking at. "Anytime you're finished swooning over those dogs, missy, we could use some help over here."

She laughed, moved to the table to rejoin the others. A sudden breeze blew up, rustling the tops of trees and scattering her paperwork. Billie scrambled to hold everything down.

And all hell broke loose.

Hank caught a scent in the wind, started baying like a banshee and straining against his leash. McGee either picked up the same smell or trusted Hank to know the score. They both got agitated, wanted to beat paws into the woods straight away.

"Shit, Nick, looks like we've got trouble."

"With a capital 'T', my friend." Rizzo spoke firmly to the dogs to calm them down. "If I was a betting man, I'd lay odds there's a corpse somewhere in that stand of timber over there. It might not be Hank's specialty, but he's real good at sniffing out cadavers. I can tell by the sound he's making it's what he smells. His pitch is different."

"What about McGee?"

Rizzo glanced at the Shiloh. "For now, I think he's following Hank's lead, but that'll change once we're on the move and he picks up a trail of his own."

Reece cursed. "Law, you're coming with us. I'll get Sully over here to keep eyes on Billie."

"Don't bother. I'm going with you, Reece, and that's final." Oh, man, she'd sneaked up on him and overheard the conversation. He hated it when she looked at him that way, determined to argue unless he caved and took her with him. There wasn't time.

"Reece." Rizzo switched leashes on the dogs, snapping on their working leads. Hank and McGee knew the difference and stayed on point, their ears twitching for Nick's 'move out' command. "Whatever we find, it can't hurt her. It's already dead."

"And if McGee picks up a different scent?"

Rizzoli knew what he meant and said in a low voice, "Law can bring her back while we track the bastard."

Reece thought that might not be a bad idea, his gaze shifting to Billie again. If he left her here, he didn't trust her to stay put and had a hunch she'd join forces with the dark side—Melena and Breeana. The three of them together were trouble cubed. Given half a chance, they'd traipse into the woods like they were on a nature hike, predators be damned. "You sure you want to do this, Billie? It could get ugly, real fast."

Her skin paled, but she lifted her stubborn chin. "I live on a ranch, and I know what death looks like. Let's get a move on."

Rizzo handed him McGee's leash, just like he'd done the other times they'd worked together in the field. One dog to a handler was the way his friend worked, which meant Law was responsible for Billie's safety. When Law tucked her hand into his big mitt, Reece held onto his curse. Jealousy could be a mean bitch. He focused instead on Law's other hand, the one holding the Glock with a flashlight mount. He was primed and ready to roll; he'd keep Billie safe. That was all that mattered.

Reece reached for his own Glock and snapped the tactical flashlight onto its base. Checking for the extra clips in his pocket, he hazarded a glance at Charley, figured he wouldn't be happy to know Billie could find herself in a bad situation. Her father said nothing, tapped a hand to his forehead in salute, and swung around to continue with the registration process. A touch of pride warmed Reece's chest. Charley really did trust him to take care of his daughter.

Hoo-rah.

BILLIE COULD HEAR THE dogs howling in the distance as she struggled to keep up with Law. It was either that or risk having one arm stretched longer than the other. He had her hand in an iron grip and wasn't letting go. The ground dipped into a gully and she went down. Law swung her to her feet again and kept on moving.

"You okay?"

"Having the time of my life." No, she wasn't fine. As a matter of fact, she was scared to death. Of who or what, she didn't know. Having Law by her side in the pitch dark—except for the flashlight on his gun—was comforting, but it wasn't the same. She wanted to be with Reece when they stumbled across whatever or whoever it was he and Rizzo thought they would find. He would hold her in his arms and comfort her if it was very bad. But, she'd pushed too hard when she knew he didn't want to take her, and now she was stuck with the consequences. *Grow a backbone, quit whining, and keep up with Law.*

Twigs snapped and dead leaves crackled with each of her footfalls. Law didn't make a sound, just like Reece never did. She wondered how big men could move like that and decided it must be part of their training. Mice skedaddled when they heard her coming. A couple ran over her boots and she held back a squeal. Some ranch girl she was.

She kept moving, glued to Law like a prisoner in flex cuffs. If she slowed down, he'd probably heft her over his shoulder and carry her like a carpet. He wouldn't want to lose Reece and Rizzo, or fall too far behind them. Tree limbs snagged Billie's blouse, spider webs clung to her hair—hopefully the spiders had already dropped off—and a snake crossed their path with a toad in its mouth. *Oh, joy.* Did she know how to have a good time, or what?

Finally, Billie saw lights up ahead and realized Reece and Rizzo had stopped. When she and Law got close enough, she saw them standing side-by-side and staring at the ground. That's when the smell hit her. Something so foul, she had to cover her nose and mouth with a hand.

She shrugged out of Law's grasp, ran up to Reece, and looked down.

"Billie. No!"

He grabbed her, tried to block her view, but it was too late. She'd seen the dead man. His face smashed to a bloody pulp. *Sweet, sweet, Lord!* She reeled and stumbled out of his arms. Raced for the nearest tree and staggered behind it, threw up until her stomach was empty. When she was finished, she wiped her mouth with a tissue and looked down at a pair of men's splattered boots. Reece.

"I'm, I'm so sorry," she said. Her words barely audible, her stomach still nauseated, her airways struggling against the meaty stench in the air.

"Shh. I never liked these boots anyway." He used a hand wipe on the boots, handed her a pack of gum, kissed the top of her head and circled her with his arms. McGee stood off to the side, watching them through wise, doggie eyes. "Do you want Law to take you back?"

"N-no. I'm good for now." She popped a gum into her mouth. Somehow managed to dredge up a smile and paste it on her lips. "I'll just sit on the rock over there and wait for you. Gotta say though, I've never seen a d-dead body like that one before. I mean, I've seen animals, and a few old-timers in their coffins, but nothing like this. I, I wish I could handle it better."

"Peaches, the rest of us...well, this isn't our first experience. And we're still affected by the horror. Otherwise, we wouldn't be human. My stomach's waging a battle of its own right now, and the jury's still out." He walked her to the flat rock, helped her climb up on top, took off his jacket, and wrapped it around her. "Breathe into my jacket. It will help with the smell. And stay here."

Thank God for Rocket's jacket. It became her lifeline. Billie inhaled his sandalwood scent when she buried her nose in the lining. Closing her eyes, she pretended he sat there with her. Made believe she hadn't just seen something so horrible she would never forget it as long as she lived. A nearby clicking sound startled her. Her eyes flew open. McGee's nails scratched the rock as he hopped up beside her. He flopped down, resting his huge head on her knee. Then Hank leapt up to sit at her other side, leaning against her. They still had their leashes attached but hanging loose. She wrapped her arms around both of them and held on tight, watching the men talking below. Surprised to see them pulling on purple latex gloves.

"He's in full rigor," Rizzo said, testing the arms and legs. "He's been dead for at least eight hours."

"Shot straight through the heart. We never heard it, so the killer must have had a sound suppressor on his weapon. Sound travels up here." Leaning an elbow on a knee, Reece motioned with his other hand. "He used that branch over there to bash in the face. And he's stripped the pockets clean. There's nothing to identify the victim."

"We can forget about getting a fingerprint match, too." Rizzo held up an arm. "His hands were removed,"

Oh, God. I think I'm going to hurl again. Billie swallowed several times, forcing the bile back down her throat. Sticking her nose back in Rocket's jacket, she focused on taking shallow breaths.

"Jesus. I'll get Hawke or Sully to call it in to the local police." Law tugged his cell phone out of a back pocket. "It will be less hassle if a fellow cop reports it."

"Good idea," Reece said. "Make sure they send a forensics team and the coroner while you're at it."

A man was dead...murdered...and they couldn't identify him. Billie could only imagine what that would be like for his mother, or a wife, waiting at home and wondering where he'd gone. They might never know, and didn't he deserve to have a proper funeral? Who would bury him? There must be a way to find out who he was. His family deserved to have closure. Heck, even Rena, her taxi driver with the prison tats, had family somewhere. There would be people who loved her and cared about her, no matter what she'd done to spend time in jail. And suddenly it hit her. "Reece! What about tattoos?"

He glanced up at her and actually smiled. "Babe, you're brilliant."

"You can tell that to the coroner when you ask him to check."

Reece glanced at Law and Rizzo before saying, "We're not waiting. We'll go over him ourselves."

"But—"

"Forget it, Billie. Time is a luxury we can't afford. We'll touch him as little as possible, but we're taking a look. My gut says this murder is connected to the threats on you. I can't wait a month for the coroner's report to see if we could have identified the body earlier."

"Look, the ME will be here soon. Can't we—?"

"No, we can't, because no one will be looking for distinguishing marks until the autopsy is performed, which could be days away. A small town like Hereford will ship the remains to Calgary for processing. And you can bet our corpse won't have a high priority in their log jam."

He might be right, but she still felt sick as she watched him unbutton what was left of the man's bloody shirt to look at the perforated chest beneath. He tugged up both sleeves, didn't find anything, and slid them down again. Then he and Rizzo carefully rolled the body onto its side, while Law eased up the shirt in back. "Reece, he's got a tat on a shoulder blade. And, damn, it's a loggie tattoo."

Billie slipped down off the rock, her curiosity getting the better of her. Still breathing into Reece's jacket, she carefully moved up beside Law to study the artwork with the rest of them. It resembled two cross links of a chain with black wording etched below. *Servitium Nulli Secundus.* "What does the writing say?"

"It says *Service Second To None.*" Law glanced up and grimaced. "I recognized it because it's the logistics' emblem in the Canadian military. I'm a loggie, too. See the two links of chain? We call them cross paperclips."

"What do you think? Can we identify him with this tat?" Rizzo asked.

"Maybe, but it will take time," Reece said. "Men and women in the military are supposed to report their tattoos when renewing their ID cards. Let's hope this is an old tat and it's listed on his personnel file. Even so, it could take months to track down every male logistics officer, both in country and on assignment, to see who's missing."

They carefully laid the body back in the same position. Reece re-buttoned the man's shirt. Billie looked off into the woods. She didn't want to see the man's face again, or his handless arms.

"Slide up his pant legs," Reece said. "Let's be sure we haven't missed anything."

"That's one hell of a scar on his left knee." Rizzo drew fast sketches in the small notebook he carried, recording both the tattoo and the scar.

"Ouch." Law traced the scar with a finger. "It goes from the knee to the outside of the leg and down to his ankle. The scar is faded, an old wound."

Reece agreed. "This could have happened when he was a kid."

Billie heard a snap. She turned her head to see Reece standing in front of her, removing his latex gloves. "Where did those come from?"

He took her hand and moved her several feet upwind of the body.

"I keep a few pairs in the mini first-aid kit in my cargo pants. We all carry them." Billie watched his eyes, not sure she believed him. After searching the body, she wondered if he didn't carry them for other reasons too, and not just to patch up an injured buddy in the field. "Come on, Law will take you back. He has to meet up with Hawke and the cops, bring them out here before any animals drag the body off. The noise from the rodeo grounds has kept them away for now. But once the band shuts down and people hit their bedrolls—"

"I forgot about the wildlife." Billie shivered and leaned into him. She didn't want to leave him behind, but knew he wouldn't give her a choice. She consoled herself with thoughts of a hot shower, to scrub off the smell. "I'll see you later."

"Billie, I don't want you on your own until I get back. Please stay in the house, have a drink with Breeana and Mel, and try to relax. I'll be there as soon as I can."

She had a feeling Reece still wasn't levelling with her, but she was too exhausted to argue. Wrapping her arms around his neck, she kissed his cheek and walked back to where the others waited. Law took her hand and they turned into the forest.

RIZZO WHISTLED FOR the dogs while they waited for Law to get Billie out of the area. Then Reece took McGee back to the scent the dog had found earlier. It belonged to the killer and led away from the carnage. Blood droplets splattered at intervals along the trail, most probably from those dismembered hands. Either the bag had leaked, or the mope hadn't brought anything to put his trophies in. Reece felt sickened and imagined Rizzo felt the same way. He'd seen a lot of bad shit in the military, but this psycho had a major screw loose. He was terrified Billie might be his real target. And the guy was a chameleon.

A few good sniffs and McGee was on the move, his nose to the ground. Hank joined the party with Rizzo, both dogs scrambling to find the freak. Reece knew they were too late, since the body had been dead for over eight hours. Still he prayed for something, *anything,* that would lead them right to his door. And he was convinced; this was the work of a man. A woman wouldn't have the stomach for it. Sure, she might blow a hole through a guy's chest, but he couldn't imagine any woman beating a man's face in with a hunk of wood, or cutting his hands off. Of course, he might be wrong.

Reece kept pace with McGee, his mind continuing to spin. A military connection—maybe that was the key—was their corpse one of the good guys? Was it someone he knew lying dead back there, his body desecrated beyond recognition? A man the killer didn't want identified. Why?

He stumbled when McGee veered off course and pulled his mind back to his surroundings before he broke his freaking neck. McGee and Hank spent a few minutes sniffing around a tree stump.

Rizzo waited beside him. "The perp probably stopped here to take a leak. We'll give the boys a minute to figure it out and pick up his scent again."

And they were off.

A couple more minutes, and they reached the end of the trail. Reece banked his anger, wanted to hit something with his fist, but didn't want to upset the dogs. He stood at the edge of asphalt and silently cursed. The shooter had escaped in a vehicle, leaving no trace behind for them to follow. The highway moved east into the mountains and west into Hereford. Hell, he could have gone either way.

Unless he drove back to the *Circle B*.

Chapter 13

Foley sat in the hotel lounge nursing a bourbon and watching the ice melt in his glass. He had a good view from there, could see the sexy little number working the reception desk. Jenny Lee Calhoun, the woman who'd hooked up with Banyan. He glanced at his watch. Her shift ended in ten minutes. After that she'd head home to her mama, believing Banyan had stood her up.

He wondered what she'd say when he told her lover boy wasn't coming back. Described in detail what he'd done to him. He liked sharing those kinds of things with a captive audience. He was especially looking forward to telling her how he'd tossed the man's hands in a trough at a nearby farm. Watched the pigs chow down until every scrap was gone.

Chuckling to himself, he ordered another drink to calm the excitement jangling his nerves. He thought about tomorrow's festivities, could hardly wait, making a mental note to make sure his costume fit perfectly. *Details.* Everything in life depended on the details. He laid a twenty down on the bar for his tab with enough left over for the tip. As soon as the pretty blond with the big hair and bigger tits started gathering up her stuff, he'd be on his way. *And on her trail.*

Yup, she was on the move, chatting to the clerk coming on duty as she reached for her sweater and purse.

Foley beat her to the stairs and down to the garage. He took a quick glance around to make sure he was alone. The place was deader than a crypt. Walking straight to her car, he pulled the ice pick from the sheath strapped to his wrist beneath his shirtsleeve and stabbed two of her tires. Air hissed out. He loved the sound. They'd be flatter than pancakes before she was halfway home. Then he'd ride to the rescue.

Jogging to his pickup, he sprang the door and slid behind the wheel. The canvas bag on the floor beside him contained everything he needed for a first—and last—date. The scalpel, pliers, cigar cutter, and lighter lay within easy reach. And if none of those pleased the lady? There was always the vial of sulfuric acid he kept for special occasions. Like his upcoming date with Billie Bradshaw. But she was tomorrow's prize and his *pièce de résistance*. Jenny Lee was the entrée, something to take the edge off his appetite until then.

Right on time, the blond popped out of the stairwell looking cute as a button in her hotel uniform, eased into her car, and cranked the engine. Too bad for her, she didn't notice the deflating tires. Not surprising, since she was a broad. The bitches never looked, wouldn't have a clue if there was an ax murderer perched on their back seat.

Tsk, tsk, Jenny Lee.

He settled in to wait, giving her a chance to exit the garage and be on her way. No point in kissing her bumper and raising alarm bells. She'd use her cell phone if he did. He had to play the Good Samaritan when he pulled up to see what the problem was. Aw shucks, two flat tires and only one spare. He'd offer her a lift. What a kick.

He drove slowly, tailed her from two car lengths back. Watched her leave the town limits and press on the gas. The Harley between them signalled, rumbling up the drive of a local billiard bar. There was no one else on the road, just him and sweet Jenny Lee. He switched on the radio, shutting it off again when fiddle music blasted his ears. Better keep focused on her car. It wouldn't be long now.

Bumpety-bump-bang! The front tire ruptured, chunks of rubber flying in all directions. Jenny Lee lost control, fought the steering wheel in an attempt to pull up on the shoulder. *Bam!* The back tire spun off and flew through the air. She swerved on metal rims and two inflated tires. Sparks flew as she careened past vehicles lined up at the *Circle B* gates. The road curved. Jenny Lee didn't. She headed straight for an oak tree. *Wham!* The car dinged the tree, shuddered, and steamed. Jenny Lee pushed the door open. She fell on the ground.

Foley felt the pull of his jeans as his cock roared to life. Another few minutes and he'd be feeding the beast what it craved. Once Jenny Lee was flex cuffed with her mouth duct taped, he'd toss her in the truck and take her somewhere private for his personal brand of first-aid.

Eyes on the rear-view mirror, his hands froze on the wheel as he braked to slide in behind her. An SUV filled his rear window. Bar lights blazing, close enough for him to make out the silhouette of a big man behind the wheel. He stepped on the gas, the piece-of-shit truck chugging in response. The cop ignored him, parked the SUV behind the wreck, and ran for Jenny Lee.

Foley pulled off the road up ahead and hauled out his binoculars. He adjusted the lenses. Nope, not the cops; it was one of Morgan's goons assessing the damage to both Jenny Lee and her car. He carried her to his ride, tucked her inside, and hauled out a cell phone.

Foley understood his mistake.

Two flat tires equalled one too many for the average road hazard. The prick had figured it out, knew someone had sabotaged the car to get to the bitch. *Shit.* He tossed the binocs, gunned the pickup across the highway, and headed back toward Hereford. Shoved on a ball cap and didn't turn his head when he passed the jarhead still yakking it up. Felt his icy stare drill the back of his skull. He held off flooring the accelerator until he'd rounded the bend. The slightest suspicion and Morgan's goon could radio ahead and have him picked up.

He thanked the saints his ride was rented to the film company and was damn sure Morgan was already running the plates. He'd been the only vehicle for miles behind Jenny Lee's car—that's what the chitchat on the cell phone was about. A few minutes later, Foley swerved into the parking lot of the billiard bar he'd spotted on his way out of town. He had barely cut the lights when sirens screeched past him on the highway, heading out of Hereford.

How many cops did Jenny Lee need, for crap's sake? You'd think he'd already murdered the witch. Unease mounted his spine and crawled inside his head. Had Banyan's body been found? Is that what this was about? *Fuck, no.* The coyotes would eat him before he reeked badly enough for anyone to catch the scent. By then, there'd be nothing left for them to find. *No worries.*

Climbing out of the pickup, he grabbed his canvas bag and started walking. He left the truck running with the door open. And sure enough, it sailed past him as he headed for the hotel, a bunch of teenage punks hanging out of the cab. And, oh look, there went the cops chasing after them.

A few minutes later and Foley had scaled the balconies up to his fourth-floor room. There was nothing like a little aerial action to get his blood flowing. A police unit pulled up below, the cops entering the hotel. He stripped, dashed through the shower, pulled on a bathrobe, and was towelling his hair when the pigs knocked at his door. They looked him up and down, apologized for the disturbance, and moved off down the hallway.

He guessed the joy riders had been pulled over and they were checking out their story, how someone had conveniently left the pick-up with the keys in it for them to steal. *Right.* It was nothing but a lame excuse for jacking the truck and stalking Jenny Lee.

He tried to relax after his near miss but couldn't. Fuck Reece Morgan for depriving him of his fun tonight. Yeah, he'd laugh his balls off when the prick died tomorrow. It couldn't happen soon enough or to a nicer guy.

But Billie Bradshaw, she wouldn't die until he got tired of her screams, which wouldn't be for a long, long time. Marcus's sniper would intentionally miss when he shot at her.

Morgan would still come running. Morgan would still die.

And Billie would belong to him.

JENNY LEE CALHOUN HUDDLED on a couch in the family room with a quilt wrapped around her shoulders. Billie brought her a shot of brandy while Breeana cleaned a cut on her cheek and taped it. Reece knew she was lucky to be alive, let alone sitting there with only a few minor scrapes and bruises. If Hunt hadn't followed her and brought her in, his gut said she'd be dead, but not from the car crash. Micah had scoured the highway, picked up what was left of her tires. Hawke had gone over them, piece by piece. He'd found puncture marks on the sidewalls. Someone had stalked her. The question was, why? What did she know? Or who was she involved with?

"I talked to Lorelei. I told her you were okay and we'd bring you home later." Billie took Jenny Lee's hand and held it in her own. "She said you have a new boyfriend who works on the movie set. Will you tell us about him?"

Jenny Lee laughed. "You must mean John Lakefield, but I'm not sure he's my boyfriend anymore. He stood me up tonight. We were supposed to go out after my shift."

Reece's alarm bells began to clang. He remembered Lakefield. He'd gotten a flat on the generator truck the morning the film crew caravanned in. He'd also seen him on the movie set. His body type matched the dead man's approximate height and weight.

"What happened?" Billie wrapped an arm around her, just a couple of girls having a chat.

"That's the weird part. I don't know. He never came back from the set today. I asked Spinelli, their head of security, and he said he hadn't seen John since they were at the rodeo grounds this afternoon. He didn't know where John was. I just assumed he'd gotten bored with our little fling and was avoiding me. He's been doing that a lot lately."

Use her and lose her. What a guy. Reece cut into the conversation. "Jenny Lee, there's no easy way to say this, but there was another accident this afternoon. A man is dead and the police are trying to identify him."

Her eyes rounded in shock. She looked at him, tears gathering on her lashes. "You think it's John?"

"It's possible."

"We're sorry." Billie took her in her arms and rocked gently, like he'd seen parents do with their children. "Please help us out. Tell us about John so we can clear this up."

"W-what do you want to know?" She took a tissue from a box on the coffee table, wiped her nose, and dabbed at her eyes. "I don't know why I'm so upset. I sensed he was trying to dump me, but I guess I still cared about him."

"Can you give us a physical description?" Reece asked. "Did John have any scars or tattoos?"

"Lord, it's really him, isn't it?" Jenny Lee let out a sob. She closed her eyes as more tears trailed down her cheeks. Her fingers shredded the tissue in her hands. "H-he had a tattoo on his shoulder blade. It looked like a couple links from a chain, and something was written under it in Latin. He said it was a military tattoo. Plus, one of his legs was scarred. He rode off a balcony on his tricycle when he was a kid, landed on a picket fence, and tore up his leg real bad."

So, Reece had his answer. John Lakefield was dead. And he hadn't been one of the good guys. He had used Jenny Lee to track Billie's whereabouts through Twitter feed. It was Lakefield who had blown the water tower; he'd stake his reputation on it. Why would he do it? What was the connection between Lakefield and himself? He moved away from the women and dialed Law. "I have a name for our DB. John Lakefield. Use your contacts and track him through the logistics network."

After he disconnected, Breeana went to the door to get Sully. They were taking Jenny Lee home to Lorelei. Reece thought she'd be safe as long as she stayed close to home. "The police need to find out who damaged your tires. Don't go anywhere until we have more information."

"I'm going to stay on the ranch, call in sick for a few days...try to come to terms with everything that's happened." She swiped at a tear and gave him a watery smile. "I'll be careful, I promise. And please, thank your friend for rescuing me."

Reece strode to the bar and grabbed a beer from the fridge after she left. He twisted off the cap and tossed it into the wastebasket. Billie came up behind him and ran her hands up his back, working the kinks out. "What's going on, Reece?"

"I'm not sure, but I'll let you know when I figure it out." Turning, he wrapped an arm around her waist and brushed her lips with his own. She had to be exhausted, and yet she stood with him when she could be tucked in her bed. He wished they could forget about everything for a while and catch some down time. God, they both needed it. And he needed her. To himself. In bed. Rocking his world. A selfish thought, but he couldn't seem to help it. Billie was his life, and nothing would ever stand between them again.

Except for Rizzo and Law when they plowed through the doorway. Hank and McGee followed them in and sank to the carpet.

"I got a hit on Lakefield." Law's eyes rested on Billie for a second, not sure he should continue.

Okay, mind-fuck time. Whatever it was Law had found out, it probably wasn't anything Reece wanted to hear. He took a sip of his beer, gazed down at Billie. "Tell us."

Rizzo passed them on his way to the bar. He could hear ice clink in a glass and a bottle being poured.

Law grabbed the beer Rizzo threw his way. "There is no John Lakefield in the database. But, a buddy I talked to remembered the scar on the guy's left leg. He knew who he was right away."

And here comes the punch line. The one Law has stuck in his throat. "Spit it out. What's his name?"

"Lieutenant Alex Banyan."

Jesus, Jesus, Jesus. Reece sucked in a breath, his hand tightening around Billie's waist. "It's not good news, but it sure as hell makes sense. He's changed his appearance. It's why I didn't recognize him."

Rizzo squeezed his shoulder. "You want to fill us in on the deets?"

"It's a long story, man." And no happy ending, not where Billie was concerned. He'd been right to think this had little to do with her and everything to do with him. He'd damn well caused it.

"We've got time," Billie said, looking like she'd throttle him if he didn't make his lips move. "Spill it, cowboy."

"It started six months ago, with a conversation I overheard at a dive in Iraq. I was in the area for a couple days with the team. It was late at night. Everyone else had hit the rack. The Officers' Mess was already closed so I stopped in at a local watering hole for a drink. The kind of place where whiskey and women are cheap and the lights are dimmed. Lieutenant Banyan and a Chief Warrant Officer named Foley were both stinking drunk, sitting in a corner arguing about something they called Operation Platiti. The quarrel got louder by the second, made it impossible not to notice what they were involved in. I paid a barmaid to bring them a round of drinks—and find out their names. Long story short, they were diverting tankers of oil destined for the military to the Turkish black market and making a bundle."

Rizzo whistled and took a pull from his glass. Reece guessed it was ginger ale, knew Nick never touched the hard stuff. "Did you report them?"

"I did." Reece rubbed a hand down his face. "I spoke to their Colonel, Gabe Marcus, confident he'd launch an investigation."

"From the look on your face, I'm guessing that was a wrong move." Rizzo leaned his back against the bar with his arms crossed over his chest. "He was up to his ears in it."

"Good call." Reece chugged the last of his beer, sank to the sofa with Billie, and put the bottle down on the table. "I went over Marcus's head, moved higher up the food chain, and found someone who wasn't involved. An investigation took place and the pipeline was shut down. Cost the bastards millions in revenue."

Law crossed to the fridge and hauled out another beer. "So, why come after you?"

"Take your pick." He ticked off the list of reasons on his fingers. "Because I have to testify at their trial? Because I caused them a shitload of grief and they lost a ton of money? Or maybe because the Turks are pissed off and have long enough arms to exact revenge on Banyan, Foley, and Marcus for screwing up. It could be all of the above."

He wished there was something he could say to ease the tension in the room. Billie looked shell shocked. "Reece, could this whole thing be swept under the rug if you don't testify?"

"Part of it would—the charges against Colonel Marcus. It's my word against his that I asked him to investigate. There was never any evidence tying him to the scam."

Rizzo pulled out his cell and hit speed dial, walking to the other end of the room. He talked for a few minutes in a low tone before ending the call. Dipping a hand in the chip bowl on his way back, he grabbed a few and tossed them to the dogs. "I just had a chat with my buddy in Intelligence. Word is your Colonel Marcus has retired from the military and is now a diplomat with the Foreign Service."

"Thanks for the Intel, Riz, but you're not telling me anything I don't already know."

He laughed and winked at Billie. If Reece didn't like him so much, he'd smack him one. "He's dirty, Reece. Real dirty. The alphabet agencies are building a case against him."

Motherfuck. "He's getting rid of the skeletons in his closet. Starting with me."

"Bingo. Give the man a kewpie doll."

Billie cast him an anxious glance. "What are you going to do, Rocket?"

"Handle it. Rock'n roll with a lot of kickass." He knew what she wanted, for him to disappear. Head for the hills with his tail tucked up his ass. *She can't be serious.* "We'll catch these guys."

"You're not listening." And just like that, Billie the Hammer was back. Springing off the couch and pacing the room like a dervish, she thrust a finger at Law, almost took his nose off. "Get the other men in here to talk some sense into him."

"Sorry Billie," Law said, backing up a step. "They're taking shifts patrolling the grounds. I can't call them in."

"You mean you won't."

He shrugged, looking like he'd rather be anywhere else. Her gaze jumped from Law to Rizzo. He stuck his hands in the air, palms up. "Hey, don't look at me. I'm just here to do a dog show."

"Liar. You're both idiots." She caught Reece's wrists on her next pass, dragged him up off the couch. A lot of pent-up frustration packed into one slim body. "Please. You need to leave here. Go into hiding. Right now."

"I wouldn't be much of a man if I did, peaches." He smiled into her terrified eyes. "And hell, I'd miss out on all the fun."

She jabbed him in the ribs. "You're an idiot, too!"

"Maybe so, but I'm staying to put out the garbage."

"That's what I'm afraid of." Billie stared at him, long and hard, her jaw tightening. "I don't want you to end up like Banyan. Compost."

Chapter 14

"Stupid. Dumb. Jerk." Billie sat in the entertainment tent by herself, nursing a coffee and a bad attitude. She didn't want to talk to anyone. She ignored Theo and Melena, Breeana and Sully sitting at the next table, their eyes roving the crowd. Hawke and Micah stood near the tent entrance doing the same. The team was on high alert. She assumed the rest of them were outside walking the grounds along with hired security. She pushed her plate away, couldn't swallow a bite. Her mind wandering, Billie watched folks come in to have breakfast before the qualifying rounds. The rodeo officially opened at noon with the flag ceremony, but spectators had started pouring through the gates.

"Reckless. Idiot. Butthead." Had she mentioned stupid yet? For a man with so much going for him, Reece couldn't care less about his own life. She knew she shouldn't have caved and made love with him last night. Why hadn't she stuck to her guns? Insisted he pack up his go bag and get gone. Get the hell out while he still had the chance. If he was worried about her, all he had to do was leave a couple of his team behind for a few days. Not that she needed them. No one was after her—it was Rocket they wanted. And they'd catch him, kill him if he didn't come to his senses pretty damn quick. "Moron. Nutball. Jackass."

"Morning, peaches. Are you talking to yourself?" Reece grabbed a chair and sat down beside her, a smile on his face. Dressed in black cargo pants and a T-shirt, his hair tied back with a strip of leather, he stood out from the cowboys milling around them and took her breath away. His clear, green-eyed gaze slid over her body before he planted a kiss on her cheek, moving his head lower to sniff at her neck. "Mmm, something smells good. I don't know if it's you or those flapjacks. Pass me a fork and I'll finish them before they get cold."

Billie growled her impatience, wanted to sock him one when he picked up her mug and drank the last of her coffee. "Reece, you—"

His hand touched her nape, heat rolling off him in waves. It burned her skin. Touched her soul. "Look, Billie, I said I'd end it and I will. I'll catch Marcus, Foley, and whoever else is involved. But don't ask me to do the impossible. I won't back off."

She loved Reece. Knew she wasn't helping him with her need to tuck him away and keep him out of danger. She had to stand tall, shove her fear aside, and let him do what he did best. It's not like she had a choice. "Do what you have to. Just don't get yourself killed."

"God willing, we'll get through this together." His mouth touched hers to seal the deal, warm and loving. Her lips parted, she brought him inside, put her arms around his neck to deepen the kiss.

"As I live and breathe, if it isn't Billie the psycho and the cop who dragged her back to the funny farm." Billie jumped at the sound of that voice. She'd recognize the sarcastic tone anywhere—Rena, the taxi driver. She couldn't control the grin twitching her lips at the sight of Rena dressed like a cowpoke. "It's nice to see the two of you acting so chummy. And wearing clothes is a good thing, Billie. Almost makes you look normal."

"Rena!" Reece held her back when she would have jumped up to give the other woman a hug.

"Wait." Damn. He had good reason to be concerned.

Rena wasn't alone. A hulk of a man rolled to a stop behind her. Unlike Rena, he was dressed in biker chic with a lot of tats and piercings, a hint of marijuana smoke clinging to his denim jeans and creaking leather jacket. *The real deal*, she thought, this man rode

Harleys, not horses. He and Reece stared at each other, the biker dude taking in Theo and Sully at the next table with a sideways glance. He turned slowly, caught Micah and Hawke watching him from the tent entrance with their firearms in plain sight. He swung back to Reece.

"The name's Falcone. Blue Falcone." He held his left hand away from his side and eased the other across the table for a handshake. "I'm looking for Reece Morgan. Rizzo said I'd find him here."

What the hell?

"Pull up a chair, Blue. And keep your hands where I can see them." Reece palmed his phone, wasting no time contacting Rizzo while keeping eyes on the stranger. "A friend of yours stopped by, name of Falcone."

He didn't say anything else for a minute, listening to what Rizzo had to say on the other end of the line. Reece didn't look happy. There was an edge to his voice. "What does he look like? Butt ugly mixed in with some seriously scary shit? That's him. Get over here. We need to talk."

"Trust Riz to put me in a good light." Falcone laughed, tapping Rena's hand. "You didn't tell me you knew these people."

"If I'd known they'd be here, I would have told ya." Rena rolled her eyes. "All you said was I should dress like a stupid cowgirl, come along for the ride, and pretend to be your girlfriend."

"Hell, sweet cheeks, you *are* my girlfriend."

"Yup, I guess I am at that. But you're still gonna pay for making me wear this dumb outfit." Blue wrapped his gorilla arms around Rena and tugged her down on his lap.

Reece ended his call, called off the rest of his guys with a weird hand signal, eased back in his chair, and seemed to relax. "How do you know Rizzo?"

"We served together in the marines. I'm a cop now, working gangs and narcotics. When Riz called last night and told me what you're up against, I thought I'd hang at the rodeo for a few days with five of my guys. All of them cops. All of them ex-military. All of them bikers. You won't have any trouble spotting them. We don't wear Stetsons."

Jeez. Billie figured if they all looked like Falcone, spectators would be running from the stands screaming.

"You carrying?" Reece ran his eyes over Falcone's clothing and laughed. "Stupid question, forget I asked."

"Right up to the armpits, man. The kind of company I keep? I don't take a piss without a piece in my other hand. That goes for the rest of my crew, too." He leaned toward Rocket. "Where do you want us?"

"In the stands and walking the grounds. Split up your team so you don't scare the crap out of everyone. Keep your eyes and ears open. You know what to look for. You spot someone who doesn't belong, get word to my squad." Reece hitched his chin at Theo and Sully. "They're all dressed the same."

"I get it. Look for the goons dressed in black carrying hardware." He eased Rena off his lap and stood, sliding a burner phone across the table. "Six guys, six numbers on speed dial. I'm the first number. Something goes down, we'll guard your six. All you gotta do is call."

Reece nodded, spinning the phone between his fingers, an indefinable look on his face. "Thanks, man."

Billie thought she understood. These people were laying their lives on the line for someone they didn't even know. She realized Rocket's team had done the same for Melena, Breeana, and herself. It was more than a brotherhood they shared—more like a miracle. Tears caught in her throat. She swallowed hard and took a deep breath in and out. Better.

Falcone tucked Rena behind him as he headed for the exit. He protected her; any fool could see how much he cared about her. Billie was glad. Rena's life wasn't empty at all, not like she'd first thought.

She waved to her as she walked between the tables, her hand in Blue's. "Glad you're feeling better, rodeo girl. Catch up with ya later."

At the tent entrance, Rizzo and Falcone passed each other like ships in the night, neither acknowledging the other. McGee and Hank sniffed at Blue on their way by. Tails wagged. *Oh yes, they knew him.* The dogs edged close to her when they reached the table, eyeing the pancakes she had left on her plate.

"Don't beg. You're embarrassing yourselves." Rizzo's butt hit the chair across from Reece and the dogs hit their haunches.

"You should have told me." Reece leaned back, crossing an ankle over a knee. "I might have killed him."

"But you didn't." Rizzo's brows puckered in a frown. "If I had told you, you would have said no."

"Damn straight. I don't know these guys. And I don't know if they can hold their own."

"They can. I've seen how they work." He shrugged his shoulders. "Look, Rocket, I know you can take care of yourself, and God knows, I'm not questioning the size of your gonads. But if you're planning a party, it makes sense to have a few friendly faces on the invitation list. Just sayin'."

"You trust him?"

"As much as I trust you. Falcone feels the same way about his team as you do about yours." He patted McGee and Hank. "Besides, the dogs like him."

"The dogs like him?" Reece cracked a smile, signalling the waitress to bring them some coffee. "That makes all the difference, my friend. It looks like we're in excellent shape."

REECE HELD BILLIE'S hand as they stopped at the farrier's booth to admire the display. The smithy didn't just shoe horses or trim and balance hooves; he forged wrought iron fireplace tools and created copper weathervanes as well, each of them beautiful and unique. They left his shop, strolled along the row of boutiques as if they had all the time in the world. Like any other couple looking to strike a bargain.

At the saddlery, a custom barrel-racer saddle caught Billie's eye. The rich chestnut leather inlaid with turquoise and silver was exquisite and carried a four thousand dollar price tag. She trailed a finger along the intricate tooling in the leather. Wished she could afford to buy it. But, this had nothing to do with needing the saddle. More like she should have her head examined. *Where's the psychiatrist's couch? Move out of the way people, compulsive shopper coming through.* Some women bought shoes or ate chocolate when life gave them a scare. Her weakness was saddles, fancy headstalls, and breast collars for her horses.

"It suits you," Reece said, tempting the devil riding her shoulder that screamed *buy me now!* "And it'll look great on Cedar."

"I don't think so." She laughed, grabbed his hand again, and headed out of the concession stand. "I could buy another horse for my riding school with that kind of money. I don't even need the saddle."

Digging his heels in, Reece pulled her close and wrapped his arms around her, pinning her wrists behind her back. A smile tipped his mouth. "What *do* you need, peaches?"

Should she keep it light? Come up with the usual clichés that meant nothing and went nowhere? Hard to do when he smelled wicked sinful and looked even better. Here goes. "I need you in my life, and not just for a couple of weeks. I want you to come home to me at night, *every* night. Or, golly gee, how about we have a real relationship without bullets flying and bombs exploding? That might be fun."

"I'm glad I asked." Green eyes stared into hers. Unwavering. Serious. He let go of her hands to cup her face, a thumb lightly tracing her mouth. She felt him tense. Had she upset him? As the crowd shuffled around them, Billie noticed the curious stares and smiles from the ladies as they drooled over Rocket. "You go, girl. Stick to your guns!"

Holy kasmoly, people probably thought they were newlyweds having their first argument about buying dinner settings, like should they buy the cutlery with the antler handles or not? And what about those four-of-a-kind deer hoof ashtrays? How could anyone resist the little beauties?

Reece didn't seem to notice anyone gawking, his focus only on her. "Is there anything else on that wish list of yours?"

The hell with it, she might as well go for broke. "As a matter of fact, there is. I don't want you leaving me for months at a time, rushing off to some godforsaken hellhole to build God knows what for the military. There, that about covers it."

"Billie, I—"

In the next instant, she almost swallowed her tongue. A big guy with long dark hair, an eyebrow stud, and a grin on his face bumped Rocket's shoulder. It must be one of Falcone's men. Hmm, she couldn't help noticing he had a great smile and pearly white teeth that didn't compute with the filthy denim jacket. Its sleeves were ripped off and it was open in the front revealing a skull and crossbones logo on his faded Tee. "The name's Pax. Just thought you should know there's a cowboy dressed as a cowgirl who's been shadowing you for the last twenty minutes. He's hiding over there behind the lemonade stand."

Reece turned to the biker. "He's harmless."

Billie beamed at Pax, couldn't resist stirring the pot. "Yeah, and he's got a thing for Rocket...*real bad*."

Pax nailed Reece with a quizzical look, his smile slipping a notch. "Blue says to watch your back and that's what I'm doing. But I don't wanna know what floats your boat. Got it?"

Reece scowled and bellowed, "Maurice!"

Biker dude melted into the crowd as Maurice scurried toward them. He wore tan suede culottes with fringe along the bottom, a matching Navaho beaded top, and snakeskin boots. A leather cowgirl hat rode his luxurious hair; he wore a long blond wig today. Bird feathers dangled from his ears and hung from his leather wristbands. And, oh yes, his makeup was perfect, while Billie had raced out of the shower this morning, slapped on a little lip gloss, mascara, and called it a wrap.

"Sugar bear!" Maurice galloped straight at Reece and came in for a landing. Yup, in Rocket's arms again and pressed chest to chest. "I'm so glad I found you. There are some really scary guys here today, wearing chains and lots of leather. I'm pretty sure one of them *wanted* me, if you know what I mean. I'm staying out of the John as long as he's around. He might pull a sneak attack."

Reece rolled his eyes as Maurice gazed at him doing the eyelash flutter thing. Gosh, he did it better than Lorelei Calhoun had when she was batting her baby blues at Billie's father. And that spoke volumes. She grimaced, hoped Lorelei's eyeball action would cease and desist once she received notice Dottie was marrying her dad. Otherwise, they might have to bury her on the back forty if Dottie got a hold of her before those sessions with the therapist. Billie suppressed the thought and refocused on Maurice and Rocket.

If Reece had received a lot of drooling glances from the fairer sex before, he now got shifty glances from the men in the crowd, more shocked than approving. He dropped Maurice like a hot potato and backed off a few feet. "Now cut that out. You don't need to worry about bikers, so put them out of your head. I doubt they're interested in you. More like they came to see a rodeo, close up, and were startled to see someone with your...unique sense of fashion...in the crowd."

"Really?" Maurice let out a sigh, tucked a strand of hair behind an ear, giving his earring a shake. "Why don't I hang out with you anyway, just in case? We can head over to the refreshment tent and find a quiet corner. Sip lattés and watch the world go by. What do you say, super stud?"

"No can do, pal. Enjoy the rodeo." He wrapped an arm around Billie's waist and moved them back down the path toward the rodeo action and away from the little guy.

Maurice pushed the hat off his head and waggled a hand in the air. "Wait. Billie? Does your costume fit okay?"

"It's fine. I'll be dressed and ready in two hours." Reece kept on moving so she couldn't slow down.

"I'll see you before you enter the ring for the grand opening," Maurice shouted after her. "Be sure to tuck your hair up in the hat. Savannah's hair is darker than yours."

"Will do." She flashed him a smile and waved. "I'll see you later."

Reece ate up the dirt with long strides, eyeing the throng as they passed in the opposite direction. Another motorcycle jockey sauntered by without making eye contact, probably a member of Falcone's team. Rocket scanned his phone for incoming messages. "Damn, Micah's supposed to send me photos of Marcus and Foley as soon as he gets them. I wonder what's taking so long."

She laughed. "If the military is like other branches of government, I imagine the wheels don't turn too quickly."

"Not unless it's a matter of national security, which it isn't," he agreed. "But I only saw Foley once for a couple of minutes in a badly lit bar and I've never met Marcus, so I need those pictures."

His hand touched her nape as he planted a kiss on top of her head and whispered in her ear. "You know, we have a lot of the same things on our wish lists. Tonight, babe, we'll work it through when we're alone."

Her heart did a silly happy dance against her rib cage, shouting, *oh yes, please let's talk about it.*

Chapter 15

Reece stood with Sully watching the crowd. Five minutes to show time, the official opening of the rodeo. "The air's too still. I don't like it."

Sully watched the trees sway around them, a gentle breeze picking up. "Maybe there's a storm brewing, or it could be you're on edge."

"Is Theo in position?" Reece scoured the hillside where he knew he'd be, but couldn't make him out.

"He's up there somewhere in the dirt, wearing full camo gear. Hunt's with him."

"He's operating the parabolic mic?"

Sully nodded. "They'll be on the first shot fired like white on rice, once the microphone picks up the location of the sound waves. Hunt will give Theo the coordinates to return fire. A second or two, that's all it takes."

"A couple seconds can be one hell of a long time." Reaching under his jacket, Reece adjusted the Kevlar vest. "I just pray the bastards leave Billie alone."

"Reece, we've been over this a hundred times, and she's wearing a vest." Sully placed a hand on his shoulder. "Marcus and Foley have no reason to go after her. Not when you're here, with a big fucking bull's eye on your back. Besides, the announcement was made over the P.A. system. Everyone in the stands believes she's the movie star she's doubling for."

"Don't feed me that shit, Sully." He shoved his hand away. "What if it was Breeana out there?"

"I'd be fucking insane, pal, just like you. Let's not go there." Sully gazed at the judge's booth. "Bree's with Melena, Charley and the other judges up there. And I'm none too comfortable with that."

"Billie's dad will take care of them." Reece turned to walk away. "See you later."

"Count on it." Sully watched the stands, talking through his headset to other members of their team. "Hang tough, man. We'll get 'em."

Feet thudding the dirt, Reece made his way to the alley that gave riders access to the corral. Horses and riders were lined up for the flag ceremony. Billie sat on Cedar in the first position. He scaled steel tubing to reach the top of the guardrail, making sure her flag pole rested in the leather cup attached to Cedar's saddle. "It's not too late to change your mind, peaches. I wish you'd sit this one out."

"We've already discussed it. The team agrees there's no danger to me. Not anymore." She wouldn't look him in the eye. He knew it was her way of dealing. Guessed she was scared out of her gourd, but not for herself. Yeah, she was terrified for him. Like he was for her, the two of them bloody wrecks on the inside, but calmer than hell on the outside. She pulled the Stetson down over her eyes and gave him a curt nod. "Tonight. We'll talk about our wish lists."

Hell, if he didn't say it now, he might never get the chance. "Billie. I love you."

"Oh, great. Now you've gone and jinxed yourself." The national anthem began. The gate opened. She held his gaze for half a second before nudging Cedar with her heels. "Tell me later. I love you, too."

Fourteen riders circled the arena, ten flags representing the provinces, three for the territories, and Billie out in front with the Canadian flag. The riders broke into a trot, moving to a canter. The flags flew proud. Reece held his breath. Spectators stood and sang the anthem at the tops of their lungs.

Billie circled the arena once. Twice. *Almost home, baby.* She came around for the third time. Passing Micah on the rails, she curved into the turn. A shot fired. Reece could barely hear it over the roar of the crowd. He saw blood fly. Micah hit the ground. Billie came out of the turn. She kept on riding, hadn't heard the shot or seen Micah go down.

Jesus! Reece ran full out. Would the parabolic mic separate the blast of sniper fire from the din of voices and music? Theo had to nail this bastard before he turned his sights on the crowd. Heart thundering in his chest, Reece prayed, knowing the next bullet had his name written on it. Begged God to save Billie whatever happened to him. Another shot rang out. *Fuck!* He was still alive, wrenching her from the saddle. "Move! Move! Move!"

He dragged her, half carried her to the gate. Shouted at her about Micah. Screams filled his head. People in the stands stumbled over each other and fell. All of them frantic to reach cover. Maurice opened the gate. "The barn! We can hide in the barn!"

"Help Micah, Reece! Go!" Billie latched onto Maurice's hand, the two of them barreling for the barn doors.

"Stay there!" Reece spun, thundering for Micah. More shots fired, but not from a sniper rifle. Whoever it was, he was on the ground. Blue's team worked the crowd, all of them armed. They scooped up terrified children, hiding families beneath metal bleachers. Hawke and Law pulled the other riders from their horses, using their mounts for cover as they pushed them under the rails to hide behind the ambulance standing by for the show. Sully scaled the ladder to the judge's booth, hell bent on reaching Bree and Melena.

Reece reached Micah, ripped his jacket sleeve away from his arm. The bullet had caught him below the shoulder on the outside of his arm. A freak shot. He tore off his own jacket, working it around Micah's deltoid muscle to apply pressure. A laugh behind him raised the hairs on the back of his neck. He slid Mic's Glock from his waistband, swung around. A clown. A goddamn freaking rodeo clown raised a Walther PPK380 chest level. Reece fired, dropping him with a shot through the forehead.

He reported it through his headset, turned back to Micah, and applied more force on the wound. Micah opened his eyes, flashed him a pain induced grimace. "I didn't know you cared, big guy."

"Don't get your hopes up." Reece rechecked the injury. The blood flow was slowing and not spurting, no major veins compromised. While Micah was missing a chunk of flesh and muscle, he didn't see bone splinters. Also a good sign. "You're ringing, pal."

"My cell phone," Micah grunted. "In my pocket."

Reece reached for the phone and hit the ON button. A picture flashed on the screen. Marcus. Reece glanced at the clown sprawled at his feet in the dirt. In spite of the makeup, he knew he'd killed the kingpin. The jagged scar on his cheek couldn't be disguised by makeup. "It's a photo of Marcus. He's dead."

"Thank Christ." Micah fumbled for the phone, hit the NEXT button. "Here, this is Foley."

Reece kept pressure to Micah's wound, turning to see the screen. His heart lurched, his brain exploding as he slowly made the connection. He added makeup and women's clothing to Foley's image. "It's Maurice. The goddamn fashionista is Foley!"

As the paramedics swooped in to care for Micah, Reece shouted into his headset, his legs churning like pistons for the woman he loved. "Foley's in the barn. Jesus, he's got her. He's got Billie!"

BILLIE REACHED THE barn with Maurice, her whole body shaking. She bent at the waist to catch her breath; could still hear the screams coming from the corral. Children crying for their parents. The rush of feet stampeding like frightened cattle. *Sweet, sweet Lord.*

She should be out there helping Reece and his men. Her dad, Breeana, and Melena were stranded in the judge's box. Micah lay out there bleeding. More shots could be fired. They could all die. *Stop it! You'll make yourself crazy. Calm down, do what Rocket said, and stay with Maurice.*

She searched the barn, looking for places to hide. It was empty, except for a wrangler's horse standing inside the doors; probably one of the horses used in the arena to deflect bulls away from fallen riders and the rodeo clowns protecting them. The bulls were penned outside; the wild broncos held in the paddock until it was time for their event. Still, the scent of fear hung heavy in the air; perhaps it was the horse, shifting from foot to foot with coltish energy, or her own fear dissipating. At least Maurice held it together for a change. He tugged her toward the mount. "Quick, Billie. Hop in the saddle and we'll make our escape."

"No." *Is he crazy?* While, she might give the little guy an 'A' for effort and bravery, she wasn't budging from this spot. They wouldn't stand a chance on their own. "Rocket told us to hide in here. If we leave, he'll never find us. We can cover ourselves with hay in a stall, or climb up to the haylo—"

Maurice struck with the speed of a cobra, stabbing a syringe into her thigh with a painful jab. Surprise at his action transformed to panic. *He's drugged me with something.* "Get away from me, you sick freak!"

Maurice stared at her through the flat eyes of a predator, camouflaged by iridescent eye shadow and mascara. He came toward her. And she knew. He was one of the men Reece hunted.

Her legs folded without warning. She collapsed on the ground. He tossed the hypodermic, hoisting her up in the saddle with little effort. Her mind told her to fight. It was already too late. Her body wouldn't cooperate. He climbed up behind her, wrapping his arms around her. She leaned to the side, praying she'd tumble over and hit the dirt. He held her fast. "Oh come on, Billie, what's a little ketamine between friends? Another few minutes and you'll be in the K-hole. By then, we'll be long gone."

Ketamine? Her foggy brain caught and held, remembering a discussion with her vet. The drug in combination with xylazine was a short-term anesthetic for horses. But, it had other uses...horrific ones. Panic flooded her bloodstream as trivia surfaced from articles she'd read. *Oh. My. God. It's a favorite choice of rapists and psychopaths to control their prey!*

With that final thought, her brain left her body in a dizzying haze of confusion.

The horse bolted out of the barn, past the broncos in the paddock to open fields. Billie flopped along in the saddle, unsure how she'd gotten there. Into the trees and through the forest. No one followed. No one cared. Not true. Billie vaguely remembered that someone cared about her. She just couldn't remember who. She heard a shot in the distance; people shouting. Trees mocked her as she rode beneath them, tried to pluck her from the horse. *Yes, please, take me away.* They laughed, curled up their limbs, and allowed her to pass.

Drool pooled from a corner of her mouth. She could feel it, but couldn't swipe at it. Her hands grew to ten times their normal size. They twisted into gnarled claws, wanting to gouge out her eyes. She flopped one hand against the other, pushing them down, felt something jangle and slide. Her watch flew. Hovering in mid-air, the pony on the watch face whinnied before it grew into a full-sized stallion and galloped off.

"Having fun, Billie?"

Her insides jumped. She wasn't alone. Inhaling the sickening scent of perfume, she trembled. A hand moved, groping her breast.

She felt the assault, a brutal twist of pain. And she remembered. *Maurice. I'll knock his teeth out with the back of my head. I can do it.* She willed her brain to control her muscles, allow her this one act of freedom. Nothing happened, only the saw of her lungs reacting in alarm. He didn't seem to notice. "You figured out where we're going yet?"

Where are we going? Climbing higher past the tree line, the air around her cooled. The horse picked its way over rocks, climbing higher on a makeshift trail. Twisting back and forth, all the time going higher and higher, she closed her eyes to block out the view below. When she did, monsters crawled from her brain and filled her eyelids. She opened her eyes again, terrified and dizzy. Better to see what's coming than the creatures inside her head. One slip, one sway in the saddle, and she would tumble to her death. Paralyzed by drugs and fear, she knew she was at the mercy of a madman. *Let me go!*

"What's that, Billie? Did you say something?" Maurice chuckled behind her, the ebb and flow of his upper body moving with the gait of the horse churning her like a tidal wave. Her stomach roiled.

Don't throw up. I'll drown if I throw up. She swallowed hard, again and again, forcing the muscles in her throat to work.

"We're headed to Daddy's cabin, sweet pea. I think those memories of happy family times should be replaced with some new ones. Don't you?" He yanked her hair. A handful stuck to his glove, writhing like worms. "Just another three hours to wait. By the time we get there, the 'K' will start to wear off from a second injection. Or I might give you some more. Depends if I'm feeling generous or not. Then we're gonna have ourselves a real good time. Party like you have never partied before."

Nooooo! She screamed inside her head. Did the sound reach her lips? It must have. A hand came up and squeezed her throat. Was it her hand or Maurice's? She didn't know. Fingers tore at her flesh. She couldn't breathe. Something gurgled. *Is that me?* The earth spun, tunneling into swirls of fog. Thoughts surfaced through the dark, vague memories of better times struggling to set her free.

Maybe I don't need to breathe after all. Nothing will hurt me anymore. No more scary dreams. No more monsters dressed as women. I can see Mommy and Daddy and me at the cabin. Wait, Mommy's reaching for me. She's taking me away from the bad man. I'm coming, Mommy!

The hand let go of her throat, the image of her mother vanishing. Air pumped into her lungs. She coughed, reeling for her next breath. Maurice laughed, tugging her closer, whispering in her ear. "I'll rip your larynx out if you scream again. Save your voice for the cabin. You'll need it—when you beg me to kill you."

Fat chance of that, you piece of shit. When the ketamine wears off, I'll find a way to get free. He'll help me, you'll see. There is someone...someone who loves me...I just can't remember...

As if reading her thoughts, Maurice supplied the answer. "Morgan can't save you. He's already dead. You're his legacy to me—to do with as I please. And believe me, Billie; before you die, nothing will save you from the pain. Not even ketamine. Morgan's the one who fucked me over, but you'll pay the price."

Morgan? Reece Morgan? Yes, that's who loves me. That beautiful man is dead? No, he can't be. I'd feel it in my soul. What I sense is his anger building like a thunderstorm. What I see is your death, slow and agonizing. Reece is alive, you son of a bitch. He'll find me, and when he does, he'll destroy you!

REECE CHARGED THE BARN with one thought in his head—save Billie. Screw personal safety. Screw his team. Screw everything but killing the rat bastard before he hurt her. Too bad Hawke had other ideas. He tackled him twenty feet from the door.

Felled him like a giant sequoia. Grabbed him by the shirtfront and ripped off his headset, hissing in his ear. "Get your shit together!"

Reece shoved him hard, sprang to his feet, and lunged for the doorway. Hawke slammed him up against the wall. "You wanna go in hot? I've got no problem with that. But you *don't* do it alone."

Screw Hawkins and his take-charge attitude. Billie needed him. He didn't have time for this shit. "I know what I'm doing."

"Then quit acting like a goddamn rookie." Hawke took a breath, released the hold on his shirt. "On the count of three. One."

Reece dove through the entrance and rolled to his feet. He swung his Glock wide, circling left. Dust mites floated through an empty barn, the only sounds coming from the chaos outside. Hawke moved inside behind him, going right. They travelled in sync, down opposite walls to the stalls in back. Reece cleared half of them in under a minute. Hawke had four more to check. Reece left him to it and leapt the ladder to the loft. Reaching the top, he scrambled through the hay with a pitchfork in one hand, his piece in the other.

Nothing.

Billie was gone. Foley had taken her. It was his goddamn fault. "*Motherfuck!* I should have known."

"How could you?" Hawke met him at the bottom of the ladder, sliding his gun in its holster. "We all saw Maurice and none of us guessed. Foley's a master of disguise."

"He played me and I bloody well let him." Reece turned and paced across the floor, looking for a clue, anything to help him find Billie. "Every time he hit on me, I backed away. Like he knew I would. Didn't know how to deal with him. I didn't want to hurt his freaking feelings. Didn't even bother to check him out!"

"Rocket, we don't have time for this. Let's get Billie back first."

"How will we get her back? Dead and cut up in little pieces?" Reece rammed a fist into the ladder. He needed the pain to know he was still alive. Seemed the gung ho, kick ass, in your face part of him had left the building along with Billie. Her loss laid him open like road kill. Heartache and grief chewed up his insides. "You saw what the bastard did to Banyan."

"We don't know for sure it was him." Hawke shoved him hard with his hands. "But know this. The longer you stand here with your wheels spinning, the longer he has to hurt your woman."

"Fuck you!"

"You first, cream puff!"

Hawke's fist flew. Hard knuckles connected with his jaw. Reece countered with a slam to Hawke's gut. Tripping him up, the two of them pitched and rolled across the floor, matching jab for jab. Reece gained the top, snapped an arm back to bash Hawke in the kisser. A syringe rolled by him in the straw, stopping him cold. "Hold up!"

"Not until you pull your head out of your ass," Hawke grunted.

"I'm good." Reece gained his feet, flexed his hand a couple times, and picked up the syringe. Empty. He held it up to the light.

Hawke studied it beside him. "You figure it was used on one of the horses?"

"It's too small. The freak used it on Billie."

"He must have sedated her to take her somewhere. That's a good sign, man."

"Where do you get off? It sure as hell isn't a good sign for Billie!" Reece glared at him, wished they had time to continue their 'Come to Jesus' meeting of the minds.

They both turned when Rizzo crossed the threshold, McGee and Hank on their work leads. The dogs went wild and flew at Reece as if they wanted to attack him. Barking, snarling, and baring their fangs. "Good boys. Down."

Good boys? Reece stared at the dogs as they dropped to the floor. "Nick, what's the matter with them?"

"The syringe in your hand," Rizzo said. "Both of them are trained for drug detection. Whatever was in there, it's not sugar water."

"What are the possibilities?"

"Cocaine, meth-amphetamines, ketamine, heroine...the list goes on, pal."

God, Billie, what has Foley done to you? I'll rip his heart out!

Reece fought the urge to lose it completely, forced himself to calm down. "Okay, so he's drugged her with something. They can't have gotten far." He glanced back at the floor and moved to the far doors. Wild broncs watched him from the paddock, grouped in twos and threes. A battered hat lay in the dirt between their feet. "Jesus, there's Billie's Stetson. They went out this way."

"Don't touch it." Rizzo stepped in front of him. "Get some horses saddled. Then we'll let Hank and McGee have a whiff."

Reece heard a noise behind them, turned on a dime, and leveled his weapon. Hunt came through the doorway on the fly, his own Glock in play. Both of them stood down.

"I'll get the horses." Hawke nodded at Hunt and ran by him.

"What's wrong with your equipment?" Hunt held up their headsets. "Sully figured you were both dead in here."

"Forget it." Reece jogged for the paddock. "Give me a status report."

"Theo's on the hillside with the dead sniper, filling the local police in on what went down. Law went in the ambulance with Mic. EMTs say he'll make it, but he needs surgery. Sully's with the sheriff. He's got the girls with him. Falcone and his crew are standing by in case we need 'em. We also caught a few more mutts working for Marcus. Spinelli was one of them, and a guy on the camera crew. That's about it."

Hawke rode to the paddock gate with three more horses. Rizzo took the dogs over to Billie's hat. "Let them take a good sniff." He grabbed the hat, released the dogs, and ran for the horses. Hunt mounted up.

Reece put heels to his horse's flanks. "Let's move."

The rain started an hour into the ride. Just a few splatters at first but turned into solid sheets by the time they reached a trail up the mountainside. The dogs lost the scent. The rest of them rode up to Rizzo in the lead, knowing they'd reached the end of the line.

"Shit," Rizzo said. "They can't track her any farther."

"There's no need." Reece turned his mount, putting the sleeting rain at his back. He looked up, couldn't see anything but fog after the first several hundred feet. "There's only one thing on that mountaintop. Charley's hunting shack."

"You're sure?"

"Hell, I'm positive. Billie and I snuck up there once when we were kids. Thank Christ, Charley never found out." He pulled the brim of his hat low to protect his eyes from the sleet, or hide the tears brimming on his lashes.

He remembered the day he and Billie had gone off together. Jeez, they'd rode halfway up the mountain to take a dip under a waterfall. Innocent fun, but Billie was special to him even then. She could always convince him to do anything for a kiss and a hug in those days. *And now?* Multiply those feelings a thousand times. He loved her. He'd get her back. Otherwise, he'd die with her on that mountaintop. He wouldn't come back without her.

"We'll have to take another way up," Reece said. "Anyone at the top can see for miles. The bastard could pick us off like ducks in a shooting gallery."

The men exchanged glances, their minds in sync. He tossed Hunt the burner phone. "Tell Falcone to pick us up. Have him bring Charley and Pike to take the horses back to the stable."

Reece pulled out his own phone, connecting with Sully. "Change of plans. Let's get this fucker."

Chapter 16

The second dose of ketamine was wearing off. Fighting the backward slide into oblivion, Billie struggled to hold on, knowing Maurice didn't have a clue. He was focused on other things, distracted by how he would torment and kill her. She knew it wouldn't be long now. The sky had darkened with more than just storm clouds. Birds that should be chirping were silent, even under the protection of trees, a sure sign they were settling in for the night. Another hour at most and it would be pitch dark.

With rough hands, Maurice pulled Billie off the horse. She crumpled in the mud at his feet. They had reached the hunting cabin. It was the end of the line for her.

Or maybe not.

"Bath...bathroom." She lay back in the mud, determined to make herself as unappealing as possible. Her stomach rolled, tossing bile up her throat as the strength in her muscles went from little to non-existent. And her head? If she didn't focus with all her might, she knew the monsters would worm their way back inside, along with the terror. No, the only way she would survive and find a way to escape was to think of Reece. Of what they shared, and what they could have again, if she somehow lived through this. God, it tore at her soul and broke her heart. "Pl...please...outhouse."

"Fucking bitch." Dragging her upright, he threw her over his shoulder and followed the path around back of the cabin. Propping her against a tree, he removed the bar that kept the door secured. "Make it fast. I'll be back after I unsaddle and feed the horse."

Yes, Billie knew he would care for the horse, his only way out of there...after he was finished with her.

Maurice tossed her inside and slid the bar home, locking her in. But not for long. She remembered the loose boards on the side of the structure. When she was little, she would pretend to need the bathroom in the middle of the night. While one of her parents waited for her outside, she would squeeze through the opening and sneak off to see the horses in the corral. Of course, she'd always gotten caught...but not this time.

Resolve strengthened her spine as she worked her way between the boards. A tight fit, but she was out the other side in under a minute, staggering to the creek on unsteady legs, clutching at saw grass and tree trunks to hold her upright. If she followed the stream to the waterfall, she could hide behind it. She and Reece had tucked themselves in there once, watching deer drink at its edge. A cherished memory she held close to her heart. She wanted more of those. But the waterfall was still a long way off.

She could make it if the rain continued to pour down. If Maurice lost her in the dark. If he didn't hear twigs snapping beneath her wobbly feet, or the creak of her boots. A lot of ifs. Nothing but uncertainty.

She tripped and stumbled down a slope, sliding the rest of the way to the creek below. She lay in the muck, out of breath, bracing against the stab of pain in her side. Pulling up her shirt, she lifted her head to see a bloody gash along her ribs. Realized she must have hit a rock. She lay back down for a second, noticing the rain had stopped.

"You fucking whore." *Maurice!* Coming out of nowhere, he grabbed her collar and punched her in the face; the viciousness of his strike bellied the makeup and she-clothes he wore.

Billie fought like a wildcat, raised a boot, and kicked his balls halfway to Alaska. He rolled away from her, didn't move. Scrambling to her feet, she found the rock she'd landed on, struggling to raise it high enough to bash him over the head. Whipping around, she plowed straight into him, the rock tumbling between them.

Evil stared her down, a sickening grin on his painted lips. "You lose, rodeo queen. I'm wearing a cup. How else do you think I dress in these fabulous clothes?"

Maurice slammed her in the stomach. Billie hit the ground. Grabbing her ponytail, he dragged her through underbrush and up the hill. Back to the cabin to be raped, tortured, and murdered.

REECE LISTENED TO THE drone of engines as the Hercules banked. She was a four-engine turboprop that could land on a short runway which was the reason Nick was able to park her at the local airfield. Hawke sat in the cockpit punching in the longs and lats, and coaxing the bulky bird up to ten thousand feet. Once the plane leveled off, he circled back toward the target, sounding the two minute warning.

"Thanks for the use of your gear, Rizzo," Reece said, zipping up his flight suit. "We didn't think we'd need our own on this op."

"No problem, as long as you help repack the chutes. I keep the Herc fully supplied for training sessions with the military dogs and their handlers." He looked around, apparently satisfied everyone was ready to make the dive. Hunt and Sully stood by the door aft of the wing. They would go out that way rather than raise the cargo door at the rear. "Come here, McGee. Good boy. Ready to dive?"

The big Shiloh gave a yip and wagged his tail. While Nick covered his nose and mouth with his mask and adjusted his eye goggles, Reece did the same for McGee. Free-falling was fast. Airways and eyes needed protection from extreme wind conditions. Hoisting McGee up in his arms, he helped Nick attach the dog's harness to his own. They'd be strapped together for the jump.

"One minute," Hawke announced over their headsets.

"Roger that." Reece donned his own goggles and mask, joining the others at the open doorway.

"Keep eyes on your altimeters. We'll pop the chutes at five hundred feet and not before," Sully said, glancing at his own gauge to make sure it worked properly. "There's less chance of Foley spotting us with closed chutes if he's watching the skies."

"Stay out of the prop wash on your way out the door," Hawke added. "She'll toss you around like a vengeful bitch."

Hunt rolled his eyes. "Jeez, Mom, like we don't already know that."

Reece knuckle tapped Hunt, Sully, and Rizzo, but couldn't find the words to express his gratitude. Still, some things didn't need to be said. They already knew how he felt. Billie meant everything to him. They were putting their lives on the line for her. "Be careful where you land...no broken bones on this trip."

The green light came on beside the door. It was time to kick Foley's ass.

They dove like torpedoes, caught the wind, and sailed after each other; Rizzo and McGee led the way. Reece left the stars behind as he eventually dropped through the clouds, pulled the ripcord and felt his chute open, reeling him back. He landed without incident, stashed the chute, and stripped off his flight suit.

He moved toward Rizzo and helped him unhook the dog, shedding his goggles and mask. McGee wore Kevlar like the rest of them, except his vest also contained an infrared camera, microphone, and audio capability. Rizzo could monitor what McGee was seeing on a handheld device and talk to him when the dog was far ahead.

Sully and Hunt caught up by the time Nick pulled Billie's battered hat out of a sealed plastic pouch. McGee inhaled it, took off with his nose to the ground, searching for her scent.

"He's got something," Nick whispered a few minutes later. "Down by the stream."

"Let's go." The dog sniffed along the creek bed then shot up an embankment. They were right behind him with their weapons primed.

Thank Christ, the rain had stopped. Billie's scent was still on the ground for the Shiloh to track. A horse nickered on their left. Reece spotted the big gelding in a corral. He ignored it. The cabin loomed straight ahead in the distance.

Nothing moved. No sounds came from inside. Not a good sign. Reece's heart jack hammered against his ribcage. *Billie.* Was she still alive? He cleared his mind of everything but the op. If he thought about her now, he'd lose it. And Foley would win.

Candlelight flickered in the large window at the front. He guessed it was the living room. Smaller windows along the sides of the building were dark. Sully and Hunt moved past him, disappeared along opposite walls of the cabin. McGee crouched at the bottom of the front stairs, waiting for a command, ears straight up and fangs bared. He didn't make a sound.

Rizzo gave the Shiloh a hand signal. He tapped Reece's shoulder, whispered in his ear. "McGee's all yours. I'll take the back."

Reece had two options. He could storm the place like an idiot or wait for his men to get in position. Fear edged his spine for Billie. If he hesitated, she could die. For the love of God, Foley could be suffocating her while he stood outside. His ears strained to pick up sounds from within the cabin. *Nada.* Not a moan, not a curse, not a scream. *Are they even inside?*

He caught the faraway sound of motorcycles on the mountain trail. Falcone and his crew were coming to take Billie home. He'd just about given up on his own team when Hunt, Sully, and Rizzo came through his headset. They were in position. He gave them a "Go!"

Reece inched closer to the front porch. Held up when he heard voices inside. He strained to get a fix on their location.

"It's about time you woke up, you worthless bitch." *Foley's voice.* "Spread your legs, or I'll knock your teeth down your throat."

Fucking bastard!

Billie laughed. He recognized the terror in her tone, although she disguised it well. "You wish. I only sleep with Rocket. He's a *real* man, M-Maurice, not some caricature wearing frills and makeup."

He heard the sound of a bed squeak, a hand strike out. Billie's muffled cry. "I'd rather die, you son of a bitch! I'll never let you touch me!"

Reece scaled the guard rail in a flash, landing on the balcony. McGee leapt up beside him, his whole body shaking with the urge to attack.

"Billieeeee! You don't wanna play nice with me? Let's see if sulfuric acid will get you in the mood!"

Motherfuck! Reece took in the horror on the other side of the windowpane with one glace. Billie was tied to a day bed. Foley leaned over her, a glass vial in his hands. He removed the cap. Reece smashed the window with the stock of his M25. One quick hand signal and McGee attacked.

Foley spun at the sound of breaking glass. McGee flew through the air, rammed Foley in the shoulders, and slammed him backward to the floor. The Shiloh bounced off the wall, reversing direction to rip Foley's throat out. Reece leapt over the casement and shouted, "Down!" McGee obeyed, dropping like a stone. *Thank fuck.* He didn't want him burned by the acid.

Foley lay on his back, covered in it from chest to groin. He let out a bloodcurdling scream, rolled over, and managed to drag himself off the floor. *Christ!* He was heading for the bed again. Reece caught him from behind—grabbed his head. He snapped his neck like a twig, dropped him where he stood, and stepped over the body to reach Billie.

Jesus, she was a mess. The prick had beaten her. Reece pulled out his KA-BAR, cutting the flex cuffs from her wrists as gently as possible. He kept the conversation light. If he didn't, he knew he'd bawl like a goddamn baby. She needed his strength now, not his tears. "You still styling your hair with that stun gun, peaches?"

She grinned up at him through bloody lips. "Like I said before, I haven't had time for the salon."

His team gathered around them. They'd stormed the cabin at the same time he had, each of them pouring from different rooms of the house. Hunt hit his haunches, covered Foley with a coat he'd found in the hallway. Nick examined McGee for acid burns or glass shards. He seemed to be fine. Sully put a hand on his arm. "Nice job, Rocket. I'll tell the sheriff he can call off the search."

Reece scooped Billie up, stepping over Foley's body again to carry her outside. She curled into him, burying her face in his neck. "Please take me home."

"On our way, babe."

Falcone was already out in front. He climbed off a Harley, one with a side car. Crossing his arms over his chest, the cop shot him a questioning glance. Reece nodded. *Yeah, we got the fucker.* Falcone squeezed his shoulder. "Your limo's waiting."

The biker cop thought of everything. Hell, he had even supplied blankets. Reece tucked Billie in the side car, checking her over, at last satisfied her injuries weren't life threatening. She could handle the trip down the mountain. He knew Charley waited at the bottom with an SUV to make the rest of the drive easier.

Reece circled round and started the bike, noticed Pax behind him on another Hog with a side car. Rizzo gave his dog a command and he hopped in with Pax. The rest of his team piled aboard with members of Falcone's crew. Reece felt the burn in his chest. These were all men he was damn proud to know.

"We'll come back tomorrow," Reece said as they started down the trail. It would be soon enough to bring the police, retrieve their equipment and pick up Foley's body. Right now, he had only one priority. Billie.

BILLIE RAISED HER FACE under the spray, washing away the dirt. She wanted to shower with Reece but was outvoted by Mel, Bree, and Rena who wanted to help her clean up. But her chest felt tight, and she knew hysteria was just around the corner. Damn, she'd be hyperventilating in another few seconds. "Please. I want Reece!"

"You can see him after you shower," Rena said. "There must be twenty pounds of mud on you."

"No. I need him *now*!"

"Of course, she needs him now." Breeana exchanged worried glances with Mel. "Hell for breakfast, what were we thinking?"

They hollered. Reece shot through the bathroom door. He saw the tears in her eyes and grabbed the facecloth from Rena. "Thanks. I'll take care of her."

He stripped down and joined her in the shower. When he wrapped himself around her, the dam broke and she cried like a baby. Wracking sobs poured out of her. All she could do was cling to him and ride out the storm. "That's it, honey. Let it out."

"God, I was so s-scared. I thought I'd n-never see you again. Maurice, h-he was so sick, and no matter h-how hard I tried, I couldn't get away. And then you c-came for me."

He rubbed lazy circles along her spine, unknotting the tension there, helping her relax. The shower reminded her of the waterfall, the happy moments they had shared so many years ago. She sighed against him.

"Sweetheart, of course, I came for you—me and a lot of other people. There was no way I'd let him take you from me."

"But, he c-could have killed you and your friends. And he shot Micah."

"He could have killed all of us, Billie. But he didn't. Micah will be fine after some R and R. So now we move on. We lean on each other and give ourselves a chance to heal. You up for that?"

She nodded, her lower lip still trembling. Yes, she was up for that.

When she finally stopped crying, Reece tipped her chin and kissed her battered face. Washed her hair, soaped her up, rinsed her, and dried her off. He even, very carefully, brushed her teeth. Then he applied lotion to her aches and bundled her into a sleep Tee and shorts. Billie felt cherished. She felt safe in his arms and knew everything else would work itself out.

After hopping into fresh clothes he grabbed from his room, Reece swept her up and carried her to bed. He never took his eyes off hers. "I love you. I only got to tell you once, before the flag ceremony. Just wanted to say it again, in case you forgot."

"How could I forget?" she whispered. "It's what kept me going when I was with Maurice."

Reece brushed her temple with another kiss, settled her gently on the mattress, covering her with a quilt. A doctor waited patiently; the same man who had treated Rocket when he was gored by the bull. He took one look at her and shook his head. "Good grief. Are you two trying to outdo each other, or is this just a regular Saturday night at the *Circle B*?"

She and Reece burst out laughing, but her giggles soon dissolved into tears again. Reece held her while she cried...and cried...and cried. Billie thought her emotional outbursts were because of the ketamine injections. The doctor said it was because of the trauma, of being held captive. "You don't know what you're talking about. I'm fine!"

"Sure you are, peaches." Reece made her smile as he whispered in her ear. "It's the doc who's a little squirrely."

He gathered her to him while the nut-ball added a stitch to her bottom lip and bandaged the cut along her side. After a shot of antibiotics—her tetanus was up to date—the doctor gave Reece instructions. "Keep applying ice packs to her face so her eye doesn't swell up. And make sure she stays in bed for a few days. She's been through a lot."

"Doc?" Reece smoothed a hand along her hair, adjusted the ice pack beneath her cheek, and snuggled her under his chin. "Can you give Billie something to help her sleep?"

"I'd rather not." He packed up his medical bag. "Not after the ketamine."

Reece waited until the doctor left the room and tipped her chin up. "I know it's not the time, but I want you to know I'm not taking on any more engineering projects with the military unless I can send someone else out in the field."

"You're serious?" *Oh, please, please, be serious.*

"Babe. Remember your wish list? When I said I had a lot of the same things on mine?" He kissed the corner of her mouth. "I'm moving back here, if you'll have me. I have more work as an engineer than I can handle. It's about time I hired someone to share the load. And there's no reason for me to leave you again, except for assignments with my reserve unit. What do you say?"

She stared into the emerald eyes of the man beside her—the man who completed her in every way possible. He was her protector, her lover, her best friend. What could she say, other than a resounding "Yes!"

"Peaches, you humble me." He bent his head, sealing the deal with a heart stopping kiss. "And while I'm on a roll...the Doc said I have to keep you in bed for a few days. Do you feel up to—?"

Oh, yes! A thousand times yes!

THANK YOU FOR READING this book. I hope you enjoyed it but even if you didn't, please take a few moments to go back online where you purchased it and leave an honest review. Authors absolutely depend on reviews to know how readers feel about their books and series. Thank you, it's appreciated.

For a free book, please hop over to my website at **https://www.kallielane.com**

A word about the author...

This is me in a nutshell. I was raised in Montreal and still have a home there, although most of my thriller and suspense novels come alive in my writing den, at a small cottage I love in the mountains. I guess I've always been a country girl at heart.

My constant companions these days are a Rottweiler, an American Bully, and a cat rescue. I'm widowed and have two adult sons who, I'm sure, worry about what trouble I'm getting into on a daily basis. Case in point; I've managed to break a few bones and dislocate others over the last few years when 'playing' with my dogs. While they are advanced obedience trained and a pleasure to have, I sometimes roughhouse with them a little too much. I also enjoy taking the boat out in the wee hours of the morning to see the stars and the night sky at the cottage. But, yes, I always have my cell phone handy. I'm sure if I didn't answer, someone would call 9-1-1.

I worked in the pharmaceutical and biotech industries for several years, and now I can finally enjoy writing as my real job, which I've dreamt about doing since I was a teenager. Wowzers! How lucky can a girl be? My spare time is shared with family and friends, including writer friends, and I work out to keep myself in shape, rather than dog wrestling! I'm an avid reader and spend more time with a book or tablet in my hands than watching television. Oh, I also like to travel, whether it's for business or pleasure, but I'm mostly found at the keyboard fulfilling my passion for writing.

I love to hear from readers, so please drop me an email at kallie_lane@ymail.com and I promise I'll message back. Lastly, I hope you enjoyed what you read. I would love it if you would leave a review where you purchased this book. It matters to me (and all authors) how you feel about our stories. Wishing you the very best!

To learn more about Kallie, visit her website at **https://www.kallielane.com** or follow her on Facebook at **http://www.facebook.com/KallieLaneAuthor**

Here's a sneak peek at book 4 in the Shadow Soldiers Suspense series, available wherever you purchased previous books in the series...

Lethal Abandon
Chapter 1

Remy Renaud wanted out of the Everglades. She hated the swamp so much she begged Saint Christopher, the patron saint of travellers, to please get the lead out and transport her somewhere else. Make that anywhere else. And could he manage it before the crocodile bumping her canoe killed her? Because now would be a really good time.

The whopping croc stared at her through yellow, iridescent eyes. Toyed with her like a cat with a gerbil. No doubt enjoying the game before it flipped her out of the canoe and dragged her under in a death roll. One swish of its powerful tail, that's all it would take.

Please, whoever's listening up there, find this frickin' carnivore something else to eat and make him leave me alone!

Inhaling a steadying breath, Remy attempted to center herself, knowing she had to get out of this mess on her own. Not easy to do. Everglades National Park was nothing like the nature reserve where she worked as a wildlife biologist. The bogs here overwhelmed her, not to mention the reptiles—alligators, crocodiles, water moccasins, and rattlesnakes to name a few. And would she ever forget the roughly fifteen-foot python she'd seen slithering through a cypress grove that afternoon? It had shattered whatever was left of her Pollyanna sense of adventure, never mind the croc currently stalking her every move. She was unnerved and fresh out of brilliant ideas. Could life possibly get any worse? Don't even go there, she decided.

Instead, she reminded herself how she had gotten into this mess. It hadn't been difficult, not after she refused Pete Mandel's offer to be her guide. Her obstinate streak rearing its carrot-topped head, she'd insisted she could find her own way in almost twenty-four-hundred square miles of protected acreage with only a map. Well, it had seemed logical at the time, but now, not so much.

Still, why would she allow the head park ranger to babysit her when she was trained in wilderness survival herself? And she was, just not this kind of wilderness. Pete had tried to tell her this before she'd paddled off alone in the canoe, and forgotten the two-way radio on the dock. So this was her mess and her fault.

A swarm of mosquitoes mocked her, dive bombing in the fading light, reaffirming how much she loathed this place and situation. She was here to gather information on the Canadian Sandhill Cranes that normally migrated north, and discover why some of them had summered with their Florida cousins instead. But the cranes hadn't cooperated with her visual headcount, flying farther inland. Drawing her deeper and deeper into the Glades, a bonafide suicide mission for a greenhorn. She knew she needed to make tracks out of there right away. She sighed, eyeing the crocodile. If only she knew which way to go.

No one else was around. Nature seekers and hikers weren't allowed in restricted areas of the park, which made perfect sense considering predators roamed the wetlands. The eerie sounds—a deep-throated panther growl being the obvious one at the moment—the smell of decay, the stillness in the air all caused her to sweat with fear while her insides froze with dread. She should have headed back an hour ago and hadn't, a rookie mistake of disastrous proportions. There was only a little daylight left, barely enough time before she lost the sun under the thick canopy of trees.

She paddled in a wide arc away from the prehistoric beast tailing her. He wasn't fooled, turning along with her as she altered course. Alone in the marsh with only a meat-eating stalker for company, the irony hit home. She normally preferred being by herself, enjoying the science of the job, the peacefulness of nature. Not today.

Give her bears, wolverines, and mountain lions any day of the week. At least she was armed at her own park in Alberta. But here? She imagined the dinner bell clanging as the massive reptile kept even with her, its eyes and snout skimming the algae-slicked water. She was lost in a strange place with night closing in, and hope fading to a whisper inside her head. A pitiful scream worked its way up her throat. She swallowed it back.

Forget it. I will not shriek like some scared-y-cat, little girl.

She would never live it down if someone heard her cries for help and park rangers rode to the rescue. They would inform their boss and Pete was a family friend. Crap, he'd tell her brothers and she'd be a laughingstock by the end of the day. So, no, she'd use her compass, her skills, and find her own flippin' way back to civilization.

She heard something in the distance. The drone of a motor broke through the sounds of frog ribbits and crickets chirping. Another few minutes and a beat-up boat crossed her bow. An old man hunkered at the throttle, a faded ball cap on his head. A cigar bobbed between his cracked lips. Definitely not a lost tourist, she decided, waving her paddle to flag him down.

He cut the engine and doffed his hat. "Evenin' miss. They call me Papa Joe."

Remy studied the lean face tanned to the consistency of shoe leather. White whiskers stubbled his chin, gray hair tangled to his shoulders. It was his blue eyes that held her attention, though, their gaze razor sharp. She judged his age to be somewhere between sixty and a hundred. It was impossible to tell. "My name is Remy Renaud."

"That's a right fine French name. Cajun, are ya?"

"I don't think so. I was born in New Brunswick, Canada."

"Acadian roots then. Explains the red hair and freckles." He stroked a palm along his jaw. "Ain't none of my business, Remy, but you should be headin' back afore nightfall. Lots of unfriendlies out here in the Glades. Are ya lost?"

What the heck, there was no point in ignoring the obvious. "A little. Do you think you can help me?"

"I reckon I could, since I'm headin' back myself." He grinned, chomping on the unlit cigar. "You follow me and I'll have you home in the time it takes to cut off a rattler's tail. I won't go too fast."

The tension drained from Remy's muscles, although she wasn't quite sure how long it took to "cut off a rattler's tail." Still, she instinctively trusted the man. He instilled confidence, and...

"Walter! Get the hell away from her before I bop you with the bang stick!" The old man grabbed an elongated steel rod from his boat, thrusting it in Remy's direction.

She followed his gaze to where her hand rested. The crocodile's jaws were an inch off the gunnel heading for her fingertips. Holy hell in a hand basket!

"Get out of there, ya filthy beggar!" The croc recoiled after a shot from Papa Joe's weapon and moved off. The man tossed the pole in the bottom of his skiff, shaking his head. "Rubber bullets. They won't kill him, but they sure pack one hell of a wallop. Just don't pay him no mind, missy. Old Walt has been livin' in these parts goin' on forty years. He likes to fool with the tourists some, but he ain't chewed on nobody yet, far as I know. And he won't follow you no more."

"Th-thank you." God in heaven, please get her out of there in one piece. She needed a stiff drink, a hot bath, and room service to shore up what was left of her sanity.

"Here, hang this around your neck." Papa Joe tossed her a battery powered lantern with a lanyard attached. "I'll be watching for that there light so I know you're still behind me. Otherwise, I'll double back."

As darkness closed around them, Remy did as he asked, picked up the paddle, and followed his slow-moving boat heading west out of the swamp. She backed off enough to stay out of its wake, not difficult to do after Papa Joe picked up a little speed. Before she knew it, he was quite a bit ahead, her arms churning to keep up and losing the battle. Still, she could see the stern light on his skiff, so she knew he hadn't left her alone. And while distances could be deceiving at night, she thought she recognized a grouping of trees on an upcoming beachhead. If so, then she was only ten or fifteen minutes out from the boat docks.

A flash of movement caught her eye in the nearby shadows. An alligator slid down a bank tossing its head back and forth. Something glittered in its jaws. What was that? Remy held up the light. A woman's hand flopped between the reptile's teeth, a diamond ring on a finger. The gator dove beneath the surface and disappeared before her next breath.

Sweet Jesus! Did I see what I think I saw? She might still be alive!

Remy swung into shore, landing the canoe on an embankment beside a fancy power boat. She leapt out and tried her cell phone. No signal.

Damn it, the woman needs help now! With nothing but a couple of finger-size bandages stuffed in a pocket of her cargo shorts, she grabbed the paddle and backtracked after the claw marks and tail tracks heading down to the water from a group of mangroves up ahead. She had to find the owner of that hand before she bled to death.

Pulling her belt from its loops to use as a tourniquet, she braked to a halt after clearing the trees, stumbling across something so grisly her mind refused to accept it. The blood drained from her head, the paddle slipping from her grip. She sagged against a tree to support herself as the horror around her sank in.

A man with a shovel stood over a mound of earth. He lunged at a gator. The reptile hissed when the spade swooped and bashed its head. It charged him. Dropping the shovel, the guy pulled a gun. Shot the alligator between the eyes. The boom of the weapon ricocheted, birds screeching in treetops as the sound rolled through the swamp like cannonball fire.

He swung his weapon toward another reptile. "Get out of here, you fucker!"

"Stow the firepower before the park rangers zero in on us!" A second man stepped from the darkness; stocky, sallow complexioned, a machete gripped in a meaty fist. He swung the blade, slashing the gator through the neck. Blood sprayed, landing on his silk shirt and designer jeans. The stench and sight of gore sickened Remy.

"Wha—?" Her brain finally kicked in and registered what stared her in the face. A slim arm stuck out of the ground. The hand was missing.

No, no, no! This can't be happening!

Other body parts were strewn across loamy earth, too many to belong to one person. Someone, or something, had dug them up. Remy's heart slammed in her ribcage.

Oh, dear God, this is a body dump!

Her stomach twisted in knots. Two pairs of eyes drilled her as she swallowed bile, covered her mouth with her hands, and backed away. Not much of a strategy, considering the men had her outnumbered.

"I'll be damned. Looks like the gators brought us a present, Sig." The man with the machete leered in the lamplight as he advanced, tossing the blade from one hand to the other. "What do you think? Should I gut and filet her? Or do we have time to play?"

"Right," the man with the gun said, grabbing his crotch through his pants. "Like I want some gator ripping off my wanger while I'm shagging the bitch. Cut her fucking head off and be done with it."

Remy inhaled and exhaled as best she could while Machete Man closed the distance. Martial arts—she was trained to defend herself.

It was all about breathing and using her opponent's strength against him. I can do this.

He lunged.

Remy kicked his knife hand away, dropped her leg, and hooked him behind a knee. He fell hard, but still managed to slice her with the blade. She disengaged and backed off, feeling a stab of pain in her thigh. Uncertain how bad the injury was or how long she had before she fainted from blood loss.

Ignore the pain. Breathe in, breathe out. Focus on his next move.

She didn't have long to wait.

"Freaking cow. I'll slice you to ribbons and leave you for the wild boar to eat!" The psycho sprang to his feet, charging her head on. When he lunged, she twisted by him. Clamped her fingers around his wrist and pushed his arm into the front of his body. She rammed the heel of her other hand into his shoulder blade. The machete arced upward, slicing across his throat. He collapsed at her feet, dead almost before he hit the dirt.

Remy froze, horrified by what she'd done, knowing she didn't have a choice.

"You killed him!"

Whirling too late, a gun slammed into her forehead. She crumpled in a heap, dizzy and disoriented, blood streaming from a cut over an eyebrow. Swiping at the blood, she stared into the soulless eyes of the man above her. Prayed he'd take a clean shot and kill her outright. He aimed for her knee instead.

Bam!

Papa Joe stood over him like a wild man when he collapsed across Remy's legs. "I got him with the bang stick, but he won't stay out for long. We gotta move."

"I'll call 9-1-1," Remy pulled out her cell phone with trembling fingers as the old man wrapped her thigh with a bandanna he'd tugged from around his neck.

"That there phone won't work." He dragged her to her feet. "There ain't no cell towers on state protected land. Confuses bat radar or some such thing."

"But—"

"No time for buts, Remy." Papa Joe put an arm around her waist. Much stronger than he looked, he was able to haul her out of there and down to the water. "Get in my boat afore you pass out."

"Don't worry about me. Are the keys in the power boat?"

He shook his head. "No time to check. We gots to get out of here afore he wakes up. Turn off the lantern so he don't follow us."

Papa Joe pulled on the starter cable. He shut down the running lights and gunned the throttle. "Hang on, girl. You're gonna be fine."

"I know, Papa Joe." Her world rocked on the waves for a few seconds, the drone of the boat motor soothing her before darkness closed in.

MICAH RIVERA SAT AT the open bar on the pier nursing a longneck. Pete Mandel, his buddy since kindergarten, sat across from him with a Perrier in hand.

"Thanks for driving out here, Mic." Pete toasted him with the water bottle and took a deep swallow. "Sorry I couldn't make it to Miami like we'd planned."

"Don't sweat it, pal." Micah rotated his shoulder and felt the tug. Getting shot a few weeks ago had messed with his plans, although he was almost healed now. Still, recuperating with his folks in that retirement village in Miami had almost done him in. He loved them, they were all the family he had, but playing shuffleboard and bridge weren't exactly on his list of favorite things to do. But with the injury, he couldn't do a whole lot of anything else. Not until the muscle damage healed completely. "It's great to have a change of scenery before I head home."

"Already? You sure that's a good idea?" Pete shot him the big brother look, the one he reserved for kickass occasions when Micah refused to listen to reason. "Didn't your CO tell you to take another few weeks off?"

Like that would happen. "From my Special Ops reserve unit, yes. But I have a business to run, my friend. I can't stay here indefinitely. My customers demand the best in security, which means I have to be there to make sure my employees keep them smiling."

"Bullshit. Your company practically runs itself with all the ex-forces talent you've got on the payroll." Pete laughed. "I get it. Your mama's been introducing you around again and scaring the bejesus out of you. Only a woman batting her eyelashes with marriage on her mind could make you bolt like a jackrabbit. Who is it this time, the daughter of some Puerto Rican dignitary?"

"More like the state representative herself and Maria is both smart and beautiful. I'm just not interested." Micah leaned across the bar and grabbed a handful of nuts out of a bowl. "What about you? Do you ever have the urge to settle down?"

"Hell no, especially not since Remy Renaud landed back in the Glades." Rolling his eyes, Pete signalled the waitress for another Perrier. "Damn pretty woman, but she's a royal pain in my ass."

"How so?" Micah added another longneck to the order. Any woman who could rile Pete—the epitome of laid-back and who-gives-a-shit—sounded interesting to him.

"The family bought a vacation home here after you moved away. Her four brothers are friends of mine from way back. Remy is the youngest." The waitress brought their drinks and Micah paid the tab. "Anyhow, she's a wildlife biologist now, spending a few days at the park to study the migrating patterns of birds."

"So? How does that equate with her being a pain in your butt?" Micah took a swig of his beer, settling in to get the rest of the story.

"Remy wouldn't let me act as her guide while she's in the park. Stuck her stubborn little nose in the air, shot me a stiff middle finger, and went off on her own." Pete glanced at his watch. Micah had noticed him doing that ever since they'd sat down. "That was twelve hours ago. She's not back yet."

"Hell, it's been dark over an hour now." Micah didn't like it. A lot could happen to a woman alone in the Everglades, and none of it good. "Did you send out a search party?"

"See, that's the problem." Pete ran a hand over his buzz cut, a frown riding his eyebrows. "If I do that and there's nothing wrong, Remy will skin me alive. On the other hand, if anything happens to her, the Renaud brothers will kill me and bury me deep in the swamp. I'm damned if I do, and damned if I don't."

"Yep, I'd say she's a pain in your ass." Micah felt the grin forming on his lips. "May God protect us from strong-willed women."

"I'll drink to that." Pete tapped his bottle with Micah's. "This is why we're sitting here instead of whooping it up in some steamy Miami hotspot. I'm afraid to take a piss until I get Remy on a plane back to Canada. See, she didn't hang with the rest of us when she was a kid. Hated the Glades and stayed clear, lacks experience with what's out there. Anything happens to her and it's on my head."

"You sure there's nothing romantic going on between you two?" Yeah, Micah was playing devil's advocate and enjoying the hell out of it. On the other hand, he couldn't deny his interest was piqued, which made no sense at all. The last thing he needed was a female who sounded like a firestorm. Still, he couldn't help the twinge of jealousy when he thought Pete might be hooking up with her. "It sounds to me like you have some chemistry brewing."

"More like bad mojo." Pete shot him a disgusted look. "She's the ornery kid sister I never had. I feel sorry for any dumb bastard who decides she's worth a second look. 'Cause if Remy doesn't send him to an early grave, those brothers of hers sure as hell will."

Micah shook his head. "All kidding aside, someone has to look for her. If you don't want to grow some balls and do it, get some of your people on it. But do it now."

Pete's walkie-talkie screeched to life. "Chief?"

He answered the call. "What's up, Luke?"

"The Renaud woman is back. Papa Joe brought her in. You'd better get here quick."

"It's about damn time. What's her story?"

"She's hurt, Chief."

"What?" Pete jumped to his feet and tore for the stairs down to the dock. Micah was right behind him.

"Papa Joe says she ran into some men burying a body in the swamp. They tried to kill her."

"Holy Christ! Where is she?"

"We just carried her off Joe's dinghy. It's in the last slip down by the picnic area."

"I'll be right there. Alert the sheriff's office and paramedics."

"Already done, Chief."

Pete raced along the wooden pier, hit the ground at the other end and kept on running. Micah spotted a throng of park rangers gathered around a picnic table in the distance. A slim woman sat on top. Fiery-red hair tumbled past her shoulders in thick waves. Blood dripped down the side of her face and her expression was wild. She couldn't seem to focus on the questions being asked of her by the rangers. Shit.

He nudged Pete's arm. "Let me handle Remy while you corral your staff. They're scaring her."

"Good idea. She'll balk if I try to help her anyway, won't want me telling her brothers she couldn't handle things herself. See what you can do for her while I question Papa Joe."

They broke through the crowd, Pete giving Remy's hand a squeeze before moving off with an older man and some of his rangers. Micah stayed with her, lightly cupping her chin to catch her attention. She jumped at his touch and tried to pull away. "Easy, honey. You need to lay down so I can look at your injuries."

"I-I don't need any help." She was white as a sheet. A nasty gash oozed over an eye, a bitch of a knife wound creasing her right thigh beneath a bloodied do-rag.

Man, she was out of it if she thought she could walk away with those injuries. "You're probably right, but humor me. Okay?"

Grabbing a bedroll from one of the park rangers, Micah eased her on her back and tucked it beneath her head. She struggled at first, her breathing ratcheting up a notch. She was clearly afraid and confused. "That's it, just try to relax. You're doing great."

Violet eyes blinked wide at him through thick, auburn lashes. He pulled a mini Maglite from his belt and flashed it in her pupils, trying to ignore the pull of those gorgeous peepers. Her gaze reacted to the light, her pupils contracting normally. A good sign for eliminating potential head injuries. But damn, a man could lose himself in her eyes.

Micah refocused on the three bulkiest guys standing close by, figured he'd use them to protect her from prying eyes. Whoever had attacked her could be watching. "You men, move to the far side of the table and block the view from the water. And someone find me a first aid kit."

Grabbing the case a park ranger handed him, Micah went to work. "How are you holding up, Remy? You still with me?"

She jerked when he poured peroxide in the open gash on her leg. "I know it stings, but hang in there."

Pushing the edges of the wound together, he secured them with strips of tape. Next he covered it with a dressing.

"W-who are you?"

He placed some gauze pads over her eye to stem the blood flow. "The name's Micah Rivera. I'm a friend of Pete's."

She laughed, the sound bordering on hysteria. "That's not much of a recommendation."

Micah could see the signs. Shock was setting in, her skin clammy to the touch. Sweat streaked her temples while her teeth chattered. He found a blanket and tucked it around her, touching her wrist to gauge her pulse. Her heartbeat was rapid. Where in hell are the paramedics?

Sirens echoed in the distance, lots of them. No surprise there. A body buried on park land was big news. It would attract a lot more attention than just the sheriff and his deputies. Any TV crew worth its salt had already picked up chatter on the police band and was on its way. Not to mention the forensics unit, coroner, and FBI, since Everglades parkland was their jurisdiction.

Pete clamped a hand on Micah's uninjured shoulder, drawing him aside before he could patch up Remy's head wound. "I need you to stick with her, Mic. I'll have to show the cops and FBI where the body's buried. Papa Joe gave me the location."

Micah gazed at the old man who was back talking to Remy. He had a hunch he wasn't that old and far from feeble. He watched as the guy doused some paper towels in bottled water and cleaned off her face. Then he dressed the cut over her eye like an expert. Military trained, that was for sure—a medic, maybe?

He nodded to Pete. "Remy should leave now, before this turns into a full-blown media circus. The last thing she needs is some reporter plastering her name and face on a late-breaking news bulletin."

"I'll tell her." Pete leaned in close, his jaw tight with concern. "I'm scared for her, man. We've had a serial killer running rampant in Florida for over three years, with no leads. Nine women are missing from this area alone, never mind the rest of the state. If this is what she stumbled onto, Remy's life is in the crapper. Papa Joe told me he saw body parts, and not just from one corpse. And there were two assholes out there in the swamp. One of them got away, Mic. Papa Joe didn't see his face, but he says Remy can identify him."

"Shit. What happened to the other guy?"

"Joe says Remy killed him in self defense."

Micah was stunned. How could a small woman like her protect herself from a killer and get the upper hand? "And you believe him?"

"No reason not to. She's trained in martial arts—Russian Systema. Her parents died when she was ten. Her brothers raised her after that, making damn sure she could handle herself."

"Jesus H. Christ." Micah's gaze slid back to Remy. He knew how it felt to take someone's life. Not something you ever forgot, especially when it was up close and personal. His heart ached for her. She watched him, fear and sadness in her eyes. "Let's move her before the FBI gets their hands on her then. If the dump site holds more missing victims, they're liable to hang her out like a red flag to catch this asshole. And don't kid yourself, he'll come after her."

"My feelings exactly." Pete's gaze cemented with his. "I need you to keep her in the wind until this is over, man. I don't want to know where she is. It's better that way."

Didn't that sound like fun? The pain in the ass woman who gave Pete nightmares had just become his personal problem. Micah mulled it over, wished he could walk away but knew he couldn't. If he didn't make the Renaud woman disappear until the danger was over, who the hell would? Besides, Pete was like a brother, and Micah couldn't refuse him. "Here's the deal. I won't turn her loose until I know she's safe, but after that she's on her own."

"Fair enough."

Remy didn't take the news well when Pete dropped the bomb that Micah was hauling her out of there. She glared at him, a stubborn tilt to her trembling chin. "I don't know you. I don't need medical attention. And I'm staying with Pete!"

Micah understood. She was injured, outnumbered, and feeling coerced. Only God and Remy knew what had happened to her in that swamp, but he was certain she'd paid a terrible price. He didn't want to force her to go with him, but her life could depend on it. So... "Papa Joe, are you willing to tag along with us for the ride?"

The other man glanced at Remy and then back at him. He had to know she wouldn't go without a fight. Glancing at the approaching SUV's, it looked like old Joe had already figured out the score. He had a protective streak where she was concerned and maybe wouldn't want her used by the law to bait a dangerous trap.

"Get your butt in gear, girl. We're taking this here fella up on his offer."

"But, Papa Joe..."

"No time to argue, missy. We gots to beat boots outta here." He sliced Micah a glance. "Follow me."

Micah scooped Remy up in his arms, pulling the blanket over her face so no one would get a visual if they were spotted. As patrol cars and unmarkeds screeched to a halt and killed their sirens, they pounded for the boat and pulled away. Papa Joe drove under the pier, skimming around pylons as they made it to the far end of the dock past the bar. Reaching his rental SUV without incident, Micah settled Remy on the back seat and secured her seatbelt. Papa Joe slid in beside her.

She whispered to the old man as Micah angled behind the steering wheel. "I hope you brought your bang stick."

"I did. And it ain't loaded with rubber bullets. This time it's the real deal."

Joe's gaze challenged him from the rear-view mirror, grinning around his chewed up cigar. The smile didn't reach his eyes, and Micah figured Joe's weapon was already aimed at his spine through the bucket seat. Yep, there was nothing like riding with an armed ex-military man who felt the need to protect his sidekick—especially when the battered lady's brain wasn't firing on all cylinders.

Not much he could do about it without drawing attention to his vehicle and Remy, since they were sitting in the parking lot of the bar. He cranked the key, deciding Joe wouldn't risk shooting him once he floored it for the exit. The Denali spun on gravel as the tires grabbed and pulled out on the highway. He hit speed dial on his cell phone, splitting his attention between the road behind and cars in front of him, waiting for the line to pick up. Nick Rizzoli answered on the third ring. He was an ex-marine with ties to Micah's Spec Ops squad in Canada.

"Yo."

"Rizzo, I have a friend who needs off-the-grid medical attention in the Miami area. I`m talking X-rays, stitches, shots—nothing that requires surgery as far as I can tell."

"Hold on." Rizzoli came back on the line a minute later and gave him an address in Little Havana. Micah could practically hear his grin over the phone. "Drive around back and someone will let you in. You know, for a guy already on the injured list, sounds to me like you're mixing it up down there."

"It's one of those things that can't be helped."

"Sure it is, you crazy bastard. Wish I was there to join in the fun. I have friends in the area if you need backup."

Micah thought it over, lowering his voice. "If they're anything like Blue and his team who gave us a hand with Rocket's goat-fuck situation in Hereford, it might not be a bad idea."

"I'll reach out. Give me your wish list."

"I'll get back to you from the clinic. There are a few things that come to mind." Micah disconnected the call, looked up to see Papa Joe staring at him in the rear-view. "Is something the matter?"

"Not so far." Joe pulled the cigar out of his mouth, removing a piece of tobacco stuck to his tongue. "You better pray it stays that way."

THE DARK SEDAN KEPT pace with the Denali from three car lengths back. They rolled east out of the Everglades on Highway 41. Sig's best guess? Miami was their next stop. Anger consumed him for the woman riding in the SUV. Did she think she was invincible? That there wouldn't be payback for what she had done? Taking Blade's life was a huge mistake, and she had no idea who she was up against. Otherwise, she would have done herself a favor and begged Blade to kill her outright, a no brainer to Sig's way of thinking. But the bitch wasn't smart. She also wasn't aware of the number of men available to avenge Blade's death.

Just like the boys in Lord of the Flies, their own group had formed fifteen years earlier at a private boarding school in the Alps. A lifetime ago and so far away—Sig thought of those days as a beloved fairy tale. A case of like meeting like, recognizing in each other the darkness growing within themselves—the desire to maim, torture, and kill. Without being caught, of course.

A bunch of spoiled, troubled kids thrown together by moms and dads who thought 'boot camp' would straighten them out. Make men out of them. And it did, just not the kind of men a woman wanted for her next-door neighbor.

As adults—moving on to obtain degrees from the finest universities money could buy—they maintained close contact. Because success in the eyes of the world wasn't enough, and couldn't provide the thrills they enjoyed most.

A smile touched his lips. A great leader needed his team to focus on a common cause, victory being the end result. The woman who slaughtered Blade would be their ultimate prize, her deathblow being the *coup de grâce*. He'd take pleasure in her suffering when the time came, and so would his associates.

Sig laughed, the sound mingling with the piano concerto pouring through audio speakers. He lowered the volume and hit speed dial on his throwaway phone. "Inform the others, Blade was murdered tonight. We're going after the woman who killed him."

The line stayed quiet for a few seconds. "You want us to fly out there?"

"Not yet. I need the tags run on a vehicle first. It's a rental. Find out who's driving it." He gave him the plate number of the Denali and disconnected.

The highway became SW 8th Street in Little Havana. The Denali turned off and hung a left onto 12th Street. Sig hung back, pulled over, and parked when the SUV streaked into the alley behind an emergency clinic.

He reached into the glove box, pulled out his Sig Sauer—the gun that gave him his nickname—and checked the clip, shaking his head. Not enough ammo and too many people inside. Besides, he never worked alone. Better to watch and wait. Find out where they crashed for the night and who he was dealing with. Once he knew that information, he'd contact the rest of his team.

And the game would begin.